PICTURE PERFECT

Jack Dillon Dublin Tale 9
Second Edition

PICTURE PERFECT

Jack Dillon Dublin Tale 9
Second Edition

Mike Faricy

Library of Congress Control Number: 2023920390
paperback ISBN: 978-1-962080-77-4
e-Book ISBN: 978-1-962080-78-1

MJF Publishing books may be purchased for education, Business, or promotional use. For information on bulk purchases,
please contact the author directly at mikefaricyauthor@gmail.com

Published by

MJF
PUBLISHING

MJF Publishing
https://www.mikefaricybooks.com

ACKNOWLEDGMENTS

I would like to thank the following people for their help & support: Special thanks to Nick, Roy, Julie, Mittie, and Toui for their hard work, cheerful patience and positive feedback. I would like to thank family and friends for their encouragement and unqualified support. Special thanks to Maggie, Jed, Schatz, Pat, Av, Emily and Pat, for not rolling their eyes, at least when I was there. Most of all, to my wife, Teresa, whose belief, support and inspiration has, from day one, never waned.

To Teresa
"How many years have you been wearing that?"

PROLOGUE

It was a sunny Dublin morning when Killian Graham attempted to hit the snooze alarm for the third time. He missed and knocked the clock radio onto the floor. Pulling the pillow over his head didn't help, and he reluctantly slid out of bed and turned off the alarm with his foot. He took a couple of deep breaths, stretched, and cleared his throat on the way to the bathroom.

After shaving and a shower, he dressed and wandered into his kitchen area to make breakfast. He put the kettle on, took some black pudding (actually blood sausage) and streaky bacon (strips of bacon instead of a rasher) from the refrigerator, and tossed them into the frying pan. Once the kettle had boiled, he poured a tea and tossed two eggs into the frying pan.

Today was the first of the month, which meant the American would deposit two hundred euros in his account. The deposits had been going on for the past four years. He'd had his doubts initially, but they were legitimate and arrived like clockwork, not to mention the credit card he'd received. On the first of every month, he also received an email telling him where to go. There'd be a hotel reservation, a dinner reservation, a list of two or three pubs to stop for a pint, and some fool over in the states he'd never met was picking up the tab. It was crazy, but why look a gift horse in the mouth?

He dished up breakfast, sat down at the dining room table, and turned on his laptop. By the time the laptop was working, Killian had finished his eggs and streaky bacon and was about to dive into the black pudding. He logged into his bank account. Sure enough, the two hundred euro deposit was there waiting for him.

He cut into the black pudding, stuffed a piece in his mouth, and checked his cellphone. There were two text messages. The American wanted him to travel down to Wexford and spend the night in the Riverbank House Hotel. He'd made reservations for Killian and a guest at the Emerald Gardens restaurant. Perfect. A two-hour drive on the M11, and he knew someone who would make the night enjoyable. He quickly finished the blood pudding and tossed his plate in the sink.

He poured a fresh tea, grabbed his phone, and settled onto the couch in the sitting room. He hit speed dial and waited. Ciara answered on the fourth ring.

"Killian? Is that you?"

"Who else, darling? Say, my business has me down your way later today. I'll be staying at the Riverbank. Wondered if you'd be able to join me for dinner." He checked his laptop screen. "I've got an 8:00 reservation at the Emerald Gardens."

"Today? Mmm-mmm, something planned with me mum, but, well you know… Let me cancel, and if there's a problem, I'll get back to you."

"Perfect, I'll swing by to pick you up at 7:00. We can have a glass or two before dinner. Looking forward to seeing you, darling." He disconnected and sent a short two-sentence response to the text messages.

Thank you, more than happy to make my presence known. Standard procedure, leaving tips and will forward photos.

It always struck him as odd that the tour company wouldn't use stock photos, but for two hundred euros and an all-expenses paid weekend, who was he to argue? Three hours later, he had packed a bag and was on the road down to Wexford.

Part of the arrangement with the American was he couldn't tell anyone the circumstances. That was just fine with Killian. Just keep the money and the hotel stays coming, and he'd be more than happy to keep his mouth shut.

ONE

US Marshal Jack Dillon turned the corner and walked down the lane toward his house. He held onto the leash attached to Lucifer's dog collar. They were returning from making two rounds of Albert Park, just a few blocks away. Two rounds added up to two point four miles, and the walk, plus twenty minutes of chasing a tennis ball, hopefully, added up to enough exercise to keep Lucifer from causing any major damage today.

They passed Tara's house, across the lane and two units up from Dillon's. He turned to look for a moment, but only a moment, not wanting to be caught staring. Things were off and on with her, hot or cold. The last interlude had slowed to a halt when she'd told him she was interested in an older gentleman. Just now, there was a black Mercedes in the drive, the same one that had been there an hour ago at 7:00. Someone had spent the night.

He hurried down the lane, hoping his next-door neighbor Deitora wouldn't see him. No doubt, she'd open the door and rain on what was shaping up to be a sunny day. They made it safely into the house without Deitora's negative greeting. He wandered into the kitchen, tossed a biscuit to Lucifer, and then hurried upstairs to get ready for work. He showered, shaved, and pulled on pressed gray trousers and an open-collar white shirt. He strapped on his shoulder holster, shoved his nine-millimeter pistol into the holster, and covered it with a black sport coat. He draped the lanyard with his An Garda Síochána ID around his neck and headed downstairs.

Lucifer had settled into his pillow next to the fireplace in the sitting room. Dillon checked the locks on the backdoor then glanced out the window to see if Deitora was working in her front garden. Fortunately, she wasn't. He hurried outside, locked the front door, hopped in his car, and backed out onto the lane.

He was about to head up the lane when the black Mercedes suddenly pulled out of Tara's driveway. Tara was in the front passenger seat, saying something to the older gentleman driving. She glanced over at Dillon, obviously saw him, but didn't acknowledge him, and they drove up the lane. Dillon waited until they'd turned left and disappeared before he followed up the lane. He waited for a car to pass and then turned right.

Fifteen minutes later, he nodded at Dermot checking vehicles pulling in and out of the headquarters parking lot. He was able to grab a spot close to the door just as a car backed out. At the back door he waved his ID over the keypad and heard the door lock snap. He pulled the door open and walked down the hall to the elevator. He stepped inside, pressed the button for the fourth floor, and rode up by himself.

The door to the Special Branch was just down the hall on the fourth floor. Dillon waved his ID over the keypad then stepped into the office. It was a large room with too many desks and the constant hum of chatter coming from officers on the phone. Dillon headed for his desk up toward the front of the room. Prior to his being assigned to An Garda Síochána, his desk had been a collection spot for empty tea mugs, dirty plates, and the occasional sandwich wrap, along with a variety of silverware.

Nothing had changed, and Dillon started his day like every day, stacking up dirty plates and tea mugs. This morning he had the added treat of a Yorkie candy bar wrapper. He carried everything into the break room, tossed the wrapper in the trash, and set the plates, mugs, and silverware in the sink. He went back to his desk, grabbed his coffee mug, and hurried back into the break room to fill it.

There was maybe an inch of coffee remaining in the pot, which suggested it had been on the burner since yesterday. He filled his mug anyway, dumped the small amount remaining into the sink, and turned off the burner. He built up the courage to take a sip, which only served to convince him that, indeed, it had been on the burner since yesterday.

He went back out to his desk, settled in, and began reviewing his file, actually two files— both concerning missing American girls. The girls were students at DCU, Dublin City University, which coincidently was only two blocks from Dillon's home. As a matter of fact, he'd driven past it just this morning on his way to work.

The girls, Gretchen Malden from Big Falls, Montana, and Mary Ellen Schneider from Chicago, were studying for master's degrees in the International Business program at DCU for the next two semesters. Their disappearance was concerning but not alarming.

He'd been through a number of these cases where the individuals simply neglected to inform anyone of their travel plans. Usually, the travel amounted to a week or two on the continent, oftentimes with a new boyfriend. Upon their return, the girls would have to deal not only with the school but with parents who hadn't slept for a week, worried about their daughters. Over the past four years, two fathers and one couple had traveled to Dublin to aid in the search. Fortunately, in all three cases, the girls had returned to Dublin, surprised to see a parent and having to do a bit of explaining.

The odd thing with this situation was the anonymous tip that had been phoned in suggesting there may have been a kidnapping. Even stranger was the fact that the recording sounded as though whoever made it had been cut off in mid-sentence. The number had been traced to a payphone on the DCU Campus. Dillon figured he could probably count on one hand the number of existing pay phones in the city. Ten-year-old children had their own cellphone in today's world.

"Anything on those two?" a voice asked, and Dillon looked up to see Detective Inspector (DI) Paddy Suel, his partner.

Dillon shook his head and said, "Nothing, yet. I've got a call into Eric Bergman at the embassy along with Delta, Aer Lingus, and Ryan Air. Hopefully, someone will have a flight record. DCU is checking for cellphone numbers."

Suel shook his head. "Probably dragged some poor knacker off to Paris for a romantic interlude, and they broke up after the first night."

"Oh, these are smart girls, working on master's degrees in International Business. They wouldn't end up with guys like you or me."

That brought a smile to Suel's face. "Well, one can only hope."

Dillon sipped from his mug and made a face.

"Oh, bad coffee is it? I'm heading into the break room for a tea. I'll do up a fresh pot for youse."

"No, no, don't do that, Paddy. I'll make it. I thought I could get this down, but it's God awful. I'll make a pot."

"You don't like the way I make a coffee?" Suel asked and laughed.

"Right, and I'll get you a tea while I'm at it."

"Perfect. Much appreciated, Dillon. I take back some of the awful things folks around here have been saying about you."

"Yeah, right," Dillon said and carried his mug back to the break room. He put a fresh pot of coffee on, made a tea for Suel, and waited four or five minutes for the coffee to finish. He'd just brought the mugs out, set Suel's on his desk, and was heading back to do follow-up calls on the missing girls when Detective Chief Inspector (DCI) McCabe stepped to the door of his office and called, "Suel, Dillon, if you wouldn't mind."

Suel stood, shaking his head, and together, they hurried into McCabe's office.

DCI McCabe headed up the Special Branch. Not a man to spend time with fools, he ran a tight ship. He was highly respected by the force, the members of special branch in particular, and by the citizens at large. As they entered his office, he remained focused on a file and said, "Take a seat." He signed the top sheet in front of him and then placed the file on top of a stack of maybe a dozen other files.

"What's the word on the two girls?"

Dillon gave him a rundown, such as it was. They'd only received the case yesterday afternoon. "We should have a better handle on it in a couple of hours. Give the school, the airlines, and the embassy a chance to check things."

"DI Suel, you were looking into a group of women?"

"Yes, sir, the usual. They were transported here with promises of a job. Unfortunately, the job is in the sex trade. Beatings, drugs, the usual. It looks like eight women from the information we have, but they're being moved around, so it's been impossible to get a fix on them. Lots of rumors but nothing we can really act on."

"Dance clubs?" McCabe asked.

"That would be the usual route, but nothings turned up there, at least locally. I've got calls into Cork, Limerick, Sligo Town, Galway, and Waterford. So far, a big fat zero. It may be some faction of the Smirnov group but nothing definite so far."

McCabe drummed his fingers on his desk for a moment. "Okay, see if you can't yank some chains and get things moving one way or another. Thank you for the update, gentlemen. Keep me posted."

TWO

It was close to five when Killian Graham pulled in front of the Riverbank House Hotel. He'd never been there before, but that was no surprise since it was way out of his league. This was one of the great things about the arrangement. Killian stayed in the finest hotels, ate at the best restaurants, not to mention receiving favors from a number of very talented women, and it didn't cost him a cent.

The Riverbank House Hotel was located across the bridge from Wexford town, on the Slaney River estuary with a view of Wexford Harbor. The hotel was a two-story white stucco structure at least a hundred and fifty years old. Killian parked in the guest parking lot and wheeled his suitcase into the hotel. The receptionist counter was built of dark wood paneling with a black marble countertop. A smiling, uniformed receptionist stood behind the counter. Her name tag read Maureen.

"Welcome to the Riverbank House Hotel, sir. How are you?"

"Fine, just fine, I have a reservation. Killian Graham is the name," Killian said and proceeded to spell out his last name.

She clicked some keys on the computer and a moment later said, "Oh, yes, sir. Here it is. Paid in advance and you're in one of our deluxe suites. All I'll need is your signature, just here," she said, setting a 4X5 card down on the counter and pointing to the signature line.

"Perfect," he replied as he signed. "I'd like to leave a twenty percent tip to the final bill. I'm not carrying any cash, but I would like the staff to be taken care of upon my departure. If you would just add an amount to my bill, that would be fine with me."

"Only too happy to oblige, Mr. Graham. We'll debit your card. Conrad, two-oh-seven," she called.

A uniformed man suddenly appeared from seemingly out of nowhere. He took hold of Killian's suitcase and led the way to the antique elevator. After a twenty-second ride, they stepped out of the elevator into a hallway covered with thick plush carpet. Conrad led the way down the quiet hall. Occasional oil paintings in gilt frames hung on the wall. Conrad stopped at the third door labeled 207 in brass numerals. He inserted the key card into the lock, a green light flashed, and he opened the door.

Killian stepped into a paneled room with a massive, four-poster canopy bed. Red and gold velvet curtains hung from the window behind an antique red velvet couch. An elegant white fireplace was centered on the wall opposite the bed.

"Will there be anything else, sir?" Conrad asked as he rolled Killian's suitcase next to the upholstered bench at the end of the bed.

"No, thank you, much appreciated. I left my tip information with Maureen down at reception."

"Very good, sir. Enjoy your stay," Conrad said. He smiled, gave a slight nod, and pulled the door closed behind him.

Killian's brief inspection revealed the switch for the gas-fueled fireplace which he turned on. Bottles of red and white wine rested in the refrigerator. The bathroom sported a shower and a Jacuzzi. Killian walked back into the bedroom and stretched out on the four-poster bed. He snuggled into the fluffy pillows and opened his eyes only to discover a mirror across the top of the massive bed canopy. He gave himself a little wave, chuckled and thought, *Oh, this is going to be a very interesting evening.*

He pulled in front of Ciara's home a few minutes after 7:00. He grabbed the bouquet of flowers off the passenger seat and hurried up to her front door. She opened the door while the doorbell was still chiming.

"Well, look what the cat dragged in," she said. She was wearing a short black leather skirt with a large silver zipper down the front. Her blouse was black, apparently devoid of buttons, and tucked into her skirt, displaying her wonderfully deep cleavage.

"Hello, darling," he said and thrust the bouquet toward her after a quick kiss.

"Look at you, Killian, all decked out. Oh, the flowers, you always remember how much I love them. Let's go to the kitchen, and I'll place these in some water. I've got a glass of wine poured. I hope you're partial to the Sauvignon Blanc, nicely chilled," she said and gave him another kiss. This time, the kiss lasted twice as long as the previous one.

"Whatever wine you've got is just fine with me. So how are you? It's been too long."

"I'll say," she said, entering the kitchen. Two glasses of chilled wine sat on the counter, and a small plate held a half-dozen crackers with cheese and some sort of sauce on top of the cheese.

Killian stared as she arranged the flowers in a cut-glass vase. When finished, she pushed the vase off to the side and handed a wine glass to him. She raised her glass, they clinked, and each took a healthy sip.

"So what have you been up to, darling?" he asked.

"Well, mostly working. Keeping my head above water, thank God. But business is tough."

"You're still doing the handmade jewelry thing?"

She nodded and took another sip. "More or less. I've expanded it to some knitted items and gift cards. I've taken on a line of crystal from a guy out in Carrick on Shannon. That's doing rather well. Being self-employed, I've never worked harder for less money," she said and laughed. "Now, what about you? What brings you down this way?"

"Meeting with some people tomorrow afternoon. I've done some online marketing work for them and hope to make that a little more permanent. We'll see what happens," he lied.

"Well," she said, raising her glass. "Here's to the both of us. Let's hope this year will be better than the last."

"Always," he said as they clinked glasses once more. They chatted for another ten minutes until their glasses were empty, then climbed into his car and headed to the Emerald Gardens restaurant.

"I thought you were going to get rid of this thing," Ciara said as Killian pulled his black Peugeot away from the curb.

"You know how it goes. You make all sorts of plans, and then life happens. A couple of bumps in the road, and the next thing you know, I'm driving it for another year."

Ten minutes later, he pulled in front of the Emerald Gardens. He hurried out from behind the wheel and ran around the front of the car to open the door for Ciara.

"Thank you," she said. Once she climbed out of the Peugeot, she stood on the sidewalk and examined the front of the restaurant. "Mmm, oriental food. I am so ready."

Killian glanced across the street at Flanagan's pub, where the email instructed him to have an after-dinner drink. "Well then, let's not waste a minute," he said and held the door for her.

The restaurant wasn't large, and it projected the sense of a private setting. They settled in at a table with a red linen tablecloth and napkins. Killian gave a quick look at the wine list and ordered the most expensive white at sixty-five euros a bottle. They sipped wine, had a starter, and lingered over their meal. He ordered a glass of dessert wine for each of them, and when the waiter returned with the wine, Killian said, "Say, would you mind taking a couple of pictures?" He held out his cellphone, and the waiter took three photos.

"Thank you. I think just the check when you have a moment," Killian said.

"Why do you always do that?"

"Do what, ask for the check?"

"No, have them take pictures. Everywhere we go, you always do that."

"Could it be because I want to remember my wonderful evening with you?"

"Oh, stop," she said and laughed.

Once they finished, they headed across the street to Flanagan's pub. Killian promised they'd stay for just one. They left after two drinks and more pictures. They had a goodnight cocktail at the bar in the Riverbank House, had two more pictures taken, and then staggered up to Killian's suite.

While Ciara hurried into the bathroom, Killian sent his text message with the photos.

THREE

Sarah Halloran called through the closed office door. "You ready to go, Jimmy? I don't want to be late,"

"Just finishing up. We'll be done in a minute," Jimmy Dugan called and then looked at the two men seated across from him. He was Jimmy Dugan to them and a handful of others. Outside in the world he went by Sarah's name, Halloran. "You tell that fat sack of shit that he either pays or an unfortunate accident is liable to happen. Got it?"

Both men nodded. There was no point in arguing or attempting to explain. Jimmy Dugan wasn't the type to listen. "You enjoy your evening," Freddy said. "We'll take care of this."

"Yeah, well, see that you do. Otherwise, we'll use him as an example of what happens when you don't follow directions," Jimmy said.

The two men opened the door and headed down the hall. Jimmy heard them call goodbye to Sarah in the kitchen. He shut down his computer, checked the desk to make sure nothing was out of place, and then stood. Just as he was about to head out, he heard the burner phone vibrate in the desk drawer. He quickly unlocked the drawer and ran his finger across the screen. Perfect, a text message from Killian Graham, three messages actually, all with photos. Well worth the investment. He glanced at the time, 7:30, which meant it was 12:30 over in Ireland.

'Hope you enjoyed your evening, Killian'

"Jimmy, I'm ready to go. I don't want to be late," Sarah said as she appeared in the doorway, placing the clip onto the back of a diamond earring.

"Just locking up. You look lovely. Look even better if you smiled."

"I'll smile when we're on our way."

"Well then, let's be off," he said dropping the burner phone back in the desk drawer and locking the drawer. He pulled on his sport coat and stepped out from behind the desk.

Sarah's eyes moved up and down, examining his attire.

"That's what you're wearing?"

"Yeah, this is what I'm wearing. I'm a guy, honey. No one cares what I wear, and no one will remember. You, on the other hand, look like a million bucks. Everyone is gonna remember how great you look."

She shook her head. "Cowboy boots?"

"I'm telling ya, no one is gonna care, let alone notice," he said, failing to mention they also covered his ankle holster and switchblade.

"All right, let's go, but one of these days…"

It was a fifteen-minute drive to the Venice Country Club. As Jimmy pulled up to the front door, an attendant appeared, pasted on a smile, and opened the door for Sarah. "Oh, Mr. and Mrs. Halloran, nice to see you again. Are you here for the Becker event?"

"Yes," Sarah said.

"They're in the Beach Room," he said as Sarah stepped out of the car. He closed the car door and hurried over to the driver's side.

"No scratches, Sean," Jimmy said and didn't smile.

"Of course not, sir. Have a pleasant evening."

Jimmy and Sarah headed into the country club as Sean pulled the car into the parking lot. He held his right hand out over the console and extended his middle finger. "Screw you, you pain in the ass," he said to Jimmy's back, as he cautiously drove into the parking lot. He debated peeing into the gas tank or in the back seat, all the while knowing for certain he'd be caught if he ever dared. He'd love to screw that prick Halloran, but he'd never be able to work up the courage. He'd get a five-dollar tip at the end of the night and then have to watch as Halloran walked around the entire car checking for scratches and dents.

He pulled into the parking lot, climbed out, locked the Mercedes, and placed an orange valet tag beneath the windshield wiper on the driver's side. He glanced around for anyone watching. The lot was empty, and he hurried to the back of the car and unlocked the trunk. He looked around once more then raised the lid. The trunk was spotless. He'd hoped to find a briefcase full of money or, God forbid, a body, but no such luck. Lights from a car pulling in front of the clubhouse suddenly lit up the short drive down to the parking lot, and Sean closed the trunk and hurried back to the clubhouse.

Jimmy leaned against the bar in the Beach room, sipping from his glass of sparkling water with a twist. Sarah was busy mingling and making the rounds, laughing and telling stories. Jimmy was content to stand at the bar until they moved to the dinner tables. He got a few nods from other guys ordering drinks. Two even said, "Hello," but didn't wait for a response. That was just fine with Jimmy. What the hell would they ever do for him? Besides, the last thing he needed was a new friend.

FOUR

Dillon was on his morning walk with Lucifer. They'd circled around Albert Park twice, and he'd been throwing the tennis ball for maybe ten minutes when his phone rang. "Dillon," was how he answered as he tossed the ball halfway across the field, and Lucifer took off after it.

"Good morning, my precious," DI Paddy Suel said. "I hope I'm interrupting something."

"Not at all, just getting out of the church service," Dillon said.

Suel paused for a second or two. "Really?"

"What do you think? What the hell do you want, Paddy? If it's bail money, I'll have to think about it."

"No, thankfully. Got a tip on where the Russian girls might be. It's early enough, they haven't been moved and probably won't be for the next hour or two. Care to pay a visit with me?"

"Yeah, I can meet you at the station in fifteen."

"Make it thirty. I'll meet you in the parking lot. We'll take my car."

"See you there," Dillon said as Lucifer headed toward him, holding the tennis ball in his mouth. He dropped the ball at Dillon's feet. Dillon picked up the ball, then turned around and made two fake throws across the walking path toward the field closer to the exit. Lucifer took off across the path then stopped maybe ten feet into the field. He turned around to look at Dillon, walking toward him. Dillon tossed the ball over Lucifer's head, and the dog took off, catching it in mid-air after the second bounce. Dillon tossed the ball two more times, each time drawing closer to the exit. After the second toss, he clipped the leash onto Lucifer's collar, and they jogged the rest of the way home. Jogging down his lane, Dillon noticed the black Mercedes wasn't parked in Tara's drive this morning.

He quickly shaved, pulled on jeans and a sweater before slipping on his shoulder holster and a leather jacket. He checked Lucifer who had settled onto his pillow, and hurried out the door. He was backing into a parking place in the Headquarters parking lot when Suel arrived. As Suel pulled in front of Dillon's car, he unlocked the car doors. Dillon had barely climbed into the passenger seat when Suel pulled away. Two paper cups with white plastic tops rested in the console of the car. One of the cups had the letter 'C' written on it with a marker.

"Please tell me that's a coffee for me," Dillon said.

"It is, and good morning to you," Suel replied.

"How'd you hear about this?"

"Where they're staying? I've got a snitch with a court appearance coming up. He's eager to help just now."

Dillon pulled the coffee out of the console and took a sip. It wasn't bad.

"Meet with your approval?" Suel asked.

"Yeah, very nice. You get this at Kennedy's or Bang Bang?"

"Bang Bang, Danny says hi, by the way."

"Thanks for this."

"You link up with Tara last night?"

"Nope, she seems to be taking a bit of a break, and I'm okay with that."

Suel glanced over for a second then said, "Yeah, but if she'd knocked on the door and wanted to spend the night, you wouldn't have turned her away."

"Hell no, I'm not crazy," Dillon said and changed the subject. "So where are we headed and tell me again who gave you the information."

"We're headed into the Liberties. The address is forty-four Reginald Street. Billy the Butler called me about six this morning with the tip."

"Isn't he the guy who worked at the hotel and was breaking into all the rooms?"

"Yeah, that's him, ended up serving three years."

"But you said he has a court appearance in a couple of weeks."

"Apparently, he didn't quite learn his lesson. If this tip works out, it could go a long way in reducing any sentence, maybe even tossing the case out."

The Liberties is a famous Dublin working-class area along the Liffey River. The area was a part of the city of Dublin but preserved its own jurisdiction from back in the twelfth century. Among other things, it's home to the Guinness Brewery.

Suel took Queen Street across the Liffey to Thomas Court and then a number of twists and turns until they finally arrived at Reginald street. They had to wait for a paneled plumbing van to turn off of the street. The truck was light blue with an image of a white sink, tub, and toilet on the side. The company name and phone number ran beneath the images of the plumbing fixtures. As the truck turned, the driver gave a friendly nod, and his pal in the passenger seat seemed to slink down.

"Come on, move, you plonker," Suel said then finished up with a colorful bit of swearing. They pulled in front of number forty-eight Reginald Street and parked. The block-long two-story brick structures shared common walls and looked to be at least two hundred years old. Each unit appeared to be about ten feet wide.

"You think they've got eight women stashed in number forty-four?" Dillon asked as he climbed out of the passenger seat.

"Probably have them sleeping on the floor," Suel said.

"Or in line for the bathroom."

"You think there's a bathroom in these places?" Suel said, laughed, and headed twenty feet down the street to number forty-four. There was a front window, maybe two feet wide, centered between the door and the shared wall. A yellowed shade, curled along the sides, was pulled down, covering the window. A sign resting on the windowsill read 'Unit For Sale.'

They stood on either side of the door. Suel nodded at Dillon and knocked on the door. They waited, and nothing happened. He knocked again and tried the doorknob. The knob turned, and the door drifted open maybe six inches. Suel pushed the door with his foot and looked in. "Hello, anyone home?" he called.

Dillon peeked into the empty front room with a small, coal-burning fireplace. A soiled pillow and a worn gray blanket rested on the floor in front of the fireplace. A steep staircase maybe six feet from the front door led up to the second floor.

"Nice of you to invite us in, thank you," Suel said louder than normal and stepped inside. Dillon followed and closed the door behind them. "Jesus Christ," Suel said and shook his head. A doorway led to a back room, and Suel walked toward it while Dillon stood at the base of the staircase. Suel peeked in the room and stepped back to Dillon. "Nothing but a broken window and an empty whiskey bottle. Let's check upstairs."

Dillon grabbed hold of the wooden railing, which was surprisingly sturdy, and headed up the staircase. A small, empty room was at the top of the stairs, no hallway, just the room. Another coal-burning fireplace was positioned roughly above the fireplace on the first floor. Pieces of newspaper were scattered around the floor. A bathtub, sink, and toilet were in a far corner. The cardboard tube to a roll of toilet paper lay on the floor next to the toilet. Lengths of heavy twine and what looked like bits of duct tape were piled in a corner.

"You think they were given that newspaper to cover themselves?" Dillon asked.

"Maybe. I'd guess they were tied up and probably gagged," Suel said, nodding at the twine and duct tape as he walked over to the sink. He turned one of the worn handles. Rust-colored water sputtered out of the fixture and a moment later ran onto the floor. He quickly turned off the water, glanced at the toilet, and recoiled. "Christ almighty, don't get any nearer to that. Nothing here to see, and if we stay any longer, we're liable to catch some dreadful disease. I'd say they were here, but we missed them. For all I can tell, they could have been here last week."

They headed back down the stairs, and Dillon stepped over to the entrance to the back room. A drainpipe stood where there must have been a sink at one time. A strip of wood ran across the wall against the ceiling for maybe four feet where a cabinet or shelves had hung.

Suel was already outside when Dillon stepped out and closed the door behind him. "You want to try the neighbors?"

"I don't see any point, but we can try," Suel said. They knocked on a half-dozen doors but never got an answer.

"I'm going back to that place for a minute. Pick me up there," Dillon said and hurried up the street. He pulled out a pocket notebook and wrote down the phone number listed on the 'For Rent' sign. Suel pulled up a half-minute later, and Dillon climbed in.

"You leaving a note?" Suel asked.

"No, but I'd like to talk to whoever is renting the place out. See if they gave the key to anyone."

"That broken window in what used to be the kitchen is probably how they got in and then opened the front door from the inside. Damn it. I wonder when they were actually in the place."

"I'm guessing last night," Dillon said.

"Care to share with me what you're basing that assumption on?"

"Well, based on your reaction to whatever you saw in the toilet, the fact that that room didn't reek to high heaven yet, might suggest that the toilet had been recently filled."

"By a lot more than one," Suel added.

Dillon nodded. "Plus, you know what else I'm thinking? What if we just missed them and that plumbing van with the two guys actually had the women in the back? Now I'm thinking that guy sort of ducking down in the passenger seat might make a lot more sense."

"You recall the name on that truck?"

"No, I was too busy listening to you bitch at the driver to pay any attention."

"I was doing that to keep him occupied so you could memorize the name and phone number," Suel said. He turned onto the main road and headed back to the station. "Hopefully, there aren't a lot of companies with a van like that. We can check it out when we get back."

Once back in the Special Branch office, Suel headed to the restroom. Dillon gathered up the plates, mugs, and spoons from his desk and deposited them in the break room sink. Fortunately, the lights were off in DCI McCabe's office, which gave them some time to try to identify the plumbing van they suspected of transporting the women.

FIVE

Killian woke to the sound of Ciara snoring. The digital clock on the bedside table read 10:20. Sunlight drifted through a slight opening between the velvet curtains. He laid in bed, attempting to recall the after-dinner hours. He thought they'd had two drinks at Flanagan's but had difficulty remembering the bar downstairs. Were they in there until close?

He pulled his trousers from the floor and took out his cellphone, ready to text the photos over to the States, then noticed he'd sent an email a little after midnight. Good, that was all he had to do today, and it was already done.

He attempted to go back to sleep, but Ciara's snoring put a stop to that. He shook her by the shoulder to get her to stop, and she slapped his hand, murmured something about 'not again,' and rolled onto her side. He finally crawled out of bed. He poured the last of the wine from a bottle into a glass on the coffee table and stumbled into the bathroom. He filled the Jacuzzi, climbed in, and drifted off to sleep again.

The sound of the toilet flushing brought him back to consciousness. He opened his eyes just as Ciara was climbing into the Jacuzzi. "Good morning, Mister Energy. God, I can barely walk. Move over."

"Are you okay?"

"Believe me, not a complaint. But I think a good warm soak is in order."

"What do you feel like doing for breakfast?" he asked.

"Breakfast? It's almost two, darling. Mmmmmmm," she said, settling into the Jacuzzi. "This will do for the moment." She leaned back and closed her eyes.

Killian phoned the front desk an hour later and extended their stay for another night. They grabbed a 4:00 late lunch in the dining room. Once again, Killian had their server take a couple of photos.

"Honest to God," Ciara said. "I don't get it. I've no makeup on. I'm hungover. You rode me like a bronco buster for two hours last night. I—"

"I don't recall any complaints."

"I'm not complaining, Killian. Merely stating a fact."

"Well, not to worry, darling. With you holding the napkin up in front of your face, no one will have any idea you're not wearing makeup. Any place special you'd like to have dinner tonight?"

"Dinner? Killian, we just pushed away from lunch."

Killian sat on the antique couch and watched her napping in the four-poster bed. His instructions were to wake her at 6:00. They had a dinner reservation at 8:00. He pulled out his phone, and despite Ciara holding the white linen napkin in front of her face, he texted the images. God bless her for resting up before tonight.

SIX

Jimmy Dugan was at his desk when the burner phone began to vibrate in the drawer. He unlocked the drawer, pulled out the phone, and clicked on the link. No message, just two images of Killian Graham and a woman. The woman was holding a linen napkin in front of her face. He started to shake his head and smiled. This was perfect. Hiding her identity after being seen with him. He added the images to a file with the previous seven, nine images in all. He logged onto the server in Eastern Europe, uploaded the images and then pulled out the sheet with the email addresses. He'd send this message to a couple of reporters and the Boston FBI.

* * *

Kevin Byrne was seated at the kitchen counter, drinking a glass of ice water. He'd just finished cutting the grass, and he would have loved a beer, but his wife had put a halt to that.

"Kevin, no, we've got the fundraiser at the kid's school tonight, and I don't want you drinking a beer before we get there."

"Honey, I just cut the grass in eighty-five-degree heat and about a hundred percent humidity out there. I'm lucky I didn't have a heat stroke. One beer isn't going to make a difference."

"Well, good, then you can just stick with the water. Things start at school at six. They're serving wine in the hopes that after a couple of glasses, everyone will loosen up and be willing to donate more. Besides, I know you want to sweep the sidewalk, and you'll do a better job if you don't have that beer."

"But—"

"No, Kevin," she said just as his phone signaled a message coming through. "Oh no, don't tell me you're getting called in today. It's Saturday."

"Don't worry. The Bureau doesn't send a text message if they want me to come in. If I had to go in, Ehrhart would have called, and I wouldn't be sitting here now, sipping my ice water."

As he pulled out his phone, she asked, "Is everything okay?"

"Relax, it's not from the Bureau. I bet it's more of those pictures of Jimmy Dugan in a bar or on the street. People take the pictures and then send them to me. I don't get it."

"That awful, disgusting person. I thought he was dead. In fact, I prayed he was."

"He's living it up over in Europe somewhere. People take pictures of him, but he never seems to get caught."

"Just as long as he stays away from us. He's an awful person."

"The word awful doesn't do him justice. He's on the ten most wanted list in the US. I get reported sightings of him living it up in Europe, Ireland, Italy, Paris. I've reported it. I'll report these, but nothing seems to happen. Come and look at this. The woman with him is hiding her face."

"Maybe it's just someone looking the other way."

"No honey, check it out. She's holding a napkin up in front of her face."

She stepped over and looked at the two images, Jimmy Dugan and a woman eating dinner somewhere. The woman was actually holding a white linen napkin up in front of her face.

"Kevin, wouldn't a bunch of people in the restaurant recognize him and call the police? Someone, somewhere has to—"

"The problem is it's not here, not in the US. These pictures were taken in Ireland. The guy is on about year number eight or ten of just taking it easy, eating fabulous food in five-star restaurants, not a care in the world. Meanwhile, there are tons of people who will never get their lives back together after this piece of shit entered it, and those are the folks he didn't kill. It's really criminal. A sad commentary on our system that let him slip away."

She leaned her head against his shoulder and said, "I'm glad I married you. Now finish up that water and go sweep the grass cuttings off the sidewalk. You may be able to squeeze in a short nap if you hurry."

"A beer might help me sleep."

"Kevin."

* * *

Wendell Murphy was a twenty-two year veteran with the Boston Globe. He loved his work so much it had cost him two marriages. He was currently unattached, which gave him that much more time to work. Just now, he was sitting behind the wheel of his 2013 Acura ZDX eating a Big Mac while waiting for State Senator Noel Bishop to step out of the Magic Touch massage parlor. The Senator, a conservative Christian, had apparently bought into the 'You must sin before you can be saved' axiom.

He set what was left of his Big Mac back in the box on the passenger seat, wiped his hands on his jeans, and pulled out his cellphone to check the text message. More photos of Jimmy Dugan having a night out on the town. He seemed to receive them every month or so. Dugan out with all sorts of different women, living it up in Ireland. The first three photos were in a restaurant. He could make out the building across the street, Flanagan's, maybe a pub. He went through the pictures. There were a total of nine in the three text messages. None of the others had a view of the outside, and two of them didn't even have a view of Dugan's date. She was holding a napkin up in front of her face. Interesting that she knew enough not to be photographed, and yet Dugan didn't appear to be the least bit concerned.

He turned his cellphone off, wolfed down the remainder of his Big Mac, and pulled his laptop out of his computer bag. He typed in Flanagan's Pub, Ireland and began searching. Fifteen minutes later, on Google's page fourteen, he thought he might have found the place. He compared the image on his laptop to the image on his cellphone. They certainly looked the same. The name across the front of a gray building looked to be a neon sign in writing script format. The neon lights were off at the moment, since it appeared to be daylight, maybe early evening. Interestingly, the place was located in the town of Wexford in Ireland.

He'd write something up, see if it might get published this time. They published the first two articles he'd written, once they had edited out a good fifty percent. That had been two years ago. The next four articles never made it to print, and he was pulled aside by an editor pal and told to give it up. No one cared.

Sage advice, not that he followed it. He'd include a couple of these images and write another article of a Boston criminal, a destroyer of lives, a murderer, living it up while everyone, at least the lucky ones, were struggling to put their lives back together.

SEVEN

At the moment, Dillon was also on Google. He was searching through images of plumbing vans in Dublin County. He searched vans, trucks, and companies and never found an image remotely matching the vehicle they saw this morning on Reginald Street. He brought up a list of plumbing companies in Dublin and started making phone calls.

"Advance Plumbing, how may I direct your call?"

"I'm wondering if I saw your van on the road today. If so, I'd like to have you in to do some work."

"Our van?"

"Yes, do you have a van?"

"We do," this drawn out response suggested she was wondering just where this was going.

"Could you describe your van to me, please?"

"Describe it? It's blue, and it says Advance Plumbing on the side with our phone number."

"Any pictures of a toilet, sink, or a bathtub on the side?"

"No."

"Would you know of a company with such a vehicle?"

Click.

A couple people hung up on him after his first question. If they didn't hang up and their van didn't match, he was able to ask if they knew of a company with such a van and crossed his fingers. Unfortunately, no one knew of such a company, which begged the question. Could the van be from another part of the country?

Dillon's phone rang. "Marshal Dillon," was how he answered.

"Hi, Jack, Eric Bergman. How's your day going?"

"I'll tell you once we're done talking. Hopefully, you can improve things. Up till now, everything I've touched seems to quickly come to a dead end."

"Well, I'm not sure I can improve on that. All I have is confirmation that the DCU girls did indeed board a Ryan Air flight for France on Sunday. The flight landed in the town of Lille and—"

"Lille? In the north of France?"

"Yeah, a little more than two hundred kilometers from Paris."

"Isn't that sort of out of the way?" Dillon asked.

"Yes and no. Remember, they're students, and they're flying Ryan air. So for maybe forty euros, they can fly from here to Lille, hop a train for fifteen more euros, and get dropped off in the center of Paris."

"Any mention of someone flying with them?"

"No. That doesn't mean they weren't accompanied. They could have traveled with boyfriends, and there would be no mention of that if everyone purchased their own ticket."

"Well, at least they're not walking around the Ring of Kerry or on some other stupid ass escapade. Any line on credit cards?" Dillon asked.

"No, and we wouldn't have that anyway. You might talk to the folks at DCU and search their rooms if they're living on campus. Otherwise, they'd have an off-campus address, and you could maybe check that. You might find a credit card statement or a hotel reservation or something."

"I'll get on it, Eric. Thanks for the call. Aren't we due to have lunch, dinner, or a night of pints pretty soon?"

"No, Jack, we're overdue. Give me a day or two to clear my desk and let's touch base then."

"You're preaching to the choir," Dillon said. "Talk to you later."

"Any luck?" Suel asked as he stepped out of the break room. He slurped from his tea mug as he stood in front of Dillon's desk.

Dillon shook his head and said, "No, nothing. What about you?"

"I've made three calls to the rental number and still no one has answered at that number. Makes you wonder exactly how long the place has been vacant. It could be years."

"Or, someone is letting them use it for a night or two and getting paid," Dillon said.

"Possibly, although the property is owned by an eighty-three-year-old woman by the name of Nora Scallen. She resides in St Margaret's Rest Home down in the Liberties. I'd guess she owns the place and probably put it up for sale when she moved into the rest home. Based on what we saw this morning, who would pay money for the place?"

"Damn it, five minutes sooner, and we maybe would have seen them loading girls into that damn van. You get in touch with Billy the Butler?"

Suel shook his head. "Not for lack of trying. I just placed my third call to him, too. Still no answer from that Gobshite. Anything from DCU?"

"The missing girls? No. I left a message and haven't heard back. I just got off the phone with Eric Bergman at the embassy. The girls took a Ryan Air flight to Lille. No way to tell if they were flying with anyone else. The flight to Lille suggests a cheap student trip. Hop across to France, take a train into Paris for fifteen euros. Stay in a hostel or some one-star hotel in Paris. Hell, they might even know a student over there, and they would all cram into wherever that kid lives."

Suel shook his head and said, "For feck's sake." He walked back to his desk, ran his hand through his hair, shook his head, and placed another call on his phone.

Dillon wasted another half-hour getting nowhere with calls to plumbing companies. He dumped what was left of his coffee into the break room sink, rinsed out his mug, and set it in the drawer of his desk. He waited until Suel hung up the phone and walked over to his desk.

"I'm going to drive over to DCU. I'm not getting anything from them, and if I leave now, I can probably catch someone in the office and hopefully get a line on where these girls live."

"You going to search their place? You'll need a warrant," Suel said.

"I know. Unless they're living in a school dormitory, then, if someone from the school should happen to let me into the room, I could at least check a calendar or maybe a notebook. All we need is something that tells us they took off on a trip and they're okay. Then I can get this off my desk. Anyway, I'm heading out."

"Can't say that I blame you. See you tomorrow," Suel said.

"Let me know if you hear anything from Billy the Butler."

"That damn knacker," Suel said and waved goodbye.

EIGHT

Wendell Murphy, the Boston Globe reporter, had just been handed a pint of Guinness from the bartender. It had been a long day, and he planned on staying for just the one before heading home. He settled onto his favorite stool, glanced around at the handful of folks in the place, and took a hearty sip. He began to relax with that first sip and licked the foam from his upper lip. He was about to reward himself with another hearty sip and thought maybe it wouldn't be that bad an idea to stay for a second pint when his cellphone rang.

He glanced at the number, Artie Doyle, editor at the Boston Globe. The same editor who'd pulled Wendell aside and told him not to bother sending any more articles with photos of Jimmy Dugan because no one cared. No doubt he was calling to give the same message after Wendell sent the article this afternoon. Jimmy Dugan with the woman holding the napkin up in front of her face. Might as well get it over with.

He took a hearty swallow of Guinness, enjoyed it for all of a second or two, and then swiped his finger across the screen. "Yeah, Artie, what's up?"

"Hey, Wendy, thought you should know. Against our better judgment we're running your Dugan article. Where the hell did you come up with that photo?"

"You're kidding me. You're actually running it? You know I've sent four or five previous, and every one of them was rejected. What made you finally see the wisdom in my excellent writing?"

"Very funny, not. Don't get your hopes up. They pulled something at the last minute, and your article just happened to fit the space. They're running it now."

"With the picture?"

"What would be the point of running it without the image? It's your lucky day."

"Gee, maybe I should buy a lottery ticket."

"Yeah, you should, and then if you win, you can split the money with me since I gave the nod to run that thing."

"If I win, Artie, you'll be the first person I call."

"That's because I'm the only guy dumb enough to answer your phone calls."

"Thanks for the call. I'll look for subscriptions to go up starting tomorrow."

"Later," Artie said and disconnected.

"Hey, Bonnie," Wendell called to the bartender. "Pour me another Guinness and better give me a lottery ticket, too. Turns out it's my lucky day." He took three large gulps from his pint, gave a satisfied gasp as he set the glass down, and licked the foam from his upper lip. Yeah, this was definitely his lucky day.

NINE

Dillon took North Circular Road into Phibsboro, drove over the Royal Canal on Cross Guns Bridge, and up Ballymun Road to Collins Avenue and Dublin City University, DCU. He parked in the visitor's parking lot and walked along the brick-paved walkway to the university offices in the Henry Grattan Building. Along the way, he took note of the CCTV cameras positioned throughout the campus.

He entered the area marked offices and walked up to the reception counter. A young woman, probably a student, smiled and said, "How may I help you?" Her name tag read 'reception.'

"I'm here to see Myra Harrison."

She nodded and turned to a blank page in a spiral-bound book in front of her. She glanced at the page for a long moment before she looked up. "Do you have an appointment, sir?"

"No, I'm afraid I don't. But I spoke with her yesterday. My name is Marshal Jack Dillon. I'm with An Garda Síochána," he said and presented the ID hanging on the lanyard around his neck.

Her eyes seem to widen for a moment, and she said, "Let me just call her now." She picked up the phone and a moment later said, "Yes, Miss Harrison. This is the front desk calling. I have a gentleman from An Garda Síochána out here who would like to speak with you. Yes, he did. Umm, Marshal Dillon. Okay, thank you."

A look of relief seemed to wash over her face as she hung up the phone and said, "Miss Harrison said you could go back to her office. Do you know where it is?"

"I do, thank you," Dillon said and headed down a short hallway. Myra Harrison's office was at the end of the hall. The door was open, and he knocked on the door-frame as he entered.

Myra was seated behind her desk and grinned. She closed the file in front of her and said, "Well, you've given our girl up front something to tell all her friends tonight. No doubt they'll be able to link me to whatever this week's major crime is."

"Good to see you again, Myra. Sorry to drop by un-announced. But I was in the neighborhood and wondered if you'd received any news regarding Gretchen Malden or Mary Ellen Schneider?"

"No, interesting you mention it. I was supposed to hear from their roommates today. I'll just place a call."

"Before you do that, let me suggest an alternative. If someone could direct me to their room, I'll knock on the door, and hopefully, one of them will be there. A couple of quick questions, in person, might eliminate any at-tempt to dodge. I did speak to a source at the American embassy today. He confirmed that the girls took a Ryan Air flight to France forty-eight hours ago. They landed in Lille and—"

"And no doubt took a train for fifteen euros into Paris. This has all the earmarkings of a getaway trip on a student budget," she said.

"One can only hope. Would you be comfortable with me talking to their roommates?"

She seemed to think about that and then nodded. "Let me get someone in here to take you over. The girls are in a four-person suite in the Postgraduate Residences, Block B."

She turned in her chair and typed something into her computer, waited a moment, and said, "The roommates are Shannon O'Leary and Meghan Morrissey." While Dillon wrote the names in his pocket notebook, she made a quick phone call. They chatted for maybe ten minutes before a gangly kid with a thin beard knocked on the doorframe.

"Oh, Brian, thank you for coming over. This is Marshal Dillon with An Garda Síochána. Marshal, this is your guide, Brian Gleeson. I'd like you to escort him over to the Postgraduate Residences, Block B."

Brian nodded at Dillon, and Dillon nodded back.

"Once you're there, Marshal, you can go in. Their room is number 206. There's an intercom just inside the entrance. Punch in the room number, and if someone answers, they can buzz you in. I'll be here for at least another hour if you wouldn't mind touching base when you're finished," she said, raising her eyebrows for half a second.

"Not a problem. Thanks for your help," Dillon replied and followed Brian back down the hall. Once they were outside, Dillon stepped next to Brian and asked, "Where are you from, Brian?"

"The west, in Roscommon. A town named Boyle."

"I'm familiar with it, near Kilmactranny?" Dillon asked, mentioning an area near the town.

The kid studied Dillon for a second or two and said, "How do you know that place?"

"I get around, spent a little time out there a few months back."

"You're American?"

"Yeah, I am."

"And you're in An Garda Síochána?"

"That's right. I was assigned a couple of years ago. I was so good back in the States that they sent me over here as sort of a reward, and fortunately, An Garda Síochána isn't sick of me yet."

The kid smiled at that, not sure if Dillon was serious or not. "That's the Postgraduate Residence just over there," he said, nodding in the direction of a five-story gray building ahead. "Just go in that main door, and the security access is right there."

"Thanks for your help, Brian. Good luck at school," Dillon said and held out his hand. They shook hands, more or less. Brian didn't really grip or squeeze. He did smile and nod then hurried back the way they'd come.

Dillon watched him until he disappeared around the corner before going across a brick courtyard with raised flower beds and heading into the building.

The entry was glass on all four sides with a digital phone mounted on the wall. Dillon was about to take hold of the receiver when two young women entered behind him. One of them swiped a keycard for access to the building. As they entered, the taller of the two held the door for a moment, looked at Dillon, and asked, "Coming in?"

"Thanks, but I'll play by the rules," he said and nodded at the digital phone.

"Suit yourself," she said and stepped inside, letting the door close behind her.

Dillon watched them head toward the elevators and thought, *so much for security*. He punched in the number 206 on the keypad, followed by the pound sign, and listened to the rings. He was just about to think it was a failed visit when a voice with an Irish accent answered. "Hello."

"Hi, I'm looking for Shannon O'Leary or Meghan Morrissey," Dillon said, reading the names from his pocket notebook.

"This is Shannon."

"Shannon, my name is Jack Dillon. I'm an American assigned to An Garda Síochána. I'm just checking on a couple of things regarding Gretchen Malden and Mary Ellen Schneider, and I wonder if I could come up and talk with you for a minute or two?"

There was a pause before she said, "Is everything all right?"

"As far as we know, everything is fine. I'm just hoping you can verify a couple of things for us. Would you mind buzzing me in?"

"And you're an American?"

"Yes, assigned to An Garda Síochána. I have an ID I'll show you." There was another pause, this time longer, before the security door buzzed and Dillon heard the lock snap. "Thank you," he said, hung up, and pulled the door open. He entered the lobby and walked to the elevator. He pressed the button for the second floor and gave a quick look around. The place was a lot higher class than the memories he had of a college dorm building.

He stepped onto the elevator as the doors opened and stepped back off on the second floor about five seconds after that. Room 206 was down the hall to the right. His college experience suggested there should be loud music coming from a number of rooms, but the place was actually quiet.

He knocked on the door numbered 206, making note of the fact that a key was required to open the door. No swipe card access to the individual rooms.

"Just a minute," a voice called from the other side. A moment later, the door opened, and a pretty ginger-haired woman with blue eyes smiled at him. He guessed her age at twenty-five, tops. The scent of perfume drifted toward him.

"Hi, Shannon?" She nodded. He held up his An Garda Síochána ID and said, "I'm Marshal Jack Dillon."

"Please, come in. Nice to meet you."

"Thank you," he said, stepping in.

She closed the door behind him and extended a hand toward a sitting area. What looked like a faux leather couch with chrome legs and two matching chairs were arranged around a low square table with a blue Formica top. The upper half of the two windows were open, and two sets of gray curtains were pulled to the side. The view out the window was a line of trees in Albert Park. A plant of some sort sat in the corner and looked like it had seen better days. A small kitchenette was just off the sitting area.

"Please take a seat. Can I get you a tea?"

"You going to have any?" Dillon asked.

"I just put the kettle on, so it should be ready in a minute," she said. He noticed there were already two mugs with tea bags on the Formica counter.

"This is a very lovely setup. I've never been in this building before. All four of you live here?"

"Yes."

"And you each have a private room?"

She shrugged and said, "If you can call it that. There's a bed, a desk, a very small closet, and a chest of drawers." The kettle started to boil, and she raised her voice to be heard. "We share the bathroom, which can get crazy on any given day."

"Are you from Dublin?"

She shook her head, "Enniskeane, County Cork. I'm working on my master's in international business. We all are, as a matter of fact. I've also got a minor in programming."

"Well, then, you're obviously smarter than I am," Dillon said just as the kettle switched off and the noise subsided.

Shannon smiled at the comment but didn't respond. She filled the mugs and asked, "Milk or sugar?"

"No, just the way it is, please."

She nodded toward the couch and chairs and Dillon took a seat in the far chair. Shannon set the mugs on the blue Formica table, stepped back into the kitchen area, and grabbed a small saucer. She set the saucer in the middle of the table and sat in the chair opposite Dillon.

"So, enjoy your tea. Now, what exactly is this about?" she asked as she lifted her tea bag up and down a few times then placed it on the small saucer.

TEN

illon said, "We received a phone message regarding Gretchen and Mary Ellen's trip to France."

"A phone message?" Shannon asked and followed up with a sip of tea.

"Yes. The person, it was a woman who called, left a message. She mentioned Gretchen and Mary Ellen and said they had flown to the continent. We've since determined they flew to France. We suspect they may be in Paris."

Shannon shook her head. "But if they were going to Paris, I think they would have said something, mentioned it to Meghan or me."

"So you were unaware they went to France?"

"I had no idea. I mean, I knew they were gone, but in the past, when they've disappeared, they rode a train to the west of Ireland. I think they've done that twice, and then one time, they went up to Belfast overnight. They were just doing some sightseeing, nothing crazy. If you're thinking they might be transporting drugs or something, I don't think they'd do that. But I can't say for sure."

"Why did you mention drugs?" Dillon asked.

"Just thinking is all. No evidence of any sort. Isn't that usually what someone would do? You know two students, they probably flew Ryan Air. They'd be the cheapest, and I don't think they're all that tough on security. At least that's been my experience the couple of times I flew them," she added.

"Are you aware of the girls using any drugs?"

"I haven't actually seen them taking any, but more than once, they acted like they were completely out of it. That could have been after a night at the pub. I'm not sure. Don't get me wrong. They're really nice, and we all get along well. It's just, I don't know, the drug thing never appealed to me. As far as I know, there isn't a very long list of people who can tell you drugs really improved their life."

"What about their personal lives? Do either one of them have a boyfriend?"

"A boyfriend? If they do, they never mentioned it to me. To be honest, the International Business program is so tough none of us really has time for a boyfriend. Of course, now that I think about it, Gretchen is gone quite a bit. I don't mean off campus or out of town. But with all the schoolwork we have, I'm one of the most boring girls on campus, and she seems to be out almost every night. Sometimes she's here in the morning, and other times, well, you know."

Dillon nodded. He did know what it was to be boring, and he liked things that way. "You mentioned you each have your own room?"

"Yeah, just down the hall. Let me show you," she said and stood from her chair. Dillon followed her down the hall. There were five doors. The door at the end of the hall, the bathroom, was open and displayed a double sink, a toilet, and a shower. It appeared nice enough, although when you factored in four young women, there wasn't all that much room.

Shannon opened the door next to the bathroom. "This is Gretchen's room. All the rooms are the same, not a lot of space. Mary Ellen's is the one right across the hall."

Gretchen's room reminded Dillon of his college dorm. Although this place was compact, it appeared to be up to date. A gray Formica counter was attached to one wall with four electrical outlets along the countertop and four drawers underneath the counter, making a very nice desk. One of the drawers was only partially closed. A single bed was along the opposite wall, and a built-in chest of drawers was at the foot of the bed. Opposite the chest of drawers was a small closet.

There wasn't a lot of room, but the place was functional, at least from Dillon's standpoint.

"You can see there's hardly any room," Shannon said.

"Yeah, I guess, but it's nice and private."

"How about I let you look around? Let me know if you have any questions. I've got a class this evening, and I have to do some prep. Just give a yell if you need anything," she said, waited a second or two, and then disappeared. A moment later, Dillon heard a door open in the hall.

Nothing seemed out of place in the room. As a matter of fact, the room appeared very neat, particularly when compared to what Dillon recalled from his college days. He pulled open the partially closed desk drawer, revealing a Kleenex box and a spiral notebook. He paged through the notebook. It was new since nothing was written in it. Two cords were plugged into outlets along the desktop. They looked like power cords for a computer and a cellphone, which maybe suggested Gretchen would be studying while traveling or, more likely, texting friends.

The dresser drawers contained nothing unusual, and other than a large number of boots and shoes, nothing seemed out of place in the closet. There was nothing unusual in the other three desk drawers. He pulled the rug halfway back, nothing. He lifted the other half and got the same result. He found nothing that suggested Gretchen Malden was involved in anything illegal. He took out a business card and left it on her desk.

He opened the door directly across the hall, Mary Ellen Schneider's room. At no surprise, it was an exact replica of Gretchen's room except that there was a laptop on the desk and a pair of jeans had been tossed on the bed. A stack of what looked like a half-dozen term papers were piled on a corner of the desk. All but two were graded in the upper nineties with a red marker. The two that weren't graded simply had a checkmark on the top sheet, again in red marker. Not quite as many boots were in the closet. He left another business card on Mary Ellen's desk.

He walked to the door, gave the room one more quick glance, and stepped out into the hallway, closing the door behind him. Shannon's door was open, and he knocked. She was seated at her desk, typing something on her computer. She turned as he knocked and said, "Finished already?"

"Yeah, thanks for letting me interrupt your day. If you should hear anything from Gretchen or Mary Ellen, I'd appreciate a call," he said and stepped forward to hand her a business card.

"Sorry I couldn't be of more help. I just don't know what to tell you. Are they in any kind of trouble?"

"Trouble?" Dillon seemed to think for a moment and shook his head. "No trouble. We just want to make sure they're okay. If you hear anything from them, let me know."

She nodded and set the card next to her keyboard.

"I'll let myself out. You take care and thanks again for your help, Shannon."

"Nice to meet you," she said.

As he stepped back into the hall, he could hear her clicking keys on the keyboard.

He took the elevator down to the main floor and walked out the way he'd come. He traced the route back to the university offices in the Henry Grattan Building. The same girl behind the desk smiled as he approached and said, "Did you want to see Myra?"

Dillon nodded and said, "Yes, Jack Dillon with—"

"With An Garda Síochána," she said, finishing for him. She picked up the phone and pressed a couple of keys. "Yes, Miss Harrison, I have Jack Dillon with An Garda Síochána here to see you again. Yes, I will. Thank you."

"You can go back," she said and smiled.

"Thank you," Dillon said and headed toward the short hallway.

ELEVEN

Myra was typing on her computer. Dillon knocked on the doorframe and stepped into the office. Without looking up, she said, "Take a seat, Marshall. I'll finish up in just a moment." Seconds later, she turned to face Dillon. "There. Were you able to talk to anyone?"

"Yes, Shannon O'Leary, nice girl. A woman, actually."

"Yes, in that residence, everyone is working on advanced degrees. I stress the term 'working,' not your usual bit of college, umm activity," she said and chuckled.

"Yeah, I gathered that from the little bit I saw. Nice lady, she seemed surprised they were in France. Maybe that suggests this was a spur of the moment adventure."

"Quite possible. It could be anything from a sightseeing trip to having an appointment with an individual or a company. We have students offered positions in companies all the time and often for a fair amount of money. If either of them received an offer, I could see both of them going over. It can be uncomfortable traveling alone in a strange country."

"A job offer wouldn't come through school?"

"Oh, it certainly could. But they may have applied directly, answered an online request, have a contact, even posted something saying they're looking for the right opportunity. The contact could even be someone they met here, another student, someone who gave a lecture. We have hiring events twice a year. They could have talked to someone at one of those. On the other hand, maybe they just wanted to see the Eiffel Tower for the first time."

"You don't seem too concerned?"

"Half-right. I'm not overly concerned, at least not yet. That said, on any given day, we have one or two girls missing. I use the term missing with caution. We're alerted by parents in a different country, or parents here in Ireland for that matter, when they don't receive their weekend phone call. A boyfriend or girlfriend calls, not realizing the relationship was ended. Quite often, it's someone doing some sightseeing, maybe on the sly since they're missing classes."

Dillon nodded and was about to mention Madeline Keller, a student who was murdered two years ago.

Myra beat him to it. "There was a tragic case, I think, two years ago, fortunately before my time here. An American student was abducted and later found murdered."

"Madeline Keller," Dillon said. "I was involved in the case."

Myra was silent for a moment before she said, "Yes, of course, you were. I'm sorry, Marshal. I didn't put it together. I was informed of the incident once I was hired, but, obviously, it was after the fact."

Dillon nodded and moved on. "Well, hopefully, this won't be a repeat. If you hear anything, please let me know. I left a business card with Shannon O'Leary and left a card on the desks of Gretchen Malden and Mary Ellen Schneider."

"Oh, so you were in their rooms?"

"Yes, Shannon let me in."

"And?"

"And they seem to keep a much better room than I was capable of doing at the same age. Gretchen Malden's laptop was gone, so I'm thinking she may have been involved in something. Possibly a job interview as you suggested, maybe writing a paper, or staying in touch with her family. I find it hard to suspect she was abducted and then brought along her laptop."

"It's sounding more and more like the typical getaway. Still, if I learn anything, I'll pass it on."

"Thank you. I'll let you get back to work, Myra. Always a pleasure, and I'd like nothing better than a call from you telling me this was a false alarm."

"If it's a false alarm, we'll have to celebrate with a pint or a tea."

"That sounds like an excellent idea. I'll look forward to it," Dillon said. He gave a little wave and left her office. "Thanks for the help," he said to the young woman seated at the reception counter as he headed out the door.

He was home not ten minutes later. He pulled into his parking area up against the front of his house and hurried inside before Deitora from next door stepped outside. He turned off his alarm and called up the stairs, "Lucifer."

The sound of Lucifer jumping off the bed and stretching could be heard. A moment later, the dog's black face appeared, doing his usual peek around the upstairs newel post.

"How about a treat, pal?" Dillon called as he stepped into the kitchen, took the lid off the cookie jar, and pulled out a biscuit.

At the sound of the word 'treat' and the lid of the cookie jar, Lucifer hurried down the stairs. "Let's go outside," Dillon said and opened the front door. Lucifer followed and stepped onto the front stoop just as Dillon tossed the biscuit in the direction of the lawn. Lucifer jumped off the stoop and snatched the biscuit on the first bounce. Dillon picked up the day's mail from the floor, two circulars. One was an offer from an internet provider, and the other was a flier from Dublin City Council with the dates at various recycling sites where paint and hazardous materials would be accepted.

He tossed the fliers into the grocery bag for recycling. He thought about a glass of wine, decided against it, and pulled out a bowl of chili and rice from the refrigerator. He guessed the bowl had been in the refrigerator for no more than a week, and he set it in the microwave and turned it on.

He filled Lucifer's food and water dishes, let him back in the house, and they settled down to dinner with the evening news playing on the TV. He went through the laundry list of tv channels four or five times, never seeing anything that caught his interest. He turned off the tv, grabbed Lucifer's leash and the tennis ball, and they headed out the door for their evening walk. Fortunately, the exterior light was on, and he was able to walk around the various piles Lucifer had deposited over the past few days.

As they headed up the lane, Dillon casually glanced over at Tara's house. The black Mercedes was there again, backed into her parking place. Clearly, whoever the guy was, he was quickly becoming a regular. Dillon's first thought was to sneak over and slit the tires, but she'd probably know he was guilty right off the bat, and besides, they'd more or less agreed to look at other people.

Of course, that suggested Dillon had the time and the inclination, which he didn't. They walked up the lane to St. Pappen's Road. Dillon took a left and headed toward the square, a grassy knoll surrounded by houses on all four sides. The closer they got to the square, the more Lucifer picked up the pace. Dillon unhooked the leash once they crossed the street, and Lucifer took off. He ran maybe twenty feet, then circled back and faced Dillon, jumping back and forth. Luckily, the streetlights illuminated the square, and Dillon tossed the tennis ball over Lucifer's head. He raced after it, catching it on the second bounce, then ran back to Dillon, dropping the tennis ball at his feet. Dillon tossed it again, and Lucifer took off.

They kept it up for the better part of twenty minutes until Lucifer returned the ball only partway before settling onto the grass and dropping the ball in front of him. This served as the signal that he'd had enough running for the night, and Dillon reattached the leash, and they headed home.

He crossed over to Tara's side of the lane and walked down past her house. The Mercedes was still there, and for a moment, he thought about memorizing the license plate number before quickly deciding that was not a good idea. Just as they were about to cross to the opposite side of the lane, a light came on on the second floor. Tara's bedroom and the shades were pulled.

It couldn't be more than 8:00, and she was already 'entertaining'? He thought about slitting the tires again as they quickly hurried home. He locked the door once inside and removed his shoes as a deterrent to running over to Tara's place. He decided a glass of wine couldn't hurt and ended up having two while he read a book of no redeeming value on his Kindle.

He woke the following morning before his alarm went off. Lucifer rolled over on the bed and went back to sleep. Dillon thought for a moment or two before crawling out of bed and heading toward the bathroom. Along the way, he adjusted the shutter on the hallway window and glanced across the street. The black Mercedes remained exactly where he'd seen it last night. He showered, shaved, and dressed then went downstairs and poured himself a cup of coffee. He resisted the urge to glance across the lane and instead mixed a bowl of oatmeal and set it in the microwave.

He encouraged Lucifer to get up with a couple of calls using the word 'treat.' After the fourth time, he heard the dog jump off the bed, and a moment later, he popped his head around the upstairs newel post.

"Come on, Lucifer, treat," he called, and the dog hurried down the stairs. Dillon encouraged him outside with a biscuit, all the while not wanting to glance across the lane at the black Mercedes. He filled Lucifer's food and water dishes, let him back inside, and ate his oatmeal leaning against the kitchen counter while watching the morning news on TV.

TWELVE

Dillon was at his desk just after 7:15. He cleared the plate and two tea mugs from his desk and made a fresh pot of coffee. Suel entered maybe a half-hour later. He gave a wave as he headed for the break room and was back in front of Dillon's desk slurping from his tea mug two minutes later.

"Good morning to you, too," Dillon said in response to Suel's slurps.

"I got a call from Billy the Butler early this morning," Suel said and slurped again.

"Describe 'early'," Dillon said.

"Just a little after four. Seems he was enjoying the company of a Russian woman until someone kicked him out. He said they're locked up in a house over in Clontarf and gave me the address. You interested in heading over there?"

"You think he was on the level?"

"Yeah, he sounded upset about his plans being interrupted. Told me this was going to be a payback for letting him see the merchandise and then kicking him out before he was able to sample."

"Must be tough," Dillon said and shook his head. "Yeah, count me in. When were you thinking of going?"

"Sooner the better. I'd like to avoid a repeat of yesterday."

Dillon grabbed his coffee mug, took two swallows, and set the mug down. "Let's go," he said.

They drove up to the north side of Dublin, headed for Clontarf, got onto Clontarf Road, and from there, turned onto Stiles Road. Suel pulled to the curb maybe a half-mile down the road in front of number ninety-four.

It wasn't just a nice neighborhood. It was a very nice neighborhood. Large, two-story homes with a red brick first floor and white stucco on the second floor. All the homes sat behind a three-foot wall. There was a hedge maybe five feet high behind the wall in front of number ninety-four. Every home had an attached garage and a long driveway leading up to the garage.

The homes in the area started at somewhere around eight or nine hundred grand and went up in price from there. Suel stared out the window for a long moment, shaking his head before he said, "This can't be right."

"You don't think they could keep eight women in that place? You could easily fit a dozen of those dumps on Reginald Street in there."

"I'm sure you could. But this is one of those neighborhoods where anyone got wind of that going on, and they'd call the guards for sure. You've probably got three or four solicitors living within sight of this place, not to mention high paid city and county officers."

"Oh, yeah, well, that's certainly a group who wouldn't be involved in crime. Throw in a couple of politicians, and you wouldn't have anything to worry about."

"It just doesn't feel right."

"Which would make it the perfect place. You said Billy phoned you a little after four. There wouldn't be any street traffic at that hour. A quiet neighborhood and that hedge gives them more than enough privacy. Pull the van into the garage and unload the women. No one would actually be able to see the activity. They're tied up inside, gagged. Think about it, Paddy. It's perfect."

Suel drummed his fingers on the steering wheel for a long moment. "We don't have a warrant."

"We could knock on the door and see who answers."

"So we knock, and whoever answers, even if they don't recognize us, they don't let us in. All we've done at that point is warn them that we know. Even if we left and got a warrant, they'd be gone by the time we came back."

"Are you suggesting we do a stakeout?" Dillon asked.

"Not exactly. What if we placed some monitor equipment here? See if there's a pattern. Vehicles coming and going at odd times, like four in the morning. In the meantime, we talk to Billy the Butler. Suggest to him if he really wants a good word put in for him, we have to know who, exactly, is working this."

"You think McCabe will go for that?"

"I don't think he has a choice, Dillon." Suel put the car in drive and continued up the road. Once back in the secure Special Branch section, they headed for DCI McCabe's office. He wasn't in, and Suel left a note. He placed a call to Billy the Butler. He ended up leaving a message suggesting they meet for lunch because he had an idea that just might get Billy's upcoming charges reduced if not dropped altogether.

"Think he'll go for it?" Dillon asked.

"I think at this stage, he'll be desperate enough to try just about anything."

It was close to an hour later when Suel's call was returned. Dillon watched him chatting on the phone for all of ninety seconds before he disconnected and gave Dillon a nod. He walked over to Dillon's desk, carrying a small plate with the remnants of a pastry. "That was Billy. He'll meet us at Haddigan's in a half-hour."

"Haddigan's? Do they even serve lunch?"

"Billy's on what you might call the liquid diet."

"How did he sound?"

"Billy? The usual, hungover. Let's go."

Haddigan's was in a bit of a dicey area of the city center. It was a dingy looking pub from the outside, and nothing really improved once you stepped inside. Dillon could only recall being in the place twice. Once he stepped inside, it became obvious why he hadn't returned.

Billy the Butler was one of four men seated at the bar, each at least four stools apart. None of them looked like the sort you'd start a conversation with. Suel headed toward Billy and gave a nod of his head toward a booth in the back corner. Billy drained his pint and followed.

Suel motioned Dillon into the booth with a wave of his finger and slid in after him. As Dillon slid into the booth, his foot landed on something and he glanced down at a red thong beneath his right foot. Billy the Butler slid in across from them. He nodded at Suel and studied Dillon for a moment.

"How you keeping, Billy?" Suel asked.

"How do you think, Paddy? I'm looking for that good word you promised me. I've got my appearance in eight days, and if you don't put in a favorable report, I'm gonna be doing two to three, mate."

"Billy, it's the same as when we first talked. I can put in a word. Happy to do so, but there has to be a reason, something that's favorable about you. Telling me the address where the women were a night or two ago doesn't really help the cause."

"A night or two ago? When I called you this morning—"

"At half-past four."

"Yeah, well, they were there. All of 'em. You just couldn't be bothered to get your official ass over there."

"You lads want something to drink?" an older man with black hair and a miserable looking combover asked. He was missing a front tooth, which accounted for the lisp.

"A round of pints," Billy said. The man left before Suel or Dillon could object.

"How long are they going to be there? Do they move them somewhere different every night?" Suel asked.

"I don't know how long. They're working on Stiles Road from midnight to four in the morning. I don't know where they are before that. I know that, at four, they get to rest up for the next night."

"How do you know this?" Dillon asked.

Both Suel and Billy stared at Dillon.

"I knew it. You're Paddy's American mate. You're that plonker what shot up them Russians a couple years ago at the airport. Paddy, you told me you weren't going to mention this, and now your man is here?" he said, pointing at Dillon.

"He's the bank," Suel said. "You'd best treat him like a gentleman if you want our assistance."

Billy studied Dillon for a long moment then gave a reluctant nod and said, "Pleased to meet ya's."

The barman suddenly appeared and set three glasses of Guinness on the table. As he set the glasses down, Guinness spilled over the top of all three glasses, leaving a small puddle on the table. "That'll be fifteen euros, lads," the barman said. When he said the word fifteen, spittle sprayed out from the missing tooth space and sprinkled into one of the glasses.

Suel and Billy looked at Dillon. Dillon took a twenty euro note from his pocket, handed it to the barman, and quickly grabbed the pint furthest from the glass just spit in. Suel grabbed the other glass leaving the sprinkled glass for Billy.

Billy grabbed the glass and either didn't care or didn't know. "Keep the change, Petey," he said and gulped down a third of the pint.

"Thirsty?" Suel asked.

"No breakfast," Billy said.

"So, you were telling us they've got the women working there from midnight to four," Suel said.

"Yeah. That's right. I don't know where they were before that. They bring them in at midnight, on the dot."

"Aren't they worried about traffic at night, noise, neighbors catching on?"

"There is no traffic. You have to park down the lane and around the corner. They pat you down before they let you walk up to the place. If someone drives past and pulls in, they're in big trouble. The meetups are by appointment only, no walk-in business."

"And how do you make the appointment?" Suel asked.

"You kidding? You've to call."

"Gee, there's a surprise. You got anything like a number?"

"I got the number for tonight, but they change it every day or so."

"So how do they service repeat customers?"

"Once you call and make an appointment, they text you the new phone numbers for the next two or three weeks."

"And after two or three weeks?" Suel asked.

"Pardon the pun, lads, but you're screwed," Billy said and laughed out loud then drained his glass.

"And you've the number to make an appointment?" Suel asked.

"Yeah, but it's only good for another day or so, and like I told youse, I'm in court in eight days."

"Then you better give me the number right quick so I can get something going."

"I'm just gonna tell you, they call you back, check the likes of you out, so don't go calling from the station thinking you're pulling a fast one. You do that, they'll shut things down in a bleedin' second, and you'll be out of luck."

"Then you better give me the number, now, Billy."

He seemed to think about that for a bit before he pulled out his cell, clicked on a link, and held his phone out for Suel to see. Suel quickly input the number on his phone then looked over at Dillon. "Any questions?"

"No, I'm good."

"Okay. Now, Billy, once I arrange something, I'm going to call you and have you make an appointment. I want you there when we go in. We'll arrest you and then let you go, but I don't want them thinking you were involved in any way. They see you arrested, you'll be off the list."

"Be nice if I had the money to make the appointment," Billy said.

"We'll deal with that just before you go in."

"You know, if I booked two of the girls for my appointment, it might make me just that much more believable."

"I'm not sure you could handle two, Billy. We'll just see about keeping it at one. You make sure you answer the phone when I call because we're going to be moving fast."

Billy nodded and then said, "Another pint might be a bit of an incentive."

"Let me see what I can do. You ready, Dillon?"

Dillon nodded, and they slid out of the booth. Dillon kicked the red thong out from beneath the table. Suel headed toward the bar and said, "Bring another pint over to that knacker in the booth."

"Five euros," the barman said.

Suel tossed a five euro note on the bar and said, "Keep the change." Dillon glanced back at Billy, seated in the booth. The red thong was on the bench next to him. He was in the process of draining Suel's glass and reaching for Dillon's.

THIRTEEN

Kevin Byrne was at the kitchen counter paging through the morning's Boston Globe. He stopped on page five and stared at the picture of Jimmy Dugan and a woman hiding behind a white linen napkin. The copy just below the picture read, *'Jimmy Dugan and an unidentified guest enjoying a recent dinner in Dublin, Ireland.'*

He pulled his cellphone from his pocket, clicked on 'images', and scrolled down to the Dugan photos that had been sent to him the other day. There it was, the exact same image that he had been sent. The article was written by a Boston Globe reporter named Wendell Murphy. The name was familiar, but Byrne was positive they'd never met.

He called the Boston Globe number listed to contact reporters. A recording came on, and after clicking a number three more times and listening to three more recordings, he was able to say Wendell Murphy's name. A moment later, another recording played, "Hi, you have reached Wendell Murphy. I'm unavailable to take your call at the moment, but if you leave a message with your name and phone number, I'll get back to you as soon as possible. Thank you."

There was a beeping sound, and Byrne said, "Hi, Mr. Murphy. My name is Kevin Byrne. I'm with the Federal Bureau of Investigation. I saw your brief article with a picture of Jimmy Dugan. I'd like to discuss the photo and any information you may have. You can reach me on my private cellphone number. The number is…" He finished up with, "Thank you. I look forward to talking with you."

* * *

Wendell Murphy was all smiles as he paged through the morning's copy of the Boston Globe. He'd read his Dugan article twice, initially a little disappointed that his closing paragraph in the article had been deleted. But then his closing line, *'Apparently, Mr. Dugan has nothing to fear living on easy street in the Republic of Ireland,'* more than brought the point home.

He quickly paged through a couple more sections before folding the paper for a closer review later. He turned on his cell phone and noticed he had six messages, no doubt complaints about the article. God bless them. They'd read it and felt strong enough to leave a complaint. He clicked onto his message center and listened. The final message he listened to was the one from Kevin Byrne. He listened to the message twice and then placed his call.

"This is Kevin," was how Byrne answered after the third ring.

"Yes, Mr., or should I say, Agent Byrne, thank you for taking my call. This is Wendell Murphy with the Boston Globe. I had a voicemail from you."

"Yes, Mr. Murphy, I—"

"Please, call me Wendell, or Wendy would be even better."

"Okay, and feel free to call me Kevin. The reason for my call was your article regarding Jimmy Dugan, specifically the picture that accompanied the article. Did you happen to take that photograph?"

"No, I didn't take it," Murphy said, wondering where, exactly, this might be going.

"Would it be possible to meet and perhaps compare notes?" Byrne asked.

"Yes, I could do that. Are you ever in Boston?"

"I'm with the Bureau's Boston office. Would you happen to be free for lunch one of these next days?"

Something clicked, and Murphy had the sense he just might be onto a story. "I could probably do that. You know where the Villa Mexico Cafe is on Water Street?"

"Yeah, I could meet you there. What's your sched-ule look like?"

"I could do today if that works. How does 1:15 work for you?" Murphy asked and crossed his fingers.

"I'll make it work. I'm wearing a navy blue sport coat and a pair of gray slacks," Byrne said.

"I'll be in a light blue shirt with my sleeves rolled up and glasses on top of my head," Murphy replied.

"I look forward to meeting you," Byrne said, and they disconnected.

Murphy went online and Googled Kevin Byrne. A futile attempt that he knew would be doomed from the beginning. He found the Consul General of Ireland at the Irish Embassy in Chicago, a car repair place in Omaha, a number of attorneys, and twenty-plus pages of people named Kevin Byrne. After wasting the better part of an hour and coming up emptyhanded, he placed a call to a friend.

"Hey, Murph, don't tell me you're calling to cancel our lunch."

"Sorry, Tommy, but duty calls."

"Actually, not a problem. I was about to call you. I can't make it either. Let's try to get together next week. If something comes up, give me a ring."

"Thanks, Tommy, hope to see you next week. Thanks for understanding."

Likewise, Murph. Chat later," he said and hung up.

Murphy was heading out the door a little before 1:00. As he walked past Artie Doyle's office, Doyle called, "Hey Murph, give me a minute, will ya?"

Murphy popped his head in and said, "A minute is about all the time I got. I'm on my way to meet a guy for lunch."

"On the Dugan bit?"

"No, another piece I'm working on," Murphy lied. "What'd you want?"

"Just wondered if you had any feedback on the article?"

He shook his head and said, "Just the usual, a couple of anonymous folks calling me names. One guy said they should string Dugan up from the nearest light post. You know, the usual. Thanks for running the article."

"Don't get used to it. I wasn't kidding, Murph. It was a last-minute filler. Just so you know."

"Appreciate it all the same, Artie."

"Get out of here and enjoy your lunch," Doyle said.

The Villa Mexico Cafe was just two blocks from the Boston Globe office. Murphy had lunch there three or four times a month. The cafe was on the ground floor of a six-story building in the middle of the block. The first two floors were adorned with a series of six arches, two-stories high. The first three arches covered the front of the cafe.

Murphy lifted his glasses on top of his head, attempted to focus, and walked in. He looked around and spotted a dark-haired guy in a blue sport coat. He was seated with his back against the wall. He smiled and waved Murphy over.

"Kevin Byrne?" Murphy asked as he approached and held out his hand.

Byrne was on his feet and took hold of Murphy's hand, shaking it with a steel grip. "Nice to meet you, Wendy. I enjoy your work. Thanks for making the time."

"Likewise, thank you," Murphy said. He ignored the comment about enjoying his work. Most people who knew he worked for the paper said the same thing, but very few could mention an article he'd ever written. "You order yet?"

"No, I wanted to make sure you'd show up," Byrne said, and they both laughed.

"We gotta place our orders at the counter. I'm partial to the quesadillas."

"Works for me," Byrne said.

They ordered lunch and Cokes and carried their cups back to the table. They chatted about the Red Sox for a couple of minutes until their quesadillas were delivered, and each took a bite.

"Mmm, you weren't kidding," Byrne said. "This is really good."

"Yeah, you can't beat it, and I can walk here. There's usually a line out the door over the noon hour. That's why I suggested the 1:15 time."

"So, your article on Jimmy Dugan. What prompted that?" Byrne said and took another large bite.

"Well, before we get too far on the subject, let me stress I don't know Mr. Dugan. I've never met him. I think I've written at least a half-dozen articles on the man. Mind you, nothing really in-depth. Of those, the article in today's paper and the first one I wrote back about two years ago are the only ones that have ever been published."

"Why is that?" Byrne asked.

"I'll tell you exactly what I was told. No one cares about Jimmy Dugan. He's yesterday's news. How many years since he disappeared, seven, eight?"

"Actually, it's closer to ten," Byrne said and followed up with another bite of his quesadilla.

"Like I said, yesterday's news."

"But yet you still write about him."

"I still write articles that aren't published."

"Then, why do it?"

"Probably, Agent Byrne, for the same reason you left me a phone message. Somewhere out there are at least nineteen families who have an empty chair at the dinner table on Christmas and Thanksgiving. Their children lost a father, their parents lost a son, and Jimmy Dugan is the worthless son of a bitch who murdered them. Those are just the nineteen families we know about.

"Jimmy Dugan is the bastard who stole money from hard-working families. Jimmy Dugan is the asshole who introduced countless individuals to cocaine and crystal meth, and God knows what else, and destroyed more lives and more families. So when someone sends me pictures of this prick out enjoying dinner with a gorgeous woman or even an ugly woman, I'm not impressed.

"I want to see him arrested and hauled in front of a judge and sentenced to the rest of his life in jail. Where hopefully, the incarcerated population will come to their senses and deal with him."

"It sounds like you have a personal involvement somewhere along the way."

"I had a high school pal, Mickey Sullivan, who died of an overdose. Dugan or some son of a bitch just like him was ultimately responsible. I'd just like them to pay up, that's all. Sorry if I went off on a tangent, but there are all sorts of responsible, educated, intelligent folks out there who look at these characters as folk heroes instead of the evil individuals they really are."

"So back up for a second. You said when someone sends you pictures of Dugan out there enjoying himself."

"Yeah, that's my only connection. I occasionally get photos of Dugan in a restaurant or a pub, almost always in Ireland, although I did get one maybe a year or so ago of him standing in front of the Eiffel tower."

"And you don't know where the pictures are coming from?"

Murphy shook his head and took another bite of his quesadilla. "No idea. I tried to track it, I even had our tech guys on it, but they're from a burner phone and probably servers out of Eastern Europe. No way to track it."

Byrne nodded as he pulled out his cellphone. "That's what I've found, too. Do these images match the ones you received a couple of days ago?" he asked and handed his phone to Murphy.

As Murphy paged through the images, his eyes grew larger and larger. "How in the hell did you get these?

These are the same ones I got, but the only one I ever showed was the one in the article."

"The woman holding the napkin up in front of her face."

"I did some checking. I'm pretty sure they're in a restaurant in Wexford, Ireland called Emerald Gardens."

"What makes you think that?" Byrne asked.

"One of these pictures," Murphy swiped his finger across the screen a couple of times. "Yeah, here it is. This image," he said, handing the phone back to Byrne. "If you look out the window, you can see that sign across the street. Flanagan's. It's a pub in the town of Wexford, and right across the street is this Emerald Gardens res-taurant. I googled the restaurant and their pictures of the place on their website match the background in some of these photos."

"Jesus Christ, and we couldn't find this out," Byrne said.

"Well, it took me almost an hour."

"So in sixty minutes, you come up with this place that our supposed top-secret super search engines couldn't find."

"I guess I never thought of it like that."

"You were on a laptop?"

"Yeah, a MacBookPro. It's about five years old and due to be replaced."

Byrne had a notebook out and was writing things down. "You said Emerald Gardens is the name of the restaurant?"

"Yeah, in Wexford, Ireland."

"So here's my question to you, Wendy. Why are you and I being sent these images? Is Dugan laughing at us?"

"I can't believe he'd even know who I was. Even if he did, why not send them to an editor or the owner of the paper? I'm just one of a couple hundred worker bees at the Globe. It's like he picked my name out of a hat."

"Yeah, and why send them to me? In fact, how would anyone even get my name? I've never been involved in a Dugan investigation. Hell, I was in high school back in Iowa when he disappeared."

FOURTEEN

S uel asked, "You eager to get home tonight?"

Dillon had the phone to his ear and held up a finger. "Hi, Myra, Jack Dillon with An Garda Síochána calling. It's a little before five. Just checking in to see if you heard anything from Gretchen Malden or Mary Ellen Schneider. No news from this end. I'll give you a call at a decent hour tomorrow."

"No news?" Suel asked.

Dillon shook his head. "You were asking about going home tonight. Don't tell me you're looking to go out for pints with Billy the Butler."

"Oh, please. No, but tangent to that situation. I'd like to pay a visit to Nora Scallen. She owns 44 Reginald, where we were the other day. She's living at St. Margaret's Rest Home at the moment."

"You think she'll know anything?"

"She'll know more than she'll let on, and it could be a link to the lads over on Stiles Road."

"Yeah, I'll go if you think it would do any good. You on any schedule? If I could stop at my place and let the dog out—"

"Your dog Devil?"

"Lucifer, actually, but not far from the mark."

"Yeah, we can do that. I might just stay in the car if it's all the same to you."

"Let's go," Dillon said, and they headed out of the office.

Suel followed Dillon and parked halfway on the sidewalk as Dillon pulled into his drive. He pulled the wrought iron gates closed behind his car, unlocked the front door, and stepped into the house. He called for Lucifer and mentioned the word 'biscuit' as he clanged the lid on the cookie jar.

Lucifer hurried down the stairs a moment later. Dillon opened the front door and tossed out a biscuit. Lucifer shot off the front stoop and grabbed the biscuit. He devoured it in two quick bites then hurried over to the front gate and began barking at Suel's car.

Dillon put fresh water in the dish, grabbed another biscuit, and enticed Lucifer back in the house. He turned on the kitchen light and locked the front door behind him. He sidestepped Lucifer's various deposits on the front drive and hopped into Suel's car.

"That thing does not like me," Suel said.

"What can I say? He's a good judge of character," Dillon replied.

It was usually a ten-minute drive under mid-day conditions to St. Margaret's Nursing Home. But this was the Dublin rush hour, so the drive took almost a half-hour. "I should have driven a squad car and turned on the lights and siren," Suel said as he pulled into the parking lot at St. Margaret's.

"Relax, we made it in one piece. Besides, a siren? Do you think anyone would have pulled over for us?"

"Mmm-mmm, I suppose you have a point," Suel said.

Based on the front of the white stucco structure, it looked to have, at one time, been an elegant home, maybe a hundred and twenty years ago. Two long three-story structures were now attached to the rear. Dillon guessed they were rooms for assisted living or independent apartments, depending on the status of the resident. He followed Suel in the main door, and they headed toward a reception counter. A number of delivery boxes from various shops were stacked behind the counter, waiting to be picked up by residents.

"May I help you?" a woman behind the counter asked and flashed a quick smile.

"Yes, we're here to speak with Nora Scallen," Suel said.

The woman wrote Nora Scallen's name on a form then said, "Your name, sir?"

"Paddy Suel."

"Jack Dillon is my name," Dillon said just as she finished writing Suel's name on the form.

"I happen to know she's in the observatory with a number of other residents. They always play cards," she said and smiled as she added Dillon's name to the form.

"And the observatory would be…"

"Oh, just down the hall, second door on the left," the woman replied.

They walked down the hall. The second door on the left was actually a set of white French doors, each made up of fifteen rectangular glass panels. Suel took hold of the brass doorknob and opened one of the doors. They stepped into a lovely long room with what looked like three apple trees, maybe five feet tall, attached to an espalier trellis. Ferns were growing in a half-dozen round glazed pots, and flowers were planted along a concrete path.

Soft music played in the background, and conversation seemed to be coming from the far side of the apple trees. As they followed the path around the trees, they spotted a round glass-top table with a half-dozen elderly people seated at it. Five women and one man, to be exact. Four playing cards were arranged in front of each individual. A stack of coins and five euro notes were piled in the center of the table. A woman with short white hair, clearly the dealer, had her back to Dillon and Suel.

"Nora Scallen?" Suel called.

Everyone suddenly looked up. The woman holding the deck of cards didn't bother to turn around. Instead, she asked, "Who wants to know?"

"An Garda Síochána," Suel said, and with that, everyone but the dealer stood, shuffled down the path, and hurried out the door.

The woman at the table turned and studied them for a moment. "Well, you might as well come over and sit down. You seem to have had the usual effect on people," she said, indicating the recently vacated seats.

As they approached, she quickly gathered the five euro notes and coins. She pulled a large white purse from the floor, stuffed the cash inside, clicked the purse shut, and set it back on the floor.

"So what is it this time? I've told your lot before, I'm retired."

"I'm D.I. Suel. This is Marshal Dillon," Suel said and held out his ID.

"Oh, please, spare me. You interested in a little game of blackjack?" she asked and began gathering the cards from around the table. Dillon grabbed three hands of cards on the far side of the table and tossed them over to her.

"Thank you, darling. What's your name again?"

"Dillon, Jack Dillon."

She flashed a quick smile and turned to face Suel. "So, exactly what is so important that you had to go and ruin my game?"

"We'd like to ask you about number forty-four Reginald."

"Oh, interested in renting, are you?" she asked and smiled.

"We might be. When was the last time it was occupied?"

"Legally? Maybe three or four years ago. With my old age, the memory gets a bit foggy, don't you know."

"And illegally?"

"Well, that's a matter open for discussion. There was the likes of Travelers in and out of the place. Not that I rented to them. They just broke in and took it over. I called you lot so many times I lost count, not that you ever did anything about it. Travelers could be living there right now for all I know. But what's an old woman the likes of me to do about it?"

"Anyone express any interest in it lately?"

"You'd have to check with the firm handling that, but once again, in my advanced age, I seem to have forgotten their name. I think they've a sign in the window with a phone number."

"Any reports of a break-in or damage to the place?"

"Not that I can remember, but then, like I said—"

"I know, your old age."

"Exactly."

"Sounds like we'd better get Dublin city inspections over there to check things out, make sure the plumbing and electric is up to standards, so you can rent the place out. Be a shame to have someone of your advanced age missing out on a nice little monthly rent payment. Well, thank you for your time Miss—"

"Now wait just a bleeding minute here, D.I. Suel. If you—"

"Mmm, you're certainly able to remember names, Miss Scallen. Well done, you. You think you might try to recall who, exactly, is handling the rental of your unit?"

She frowned and said, "It's my son, Bertie. Bertie Scallen. Like I told youse, his number is on the sign in the window."

"And the last time it was rented?"

"Honestly, I don't have any idea. As far as I know, it's been vacant for quite some time."

Suel nodded and stood. He tossed a business card in front of her and said, "All right, then, Miss Scallen. I'd like to thank you for your time. Please call if there's anything I can do to help."

"Sure I couldn't interest you lads in some cards?"

"No thanks. Oh, by the way," Suel said, "the two cards you're missing are just under your leg there."

She reached down and pulled two cards from beneath her right thigh, the queen and king of hearts. "Now, how did that ever happen?"

"Good day," Suel said and headed for the door.

"Nice meeting you," Dillon said as he pushed his chair in.

"A nice lad the likes of you. You could do a lot better," she said.

He smiled, nodded, and headed for the door.

FIFTEEN

Jimmy Dugan logged into his overseas' servers. He did a search on his name to see if anything popped up after the last batch of images he'd sent out. Usually, nothing came of it, and that was fine. In fact, it was great because it suggested no one had any interest in him. Going through the series of servers slowed down any search he was working on, and he was just about to make himself lunch when his laptop dinged, signaling a result.

He clicked on the link, and it brought up a story that ran yesterday in the Boston Globe. He read the story twice and stared at the image of the Irishman, Killian Graham, posed and smiling for whoever was taking the picture. The woman next to him held a white linen napkin up in front of her face.

God Bless her, Jimmy thought. She was the only reason the article ran. Thank God Ireland was mentioned. Just in case anyone was looking for him, they could just fly over there and waste their time.

He noted the reporter's name, Wendell Murphy, and recognized it as one of the names on his shortlist. For whatever reason, he'd apparently gotten Murphy's attention, no doubt the linen napkin photo. He debated for half a moment before he pulled out a burner phone and sent an email to Killian Graham, telling him to take another weekend trip to the same place and send him the images. In the last line, he promised an additional deposit in Graham's bank account.

There was a knock on the office door, and his wife Sarah said, "Jimmy, I'm going now. I won't be back until later this evening. There's leftover—"

Jimmy put the burner phone in the desk drawer and hurried over to open the office door. "Sorry, honey, just working on some tax stuff. You're going to Amanda's?"

"Yes, bridge game with the girls."

"Take a bottle or two of wine."

"Already have them waiting at the door. There's a bowl of chili in the refrigerator and two slices of garlic bread on the kitchen counter for your dinner. Heat the chili in the microwave for two minutes on high. I shouldn't be too late."

"Not to worry. Stay as long as you want. Good luck with the cards."

"Thanks, I'll need it. Amanda plays to win. Okay, catch you later," she said then gave him a quick kiss and headed toward the door.

* * *

Killian Graham was just leaving the Paddy Power betting shop after placing a ten euro bet on Arsenal playing Southhampton tomorrow night. He was feeling lucky and wished he could have bet more, knowing Arsenal was bound to be a sure win, but the finances just weren't there at the moment. Unfortunately, even with a win, he'd only net twenty euros on the bet.

After the trip down to Wexford, he'd wasted close to a hundred euros on Ciara in an attempt to get her in the mood on their last night. All that served to do was make her sicker than a dog. Shots of tequila and Shepard's pie turned out not to be the best combination. She was throwing up in the bathroom of the hotel when he abandoned her and drove back up to Dublin. He was wondering who he could call after he won the Arsenal bet when his cellphone signaled a text message. He pulled out his phone and ran his finger across the screen as he waited for the traffic light to change.

He read the text message, another two hundred euros into his bank account and your man apparently wanted another round of photos from Wexford. *Fine with me,* Killian thought. *I'll just—*

The blare from the car horn caused him to look up. Apparently, he'd stopped in the middle of the street to check his text message. He could read the lips of the guy behind the wheel. Not all that pleasant. Killian gave him a thumbs-up as he hurried to the curb. The guy behind the wheel gave him the finger and sped down the street.

Killian waited for the light to change and hurried back into Paddy Power. He added another fifty euro to his original bet and headed back to the street. He hadn't walked ten feet when a voice called out, "Killian?"

He turned to face a black-haired beauty with piercing blue eyes, Riona Fortane. The last time he saw her, she'd told him to never, ever, call her again. Now, here she was, calling to him on the street.

"Riona, nice to see you. Long time no see. How have you been keeping?"

"It's been too long," she said and flashed a gorgeous smile.

"Still married, are you?" he asked, knowing the answer and thinking, *Serves you right after dumping me for some knacker who took you for everything.*

"One year left on our separation before I can file for divorce."

"You working?" he asked.

"Mmm-mmm, looking. It's a tight market just now. You?"

"I've been working on investments. Took a while, but it's finally starting to work very nicely," he said, making it up as he went.

"Investments? You?"

"Yeah, who knew? As a matter of fact," he said, "I'll be heading down to Wexford in a bit. Just want to check out some potential opportunities. It's fun. I stay in nice hotels, have a couple of nice meals. Helps to take the stress off, you know."

"Mmm-mmm, I know about the stress, believe me. About the only place I've been of late is to the grocery store. Wexford sounds absolutely divine."

That was simple enough, he thought. "Well, you're more than welcome to join me. I'd love to take you to dinner and catch up on what you've been doing with yourself."

"You're serious?"

"Yeah, come on along. You can book some time in the hotel spa while I check some things out."

"You're not playing me, now, are you Killian?"

"No, I'm serious. Might be nice if you showed your appreciation," he added.

"Hah, I knew it."

"Okay, well nice to see you. Take care of yourself and—"

"Hold on. I didn't say no. I'll appreciate you, baby. Believe me, you'll be very appreciated."

"Good. I'll pick you up in two hours. You still at the same place?"

"Not anymore. That no good ex of mine sold the place out from under me. I'm actually just around the corner, number nine, Castle Terrace."

"Nine Castle Terrace," Killian repeated the address, knowing the street was a series of small homes converted to one-room units. "I'll see you in two hours."

"Mmm-mmm, thank you, darling. We'll have a great time," she said. She planted a long kiss on his lips and hurried down the street.

Killian waited a full minute before heading back to his place above the hairdressers. Fortunately, his suitcase remained unpacked on the bedroom floor. He replaced his underwear and socks with two fresh sets and hurried out the door. He flagged a taxi and took it to the Enterprise Car and Van Hire just across the Royal Canal from Croke Park. Fortunately, the American's credit card was accepted, and Killian figured since the instructions in his recent email were to live it up and take plenty of pictures, the rented Audi A4 would be just the thing to make a good impression. He was back at his apartment with thirty minutes to spare.

He grabbed a quick shower, shaved, and was stylishly ten minutes late as he pulled in front of number nine Castle Terrace.

The small stucco structure was one of a dozen attached units. Number nine appeared to have been painted powder blue twenty or thirty years ago. There were four black mailboxes hanging next to the front door. As Killian stepped out of the Audi, the front door opened, and Riona hurried out, pulling a suitcase behind her.

She stopped halfway to the shiny black Audi and asked, "This is your car?"

"Yeah, is this okay?"

"It's gorgeous. I love it."

"It's comfortable, too. Hop in while I put your suitcase in the boot."

Once he climbed in behind the steering wheel, Riona leaned over, rubbed his thigh and ran her tongue in his ear. "Oh, we are so going to enjoy this. Let's go," she said and buckled up.

SIXTEEN

Dillon had a quiet night at home. Just after 8:00, he clipped the leash onto Lucifer's collar, and they went out for their evening walk. He was relieved to see Tara's car was the only one parked in her drive. He took a left at the top of the lane, and they waited for a car to pass before crossing to the square. After fifteen minutes of chasing the tennis ball, Lucifer had had enough, and they headed back home. Dillon dozed off on the couch watching an episode of Henry the Eighth on the History Channel.

He was up at 5:30 the following morning. He made a breakfast of scrambled eggs and rashers, let Lucifer out, filled the food and water dish, and checked the American news sites on YouTube for thirty minutes before he headed into the office.

Suel was already at his desk and on the phone. He gave a nod as Dillon walked past. Dillon stacked the three plates and two tea mugs deposited on his desk. He grabbed his coffee mug and carried everything into the break room. He poured himself a coffee and took a sip, expecting the worst. Actually, it wasn't bad, and he headed out to his desk just as Suel hung up his phone and strolled over.

"That wouldn't happen to have been Billy the Butler on the phone, was it?" Dillon asked.

"I only wish, but it might be something. Bertie Scallen, Nora's son. It seems we made enough of an impression that she called him last night. I'm meeting him at 44 Reginald in about an hour. You're welcome to join me."

"Let me place a call to DCU and see if anything is happening."

Suel headed into the break room as Dillon punched in Myra Harrison's number.

She answered on the third ring. "Myra Harrison."

"Hi Myra, Jack Dillon, just checking in. You hear anything from the girls?"

"No, nothing, which isn't too surprising. They may well have their cellphones turned off, just to save money. Calls are far more expensive once they travel out of the country. The average rate is something like a euro-fifty a minute. Suddenly, even the shortest of conversations with a friend is costing you five euros. I'm guessing they're either bunking with someone over there they know, probably another student. Or, they're spending the night in a hostel, which is usually safe but not the most private of places. Again, I'm not worried, and other than that one phone call, at this stage, we wouldn't even know they were gone."

"Yeah, the phone call is the strange item. No other contact, a text message or an email?"

"No, nothing."

"Okay, just staying in touch. Anything changes, let me know."

"I appreciate your concern. Hopefully, everything will turn out to be just two more students availing themselves of Paris."

"All right. I'll check in at the end of the day."

"I look forward to it," she said and chuckled just before she disconnected.

Dillon glanced over at DCI McCabe's office. The lights were still off, and the door was closed. He walked over to Suel's desk. "You know, Paddy. If we left now, we might miss DCI McCabe for the better part of the day."

Suel gave a quick glance in the direction of McCabe's office and said, "Good idea, let's go."

They took the staircase down to the ground floor just to avoid a chance meeting with McCabe in the elevator. Suel waved at the guard monitoring the entrance and exit from the parking lot, and they drove over to the Liberties section of Dublin and 44 Reginald. This time, Suel parked directly in front of number 44. He pulled up and over the curb, covering half the sidewalk, and turned the car off.

Dillon stepped out of the passenger side and stretched. As Suel climbed out from behind the wheel, a grayish Ford Fiesta pulled in behind them. A man stepped out wearing a light blue Dublin jersey and casual black trousers. Dillon pegged him at forty, maybe forty-five. He appeared to be in reasonably good shape. He had a deep red scar at the base of his chin, maybe a half-inch long. If this had been Minnesota, Dillon would have guessed a hockey injury. Here in Dublin, it probably meant hurling.

"Bertie Scallen?" Suel said.

"Right, and you must be D.I. Suel. I recognize the voice. Pleased to meet you, sir. Thank you for making the time."

"Same to you, I'm sure you've other things to do. How's the business going?"

"Oh, you know, different day, new set of problems. Let's step inside. Youse can take a look," Scallen said and took a set of keys from his pocket. The keyring appeared worn and looked similar to a cheap one Dillon had purchased two years ago at Carroll's, a tourist shop. The metal tag on the key ring read IRELAND in gold letters on a green background. This particular one that Scallen held had all the color rubbed off.

Dillon found it interesting that someone supposedly in sales didn't bother to ask him his name. It was a ploy he and Suel occasionally used, adding some pressure without having to say anything. Not always the case, but it oftentimes suggested the individual they were meeting was nervous, probably guilty of something, and preparing a defense before anything was said.

Scallen unlocked the door, pushed it open, and said, "After you."

They stepped inside to a clean front room. The worn gray blanket and the soiled pillow in front of the coal-burning fireplace were nowhere to be seen. There was a slight scent of something, not necessarily unpleasant, possibly remnants of a cleaning solution.

"When was the last time you were in here?" Suel asked.

"Oh, honestly, I can't recall. Four or five weeks at least, maybe more. I know it's my mom's place, but there isn't much call for a rental without a workable kitchen. Come on, let me show you," he said and took a half-dozen steps into the kitchen area. The empty whiskey bottle was missing, and the broken window had been replaced.

Interestingly, the original five panes of glass had been cleaned to match the new pane that had been installed. If you didn't know the pane had been broken, you'd never have picked up on it.

"I see what you mean about having a tough time to rent the place," Suel said. "Mind if we take a look upstairs?"

"No, not at all. Follow me," Scallen said and headed back into the small front room and up the stairs.

"Any problems with break-ins? I know the area can be a bit dicey," Suel asked as they climbed the staircase.

"No, nothing like that. To be honest, it's common knowledge the place is empty and there's nothing to take, no furniture, nothing like a refrigerator or a micro-wave."

"So whoever rents would bring their own furniture?" Dillon asked.

"Yeah, exactly," Scallen said as he stepped into the second-floor room. The room was spotless. The thong, bits of twine and duct tape, the toilet paper tube were all gone. Suel casually stepped over to the bathroom mirror and glanced at himself then looked down at the toilet.

"So if someone wants to rent, would you have to install a kitchen?" Suel asked.

"We have a small warehouse where we house those items. We could have a small refrigerator and an electric burner here the same day the contract is signed. I know someone who could reinstall the sink."

"Nice," Suel said, meaning anything but. "Very nice. You must run one hell of a business."

"It's a lot of work, but I love doing it, so I consider it a labor of love," Scallen said.

"And no break-ins?" Suel said.

"None that I'm aware of. Like I said, the word out on the street is there's nothing here worth the trouble of breaking in."

"I'm sure that serves you well. I'd like to thank you for making the time, Bertie. Would you happen to have a card I can hang on to? Never know when we might run into someone who needs a roof over their head," Suel said as he handed Scallen one of his business cards.

"It would be my pleasure," Scallen said as he took Suel's card and handed one of his own to both Suel and Dillon. "Now, no offense, but I hope I won't feel the need to call," he chuckled as he looked at Suel's card. He glanced at Dillon's card and did a bit of a double-take. Studied Dillon for a second or two and then said, "Have a wonderful rest of the day, gentlemen."

Dillon and Suel headed down the stairs and out of the flat. Scallen stepped out a moment later, locked up, and then waved as Suel pulled off the sidewalk, into the street, and headed up to the corner.

"So what'd you think?" Suel asked as he turned at the corner and headed toward the river Liffey.

"He's hiding something. Estate Investments is the name of his company," Dillon said, reading the business card. "Amazing, the place was cleaned, and the window-pane replaced. Did you notice the entire window had been cleaned?"

"Yeah, and that toilet upstairs had been sorted. I was tempted to flush it but didn't want to take the chance. Your man is hiding something."

"You think it's cleaned up for another set of women to be brought in?"

Suel nodded. "Oh, I think there could be a pretty good chance of that. My guess is he's no idea we were ever in the place. With everything cleaned up, he's probably thinking he pulled the wool over our eyes. But someone got to him with a warning."

"His mother," Dillon said. "She probably had him in there, cleaning the place till all hours of the night."

"Not to mention scouring the toilet. Oh, God in heaven, but that would have been an awful task."

"So, now what?"

"We might keep an eye on the place. I'm still more focused on Stiles Road. I haven't had a chance to look up Dublin county records to see who owns the place. I'll do that as soon as we're back. In the meantime—"

"In the meantime, I'd like to do a little research on Nora Scallen and her son, Bertie. That name ring a bell with you?"

"Nora Scallen?" Suel asked and shook his head. "What is she, eighty? She could have easily been out of the biz for the past twenty years. See what you can find out. There may not be anything there. Statute of limitations has probably expired on all of her activity."

As Suel drove into the parking lot, he waved at the officer at the entrance and pulled into an open space in the far corner of the lot. They took the elevator up to Special Branch. Dillon waved his I.D. over the keypad, and the door lock snapped open. The first thing they noticed was the lights were on and the door was open to McCabe's office.

"Oops, the boss is in, best behavior," Suel said.

SEVENTEEN

Killian Graham rolled over and glanced at the digital clock on the bedside table. It was almost one in the afternoon. He took a deep breath and slowly exhaled, which seemed to lessen the pounding in his head. He rolled over and studied Riona for a long moment. He couldn't make out the bits of pink on her breasts and the pink smears on the bedsheet until he spotted the can of colored whipped cream on the bedside table next to her.

Foggy images slowly drifted back to him. They were in the Riverbank House Hotel. That much he remembered. They'd driven to Wexford, had a pleasant drive down. As a matter of fact, he recalled Riona exposing herself in the car for a minute or two as they drove down on the M11. They'd checked into the hotel and had an 8:00 dinner reservation at the Emerald Gardens. He recalled parking down the street from the Emerald Gardens and stopping for a drink at Flanagan's before dinner. They'd actually stayed for two drinks and had to hurry across the street for their reservation. He'd ordered a bottle of wine with dinner and another bottle with dessert.

It was at that point that things began to grow hazy. He knew they'd returned to Flanagan's. He remembered Riona asking some guy at the bar to join them in their hotel room. Somehow, they made it back to the hotel, talked the barman into a round as he was closing, and the rest was a big blank. Too bad, it was probably a good memory. He lifted his trousers from the floor and took the cellphone out of his pocket.

He opened the 'Gallery' site, and thankfully, there were eight new images. Two of them at Flanagan's before dinner and two at the Emerald Gardens dinner table. Another one at Flanagan's where the glazed eyes on Riona's face looked like she couldn't see more than six inches in front of her. A picture of the two of them standing at the hotel bar with a very unhappy looking barman behind them. Two blurry images of naked Riona posing on all fours back in the hotel room finished up the group. Killian deleted the last two images and texted the packet off to the American. He wasn't sure how pictures of two over-served people in a pub would work for the tourist trade, but why question the guy who was paying the bills?

He set his phone on the bedside table, quietly climbed out of bed, and made his way into the bathroom. After shaving, the long hot shower seemed to do wonders for his head. He quietly dressed and thought about waking Riona.

Sometime in the last thirty minutes, she had pulled a pillow over her head. He decided the better plan might be to leave a note. He wrote a quick message, explaining he was down in the restaurant. He tiptoed out of the room and quietly closed the door behind him.

"Ready for the room to be cleaned?" a woman pushing a white cart down the hall asked. She wore a light blue vest with the hotel monogram over her left breast. The cart was filled with a stack of clean white towels and dozens of small bottles of shower gel, skin cream, and mouth wash.

"Actually, umm, no, not today. My friend is in there napping, and we're okay for today. We're not checking out until tomorrow."

"Are you sure, sir? I could come back later," she said and nodded at the 'DO NOT DISTURB' sign hanging from the doorknob.

"No, we're just fine. Thanks for asking."

"Very well, enjoy your day," she said and pushed the cart further down the hall.

Killian settled in at a table in a quiet corner of the restaurant and ordered a full Irish breakfast. He was on his second tea when the breakfast arrived, two fried eggs, black and white puddings, rashers, fried tomatoes, and two pieces of toast. He ordered another tea and settled into his breakfast. He'd just covered the last slice of toast with a half-inch of blackberry jam when Riona entered the restaurant and made her way toward his table. Other than staff they were the only people in the place.

He thought she looked a little worse for the wear as she pulled out a chair and sat down. "How'd you sleep?" he asked.

She just stared for a moment.

The server suddenly appeared and asked, "Something for lunch, ma'am?"

"I think just some tea and some aspirin if you have any."

"Very good," the server said as if that was an everyday request and hurried off.

"How's the head?" Killian asked and took a bite of his toast.

"I think I'll make it, maybe. How much did we have to drink last night? No, wait, don't answer. I don't want to know. Thank you for the dinner and the bit I do remember. I must have enjoyed myself because I could barely walk climbing out of bed this morning."

"You were very good," Killian said, thinking *the two blurry images he's deleted suggested just that.*

"I'm sorry, but I can't recall. It all grows a bit hazy after our dinner."

"You don't recall stopping in at the church?"

"What?"

"Just kidding," he said as her tea and a small bottle of aspirin arrived.

EIGHTEEN

Jimmy Dugan walked into the kitchen and poured himself a cup of coffee. He'd gone to bed a little after ten last night, and Sarah had still been out at her bridge game. All that meant was that he had the morning hours to himself. He carried the coffee into his office, closed the door, and turned on his computer. He logged into the credit card account he had set up for Graham, the Irish guy. There was a charge for a rental car, drinks at a pub, dinner at the same restaurant as last week, and more drinks. Good, he was doing exactly what Jimmy had hoped he'd do.

He was about to log onto another account when one of the burner phones vibrated in the desk drawer. He unlocked the drawer, pulled it open, and grabbed the phone he'd used to send instructions to Graham. A text message had just come through from Graham, and he clicked on the link.

There they were, six different images. Same restaurant as the previous batch, and both appeared to have had too much to drink. Perfect. As far as anyone would know, it was Jimmy living it up. Clearly a different woman than last time, no less attractive, but everyone would think he felt free to play the field. He brought up his list of recipients and proceeded to text the images to them. He could only hope it would generate another newspaper article.

He'd never done it before, but he added a line to the text message he sent to the Boston Globe reporter, Wendell Murphy. **'Dugan was out last night living the life.'** He reread the line then pressed send.

* * *

Wendell Murphy was driving his boys to school. He felt his cellphone vibrate in his pocket, signaling a text message as he turned the corner to the school. They waited in line, inching their way toward the front entrance, where he could let the boys out of the car.

"Oh, Dad, I need five dollars for school this morning," his oldest suddenly said.

"Five dollars? What on earth for?"

"We're going on a school trip to the museum on Friday, and we have to pay before we go."

The car moved forward two lengths. "A school trip? How long have you known about this?"

"I don't know, but today's the last day to pay."

"Do you have any information on the trip," Murphy asked and pulled forward another length.

"Umm, I gave it to Mom."

He pulled forward again and stopped in front of the entrance then turned and looked at his son.

"Honest, Dad. I really did give it to her. At least I think I did. But today's the last day. If we don't pay, we have to spend the time in study hell."

"I think you mean study hall, Brenden."

"Can I please have the five dollars? Please?"

Murphy gave a long sigh and pulled out his wallet. He had a ten-dollar bill and nothing else. "I don't have it. Tell your teacher you'll bring it in tomorrow, and then you remind me tonight when—"

A car honked from two cars behind, followed by another car honking.

"Please, Dad, please. I hate study hell."

Murphy pulled out the ten and waved it at his son. "Okay, but I want the change tonight. Got it?"

Brenden nodded and opened the passenger door. His younger brother hopped out of the backseat, slammed the door, and ran into the school.

"Please, Dad?"

"Okay, when do I get the change?"

"Tonight?"

He handed the ten-dollar bill to his son. Three horns behind them honked. One guy leaned on the horn for a long moment.

"All right, go, go. I want that change tonight."

"Thanks, Dad," Brenden called as he slammed the door. He ran inside as his father pulled away from the curb.

Murphy set the paper cup with coffee on his desk and picked up the phone. 'You have fourteen new messages. First message,' the recording said, and Murphy listened to a woman complain about the Jimmy Dugan article. Among other things, she mentioned that Dugan had threatened her uncle and was suspected of burning his liquor store in 1999, although he was never charged. She didn't leave a name.

He went through the list of messages, all complaints regarding Jimmy Dugan. He listened to all fourteen messages and took notes. Five people left their names. Everyone had a story about Jimmy Dugan and the damage he had done to their business, home, or family. There were three assaults, a half-dozen robberies, and a lot of unhappy people.

When he had finished, he typed up his notes and printed them off. He took a sip from the paper cup of now cold coffee and headed for Artie Doyle's office. He knocked on Doyle's office door as he stepped into the office.

Doyle was on the phone. He smiled and pointed to the chairs in front of his desk. "Actually, he just stepped into my office. Yeah, we're on it. We'll have something at the three o'clock meeting. Right," Doyle said and hung up.

"I don't believe it, Murph. Three emails to the editor yesterday, and two phone calls to the opinion page on a page five article we put in at the last minute."

"Add to that, the fourteen messages I had waiting for me this morning," Murphy said and handed Doyle the two pages of notes he'd typed up. "Maybe someone really does care."

Doyle shot a quick look but didn't respond.

Murphy's cell phone rang. "Let me just check this, Artie, and see if… Hmm-mmm, I gotta take this. My new pal with the FBI."

"Go ahead," Doyle said and set the notes on his desk.

"Yeah, Kevin. Good morning. What's up?"

"Did you get the new batch of pictures?" Byrne asked, not bothering to take time to say hello or ask how Murphy was doing.

"Pictures? Of Jimmy Dugan?"

"Yeah, did you see them?"

"No, I didn't get anything from… Oh shit. I was dropping the kids at school when a text came through. Damn it, I completely forgot about it. Let me check, and I'll call you right back."

"A half-dozen images, same routine except that he and this woman he's with look like they were really partying."

"The woman with the linen napkin?" Murphy asked and nodded at Doyle, sitting behind his desk and all ears.

"No, different woman. Dark hair, very attractive, not that the last one wasn't. But definitely not the same one. Check them out and call me back."

"I'll get back to you as soon as I can. We got a lot of folks calling in on that article yesterday."

"What'd they say?"

"Mostly just stories about what an asshole Dugan was or is. Nothing like a current address if that's what you're wondering."

"Okay, take a look at this next batch and then give me a call. I've already put a call into my boss."

"Talk in a bit," Murphy said and disconnected.

"The FBI?" Doyle asked.

"For some reason, he gets the same images as I get. Guy's name is Kevin Byrne, originally from Iowa, of all places. He's an agent with the Bureau's office here in Boston. He called me yesterday after he saw the article. He gets the same images from some unknown source. Apparently, a new text came through this morning. I got sidetracked dealing with one of my geniuses," Murphy said as he touched his cellphone screen a couple of times to get to the text message.

"Yeah, sure as hell, here it is," Murphy said and clicked on the images, looking at them one at a time before handing the phone to Doyle.

"My call was from Megan Brown," Doyle said.

"Megan Brown? That's pretty far up the chain."

Doyle nodded and said, "They want something for tomorrow morning's front page. You just got these this morning? How old do you think they are?"

"I'm thinking twenty-four hours, but there's no way to prove that. It's Dugan at the same place as the last

bunch, but with a different woman. It just looks different. He's wearing the same shirt, I think, but he's at a
different table. That painting in the background wasn't
on the wall before. The bar picture looks like the same
place, but a different bartender. That last place where he
and the woman look absolutely shit-faced that's a different place than the other bar pictures and take a look at
the bartender, not a happy camper."

"I'm thinking we run one of the bar pictures where
they're just having a drink, this restaurant picture with
the two bottles of wine, and this one with the unhappy-
looking bartender," Doyle said and handed the phone
back to Murphy.

"Three pictures?" Murphy said.

Doyle nodded. "Our readers are hungry for it."

"Word count?"

"Give me two thousand and expect some editing.
But it's going to run on page one, below the fold."

"I'm on it," Murphy said and hurried out of the office.

"Hey, Murph," Doyle called, and Murphy stuck his
head back in. "Chat up your pal with the Bureau. See
what he knows. We can maybe run a side story on Sunday."

"I'll chat him up. I'd like to write that Sunday
piece."

"We'll see. Just get this one done for now. Might
not be a bad thought to meet up with your Fed friend, go

ahead and offer to buy dinner or better yet a lunch, and I'll okay the meal expense."

"That's awfully big of you, Artie," Murphy said.

"It is what it is. Now get to work and well done. Now go."

NINETEEN

After lunch, Dillon headed back to his desk with a fresh cup of coffee. He was surprised there hadn't been any plates or mugs waiting to be hauled into the break room sink. He settled in behind his desk and noticed the light flashing on his phone, signaling a message.

He picked up his phone and listened to his message. "Yeah, Jack, Eric Bergman. Just a heads up. The FBI sent a copy of a newspaper article from the Boston Globe to our office. The article was about some gangster named Jimmy Dugan, who was photographed at a restaurant down in Wexford. The embassy forwarded the article, and whatever information they received, I think, to Special Branch. I'm waiting for clarification on that but thought I should let you know the email is out there somewhere, and you may be the logical guy it gets dropped on."

Like he didn't have enough to worry about between missing college girls and Russian women in the sex trade. He was about to phone Bergman back when McCabe stepped into his office doorway and called, "Dillon, Suel, a moment of your time, please."

Suel glanced over at Dillon as he stood from his chair. Dillon waited for him to come over and said, "Just got a message from Eric Bergman. Something about some American thug photographed down in Wexford. The FBI sent something to the embassy then passed it on to the powers that be here."

"Shite sake," Suel said and followed Dillon into DCI McCabe's office.

"You wanted to see us," Dillon said as they entered.

"Take a seat, lads. A note from the American embassy," McCabe said and opened a file. He pulled out a copy of the article from the Boston Globe and pointed at the image of the woman with the white linen napkin held up in front of her face.

"Seems your woman was having dinner with an American gangster, some knacker by the name of Jimmy Dugan. You familiar with him?" McCabe asked Dillon as he handed the copy of the article across the desk.

"Only by name. I've never met the man. I can check, but I thought he'd disappeared some years back."

"Mmm, that may be why he was photographed down in Wexford. Either of you familiar with a restaurant down there named Emerald Gardens?"

Both men shook their heads.

"I'd like you to drive down there tomorrow. Ask around the place, show them this article. Someone took the photo. Maybe it was a staff member."

"Drive down there, sir? Couldn't we just phone them?" Suel asked.

McCabe shook his head. "This has all the earmarks of some innocuous situation that could come back to haunt us. I'd like the two of you down there in person to interview and close this up as fast as possible."

"Do we even know when this photo was taken, sir? It could have been five or ten years ago," Dillon said.

"All the more reason to have you down there in person. If that's the case, a sworn statement should serve as a nice cover should something pop up six months or a year from now. Tidy things up here and head down in the morning. Questions?"

"No sir," they said in unison.

"Bloody hell," Suel mumbled when they were back at Dillon's desk. "Let's plan on leaving early tomorrow morning. Can you pick me up?" Suel asked.

"Why do I have to drive?"

"Because I live closer to the M11. Besides, that way, you can drive past the takeout and bring me a tea."

"God. Okay I'll drive, seven tomorrow morning. Be ready," Dillon said.

TWENTY

Killian was lying next to Riona when she finally woke. She was under the bed covers, still dressed, unfortunately. He was on top of the bed with two pillows wedged behind him, watching some worthless game show.

"Oh, I must have dozed off. What time is it?" she asked and stretched beneath the covers.

"Almost five."

"Almost five? Did I miss my spa appointment? Why didn't you wake me?"

"I tried," Killian lied. "But you told me to leave you alone. Told me you didn't want to go."

"Oh, God, why do I do these things?"

Killian figured he could come up with a number of reasons but decided it might be best not to say anything. "You hungry? You haven't eaten all day."

"Yeah, tell me about it. I'm starving. Do you have someplace in mind?"

"As a matter of fact, I thought it might be nice to take you to a nice little five-star restaurant that specializes in seafood. You still have a thing for seafood?"

"Oh, that would be so perfect. Think they'd have mussels?"

"I know they do."

"Give me just a minute to get cleaned up."

"Don't worry about it. Take all the time you need. Our reservation isn't until seven," he lied. "We'll drive over once you're ready. It's maybe ten minutes from the hotel."

She was suddenly out of bed and hurrying into the bathroom. Killian thought the two and a half-hour nap and the seafood ploy just might have been two of his better ideas. He waited until he heard the shower running then looked up the number and phoned, hoping he could still get a reservation.

Fortunately, he'd been able to get a reservation for seven, but since Riona hadn't finished putting on her makeup until seven, they were stylishly late. They found a parking place just around the corner from the restaurant. The La Côte Restaurant was located in a three-story building on Wexford's Custom House Quay and overlooked the harbor. The interior was pleasant but certainly not ostentatious.

"Good evening," the woman said from behind a small counter. "Do you have a reservation?"

"Yeah, hi. We've got a reservation for seven," Killian said and gave his name. "She checked on a list and led them through the main dining area to a small back room. There was a table for two next to the window looking out on the harbor.

"Oh, perfect," Riona said once they were seated. "This is so gorgeous. Look at all the fishing boats."

"Yeah, I thought you might like it, so I reserved this table for us," Killian lied.

She shrugged her shoulders in delight, reached out, and squeezed his hand. "You are so sweet. Playing your cards right for later tonight."

"Hoping to, glad you're feeling better."

"I guess I really needed that nap."

"And those six aspirins you had. I think a white wine might be just the thing with your seafood."

"Mmm-mmm, maybe just a glass for me. I'd better watch the drinking tonight."

"May I interest you in a beverage?" the server asked. He was a tall man, maybe six feet, with close-cropped hair and a white apron that hung almost to his ankles. He had a French accent.

Killian opened the wine list, looked at the prices for the white wines, and pointed to one he couldn't pronounce that ran a hundred and twenty-eight euros a bottle. "Yeah, here we go. I like this one. We'll start with that."

"An excellent choice, sir. It will be but a moment," the server said and left.

"What looks good to you?" Killian asked.

"Oh, everything. I think I'll go for the steamed mussels."

Their server returned with the wine. He poured a small amount in Killian's glass, showed him the label, and indicated with a nod of his head that Killian should take a taste.

He did, nodded, and said, "Fill 'em up."

"But of course, sir," the server said and filled their glasses. "And have you made a decision?"

Killian nodded and pointed to Riona. When they had finished placing their orders, and the server departed, Killian lifted his glass toward Riona. They clinked glasses, and both took a hearty sip. They were finishing their second glass of wine when the dinners arrived, mussels for Riona and flank steak for Killian. He ordered another bottle of wine. It never crossed Riona's mind to object.

They each ordered the meringue dessert, and once they were finished, Killian asked their server to take a couple of pictures. He did so gladly.

They walked down the street to a pub where Killian had a whiskey, and Riona ordered a Cosmopolitan. "I hear it's big in the states," she said when Killian asked her what it was. The bartender took their picture, and after two more Cosmopolitans, they were back in their hotel room wrestling in bed.

Killian woke just after ten the following morning. Riona had a pillow pulled over her head, which was just fine with him. After two nights of blurry recollections of sex, he'd had about enough of her. He took his cellphone from his pants pocket and walked into the bathroom. He sent the photos off to the American. There were only three, two from the restaurant and another from the pub with Riona pulling her blouse open to display her attributes.

He showered, dressed, waited fifteen minutes to see if Riona woke up, and left the room. He pulled the DO NOT DISTURB sign from the doorknob, slipped it under the door, and headed down to the restaurant for breakfast.

He had a pot of tea with breakfast and ordered a second to help wash down the aspirins he took for his hangover. He'd just poured the remnants of the second pot into his cup when Riona appeared at the door and made a beeline to his table.

"How did you sleep?" he asked as she pulled out a chair and sat down. She stared down at the table with her hands on her forehead.

"My head is killing me. I could have done with the rest of the day in bed, no thanks to the cleaning staff."

"They woke you?"

"Knocked on the bloody door, or should I say, pounded. God, I thought my head was going to explode."

"Sounds like we'd better get you a tea and some aspirin."

"Please," she said and closed her eyes for a long moment.

They sat for the better part of an hour while Riona waited for the aspirin to do their job. That never seemed to happen, and Killian eventually went up to the room, packed both suitcases, and dragged them out to the Audi.

It was just after he loaded the bags into the boot of the car and closed the lid that he noticed the dent on the passenger side. Things only got worse as he approached the front of the vehicle. The headlight was broken, the hood slightly buckled, the grill was cracked, and the front quarter panel on the passenger side was going to need replacing.

No sign of any damage on cars nearby, which meant whatever happened had apparently occurred on the drive home from the pub last night. His first thought was to get out of Wexford as quickly as possible. But then he remembered Riona was sitting in the restaurant.

He checked out at the front desk using the American credit card and hurried into the restaurant. Riona was seated at the table with her head tilted back, and her eyes closed.

Killian cautiously approached and half-whispered her name, "Riona."

"What?" she replied a moment later. Her eyes remained closed.

"We're all checked out, princess. Let's get you in the car, and you can sleep on the way home."

"How 'bout I just sleep here."

"I'm afraid they're going to need the table," Killian said as he looked around. Only one other table was occupied. "Time to go," he said a second or two later.

"Help me up," she groaned.

It took a good five minutes, but he eventually got her out to the car. He held the rear door open for her. She stretched out on the back seat and closed her eyes. She was asleep and breathing heavily by the time he pulled out of the parking lot.

The Audi seemed to drive at a slight angle, and Killian had to keep the steering wheel turned about five degrees to the left on the drive home. Riona snored for the better part of the drive, and Killian decided the best idea was to just let her sleep. She woke as he pulled off of North Phibsboro Road. She groaned from the back seat and said, "Where in the hell are we?"

"Just about to turn onto Castle Terrace. You'll be home in less than a minute," Killian said, thanking God she slept during the entire two-hour drive.

He helped her out of the backseat, pulled her suitcase out of the boot, and literally ran it up to the front stoop of the dingy blue structure. She was only halfway to the stoop when he kissed her on the cheek, said a quick, "Thanks," and hurried back behind the wheel.

He thought she might have called his name, but he wasn't sure, and even if she had, two days had been more than enough. He disappeared around the corner and drove to the car rental agency.

The staff at Enterprise were none too pleased with the damage to the vehicle. He attempted to lie and told them the damage must have happened just a moment ago in their parking lot, but they weren't buying it. They ended up taking his information, cellphone number, current address, and date of birth, then made him sign a sheaf of documents, including one authorizing charges to be made to his credit card.

He could only hope the American would miss the repair bill charges. He pulled his suitcase out to the street and flagged a taxi for the ride home. He promised himself it would be a cold day in hell before he ended up with Riona ever again.

Once home, he turned on his computer and checked the football scores. *How in the hell could Arsenal have lost? That was a sure bet and now he was out fifty euros.* He kept thinking about the damage to the rental car. Try as he might, he couldn't remember running into anything on the drive back to the hotel. But then, he had no recollection of the drive home. He decided he'd better inform the American, and he sent a shot text message.

'Bit of a fender bender in the parking lot. Someone hit the rental car. Minor damage will keep you posted.'

TWENTY-ONE

endell Murphy was back on the phone with Kevin Byrne. "Kevin, there has to be something you can tell me. Jimmy Dugan's apparently living the good life over in Ireland with a different gorgeous woman every night. Isn't there some kind of treaty or legal agreement that would let you guys go over there and arrest him? It looks like he's giving the US the finger."

"It's a bit more complicated than just going over and slapping a pair of cuffs on the guy. We need a little more proof besides a couple of pictures in a restaurant before we initiate an arrest outside of the country."

"Any idea where these pictures are coming from?"

"No, that part I can give you the straight scoop. The text message comes from a server in Latvia and—"

"Latvia? I don't know anyone in Latvia."

"Neither do I. This is a pretty standard method that's used when the sender doesn't want to be traced. Purely speculation at this stage, but the images are probably sent from a burner phone. They're sent from a server in Eastern Europe, in this case, Latvia. Basically, what it boils down to is they're untraceable. I think the bigger question is who is sending them?"

"Maybe a driver or someone who is with Dugan but not in any of the pictures."

"Maybe. Based on the pictures, I'd say it's a safe bet Dugan knows they're being taken. Hell, he's posed for them, right?"

"Yeah, and in that one, the woman obviously didn't want to be seen. That's why she held the napkin up in front of her face."

"Yeah, but at the same time, Dugan clearly doesn't care. Hell, he's all smiles. The question is, why? Here's a guy who's disappeared. A guy who's been underground for ten years, and now he's sending pictures to the FBI and you. It doesn't make any sense."

"You think he just misses being in the limelight?"

"After ten years? I think he'd be thanking his lucky stars he isn't sitting in a cell somewhere for the rest of his life."

"What if someone is trying to out him?" Murphy asked.

"Okay, but then why just send the pictures? Why not send an address and a schedule with the best time to arrest this schmuck? And we're still back to the same question, why, in God's name, is he posing for these pictures?"

Murphy shook his head and said, "I'm back to thinking he's giving all of us the finger."

"Maybe. You want to know what I'm thinking?"

"Yeah, tell me, please."

"I don't think it's Dugan."

"What, did you look at the pictures, compare them with shots of Dugan over the years? We can't detect any makeup. The images aren't photoshopped. We checked them out. Really we did, Kevin."

"Yeah, and we did, too. But just suppose Dugan is living out in, I don't know, California or New Orleans or hell, back in Iowa, my home state. What if he's keeping his low profile somewhere, and these are just to get us thinking he's in the UK or Ireland or wherever in the hell these pictures are? He sends them out. We got no idea where they came from. And at the end of the day, it's not even him."

"But what would happen if we found out it wasn't him?"

"Humph, I think the first thing that would happen is whoever it is in those pictures would find himself dead, and his body would never be discovered."

Murphy was furiously writing on a yellow legal pad.

"Wendy, you still there?"

"Yeah, Kevin. Hey, I should let you get back to work. I'm under deadline here, and I'd better get to writing. Look for the article in tomorrow's paper, front page."

"What's it gonna say?"

"I don't know. I'll tell you once I write it," Murphy said.

"Keep me posted," Byrne said and disconnected.

TWENTY-TWO

Dillon was ten minutes early picking up Suel for the trip down to Wexford. Suel climbed into the passenger seat and smiled.

"What's so funny?" Dillon asked as he pulled into traffic and headed for the M11.

"Not a thing, other than I'm looking forward to resting my eyes for the next two hours while the likes of you chauffeur me down to Wexford. You find anything on your Man Jimmy Dugan?" Suel asked.

"Not really. He was up on a laundry list of charges when he disappeared in 2008. He posted a hundred grand for bail. That's ten percent of the million dollars the bail was set at. There's a question why bail was even granted. The judge that granted it was removed from the bench the following year and investigated, but that seemed to go nowhere.

"There have been suspected sightings of him over the last four or five years. Pictures were supposedly taken in Ireland and Paris. The few pictures over the past couple of years have been from here in Ireland. From what I can determine, no one has ever spoken to him or confirmed that any of the photos are actually him. Nothing like fingerprints or DNA have substantiated any photo.

"Other than the photos, there aren't any records, nothing like a passport or a driver's license. Nothing from Homeland Security or TSA. Nothing that would suggest he purchased a place to live or a car. I'm wondering if this isn't some scam to get people thinking he's living it up over here," Dillon said.

Suel glanced over and said, "Are you suggesting a restaurant would put the photo out there, hoping to get some free publicity?"

"No, if you had a restaurant, would you want that sort of press out there? Not exactly the thing to encourage people. Come and spend the evening with a major criminal and murderer. I'm trying to think of the kind of woman that might appeal to, certainly no one I'd be interested in. And another thing, Paddy. Just for the record, let's say the pictures are the real deal. Everything I've read about this Dugan guy suggests he's keeping a low profile. Pictures in a restaurant are the last thing he'd want. He'd probably attack whatever idiot tried to take a picture of him."

"So what does that mean, it's some internet scam? Are people taking pictures and maybe posting Dugan's face in there?"

"I never thought of that. I suppose that could happen. Be interesting to find out when we talk to the restaurant staff."

They drove on, not talking, just listening to the news report and an interview on a stimulus package that failed in the Dahl.

"Damn politicians. They're only in it for themselves, never doing the job they were hired to do. You mind if I turn it off?" Suel asked.

"Please, be my guest. It will only improve my blood pressure," Dillon said.

As they approached Wexford, Suel gave Dillon directions.

"I thought you said you'd never been to this restaurant," Dillon said.

"I haven't. I was online this morning looking it up. Even wrote the directions down," Suel said, pulling a used envelope from his jacket pocket to show Dillon.

"Amazing," Dillon said. "When did you stop using color crayons?"

"Ha-ha-ah, aren't you just the clever one," Suel replied. "That's the Emerald Gardens up ahead on the right side," he said, nodding at a three-story white building in the middle of the block. Dillon pulled into a parking spot half a block further just as a car pulled out.

"You think they're open yet?" Dillon asked.

"Bit early. I'm thinking it might be the wise thought to grab a tea, figure out our plan, and go in around 11:00."

"If they're even open then."

They crossed the street and went in the opposite direction toward a coffee shop on the corner. Dillon ordered a coffee, and Suel got a breakfast tea and a scone.

"You sure you don't want something to eat?" Suel asked.

"No, I had a big breakfast before I picked you up."

"Thanks for sharing," Suel said and slid his plate with the scone closer to him as they sat down. They rehashed the pictures of Jimmy Dugan some more and didn't come up with anything new. They left the coffee shop a few minutes after eleven and headed up the street to the Emerald Gardens. Along the way, they stopped twice, once to look in the window of a Lingerie store and the other time to watch two drivers arguing about who deserved the parking place.

A woman inside the Emerald Gardens had just unlocked the door when Dillon opened it.

"Oh, good morning, umm, table for two?" she asked, not hiding her surprise at the early morning guests. She was Asian, and Dillon pegged her at sixty, maybe sixty-five. She had an accent, and she smiled as she reached behind her and grabbed two menus.

"Actually, we'd like to talk to a manager. We're interested in a photo taken here recently," Dillon said. Suel handed him the manilla folder, and he pulled out the copy of the Boston Globe newspaper article.

The woman glanced at the image and said, "I get manager. You wait here." She hurried over to a swinging door they guessed led to the kitchen and disappeared.

The image of the couple with the woman holding the white linen napkin in front of her face suddenly hit both Suel and Dillon. All the tables in the restaurant were covered with red linen tablecloths. Place settings of silverware rested on white linen napkins. You couldn't see the red tablecloths in the newspaper image, but you could see a portion of a framed hexagonal mirror on a wall behind Jimmy Dugan.

Suel walked over to a table near a hexagonal mirror hanging on the wall. "Hey, Dillon, check this out," Suel said.

"This has to be the table," Dillon said, looking around. Two rectangular paintings hung on the walls above two other tables.

TWENTY-THREE

Ayounger man, Asian, possibly the son of the woman they'd spoken to, was walking toward them. "Can I help you, gentlemen?" He was dressed in navy-blue trousers and a white open-collar shirt with a button-down collar. He smiled and asked again, "Can I help you, gentlemen?" He had an Irish accent.

"Hi, we're with An Garda Síochána, Special Branch," Dillon said. "We're trying to locate an individual who may have been here recently."

As he spoke, Suel pulled out the copy of the article and handed it to the man. He studied it for a moment, nodded, started to smile, which quickly turned to a frown.

"You recognize him, the man? Do you know him?" Dillon asked.

The man shook his head and handed the copy back to Suel. "No, I don't know him, but the picture has been the talk of our waitstaff for the past week. Your man asked to have a picture taken by one of our servers, and then the woman held the napkin in front of her face. We were placing bets on whether or not she had a husband and was out on the sly."

"How long ago was this?" Dillon asked.

"Mmm, I can't be certain, but it was sometime last week. Alofie was the server who took the photo. You want to wait a minute I can check and see if he's working today."

"That would be great," Dillon said, and the manager headed back into the kitchen.

"Well, if we can talk to the server, we can confirm the image was taken recently," Suel said.

Dillon shook his head. "They asked to have their picture taken. That pretty much eliminates photoshopping Dugan's head on an image. But it still doesn't make any sense if he's trying to keep a low profile."

"Maybe he thinks he's gotten away with everything. Is there a statute of limitations on his charges that has expired?"

"Certainly not on murder charges, and he's facing a number of those."

The kitchen door suddenly swung open, and the manager walked out. "Alofie's not here right now, but he's due in little more than an hour. How about lunch, and as soon as he comes in, I'll send him over?"

Dillon was thinking about that when Suel said, "Thank you, that sounds like a wonderful idea."

"Follow me. We have a table that's nice and private. You can talk to Alofie and not be interrupted," he said and led them to a small back room. There were only four tables in the room, and he pointed to one in the corner. "Take a seat, gentlemen, and I'll send someone back with menus." As he left the room, he stopped in the entrance and clipped a red velvet cord to the opposite side of the wall, smiled, and disappeared.

"Looks like he's got us locked in," Suel joked.

"Yeah and positioned so no other customers will be able to see us. This just seems to reinforce my thought that a restaurant wouldn't want a picture of Jimmy Dugan enjoying himself in their business."

The older woman who first let them in arrived with two menus. She quickly placed them in front of Dillon and Suel and fled the scene, reattaching the red velvet cord as she stepped back into the main restaurant.

They ordered lunch, ate, and were drinking tea and coffee when two younger men stepped into the room and walked over to their table. "Hi, Bao said you had some questions about a picture I took of a couple last week."

"You're Alofie?" Suel asked.

The man nodded.

"Have a seat, lads. I didn't catch your name," Suel said to the other guy.

"Tommy," he replied.

Dillon and Suel introduced themselves. "We want to be perfectly clear," Dillon said. "No one here, especially you guys, are in any trouble. We just have a couple of questions to ask this person in the picture, and if there was any way you could help us, that would be great. What's the manager's name again?"

"Bao," they both said at the same time.

"Is that his mother who let us in?" Suel asked.

"Yeah, she actually owns the restaurant. Started it a thousand years ago with her husband," Tommy said. Everyone smiled at his comment.

Dillon pulled the copy of the article out of the file and handed it across the table. "So Alofie, tell us about this image."

He nodded as he glanced at the image. "That looks like the picture I took. There's not much to tell you. They were seated at the table, and I served them. They were on their second bottle of wine and feeling no pain," he said. He and Tommy chuckled. "They asked me to take some pictures. I think I took three. Can't remember if they ordered dessert."

"And this was last week?" Dillon asked.

"Yeah, pretty sure it was Wednesday night. We were pretty busy," he said and looked over at Tommy, who nodded in agreement.

"Did he have an accent?" Suel asked.

"He was a Dub," Alofie said.

"A Dub. Are you sure?" Dillon asked.

"You sure about that?" Suel asked, following up.

"Oh yeah, we get Dubs in here all the time. Definitely a Dub accent," Alofie said, and Tommy nodded in agreement.

"What about the woman?" Dillon asked.

"Local, I think. I've seen her in here before, just can't remember when. I know it wasn't her first time here."

"They both have been here," Tommy said. "Your man was in here two nights back with a different woman. Bit of a slapper, not that I'd ever complain, and they were both on the piss."

"Two nights ago, they were in here? Are you sure, lads?" Suel asked.

They both nodded. "Yeah, he had me take two pictures of them. I can show you the table. It's at the other end from where Alofie took their picture. Like I said, he was with a different woman than the one in your picture."

"Yeah, I seen 'em. I said hi on their way out, and he said, hi'yas. She was too pissed to say anything. Couldn't see more than an inch from the front of her nose," Alofie said.

"You're absolutely sure?" Dillon asked.

Both guys nodded. Then Tommy said, "You should talk to Bao. Your man paid with a credit card, so Bao would have the receipt."

Alofie nodded, "Yeah, he leaves a nice tip. The more he drinks, the bigger the tip."

"Course you could say that about everyone," Tommy said.

"Would you mind asking Bao to join us for a moment," Suel said.

Alofie and Tommy looked at one another for a moment. Alofie seemed to take a big swallow and said, "You want to talk to Bao?"

"Yeah, here's the deal. If you can get him to join us for just a minute, we'll put in a good word for both you lads. You've given me an idea that could help him boost his tourist business, and it won't cost him a cent. We'll spread the good word," Suel said.

That seemed to take some of the pressure off, and Alofie hurried off to get Bao.

TWENTY-FOUR

Three minutes later, Bao returned. Alofie followed close behind. "A question, gentlemen?" he said as he reattached the red velvet cord and stepped over to the table.

"More of an idea," Dillon said. "It turns out that the man in this photo was in here two nights ago, and Tommy took his picture. What we'd like to do is get a copy of his credit card receipt, and if you could find it, the one from last Wednesday when Alofie took the picture. If you could do that, there's a very good chance it might aid us in locating him. Should that happen, we can pretty much guarantee that an awful lot of American tourists would be very interested in coming here and having dinner."

"A bit like being at the Eiffel tower," Suel said.

"Exactly or Buckingham Palace," Dillon added, which brought strange looks from the others.

"And there's no charge?" Bao asked.

"None whatsoever," Suel replied.

"I'd need to see some I.D.s first," Bao said. He glanced at Suel's I.D. and studied Dillon's for a long moment. "You're a Marshal from the United States?"

"Yes, I am."

"Like in the cowboy shows?"

"You remember that shooting two years ago at Dublin airport?" Suel asked. Dillon shot a surprised look at Suel. "Well, here's your man."

"That was you? Taking on three Russian gangsters?"

"Four," Suel said

"Wait here," Bao said. "Would you mind if these gentlemen returned to work?"

"Not at all. Let me give you our cards," Suel said and dished out three of his business cards. He took three from Dillon and tossed them on top of his. "You happen see your man in here again, please call us."

"If you'll be so kind as to wait, I should be able to get a copy of that receipt for you in ten minutes or so," Bao said.

"We'll be here waiting," Suel said.

Once Bao, Alofie, and Tommy had left the room, Dillon turned to Suel and said, "Why in the hell did you mention that shooting out at the airport? I hate that."

"I know you do, and unfortunately, it's the price you have to pay for being famous with some folks. Do you think if I'd kept my mouth shut, we'd be sitting here waiting for a credit card receipt from fecking Jimmy Dugan right now? Jack, once in a while, you got to think like the other side."

It was more like thirty minutes before Bao returned, but he brought not one but two credit card receipts.

"Sorry it took me so long. I wanted to check. We had a charge to this card two evenings ago, another five days prior to that. No problem with either charge," he said and handed the receipt to Suel. Suel looked at the first receipt and handed it to Dillon. He handed over the second receipt a moment later.

The name on the receipt was Sterling, Cooper and Partners, which rang a bell with Dillon, although he couldn't remember why. The receipts for two evenings, including the tips, came to a total of seven hundred and thirty-five euros.

"We can't thank you enough for these, Bao. Very kind of you, and we appreciate the time you've taken to help us."

"It may be nothing if we become famous," he said, and Dillon couldn't tell whether or not he was kidding. "I do have one suggestion for you," Bao said.

"Yes, by all means, please," Suel said.

"The gentleman has been here twice in just over a week. Might it make sense for you to return this evening. Say 7:00, if he shows, he's here for the taking, if you'll pardon my pun. If not, you've still had a wonderful dinner, and you can return to Dublin at a respectable hour."

Suel looked at Dillon. Dillon simply shrugged. "I think that's a wonderful idea, Bao. Yes, we'll be back at seven this evening. Thank you."

"Excellent, let me get your server, and you can settle up," Bao said and hurried out of the room. This time he didn't bother to attach the red velvet cord across the entry.

"Mmm, I was hoping he was going to comp the lunch for us," Dillon said.

"Look, in the meantime, we can check around and see if anyone else saw your man. He had to go somewhere else besides here."

"There's that pub across the street," Dillon said.

They settled their bill, each handing a twenty euro note to the server and telling him to keep the change.

"Could you give us each a receipt with that?" Suel said. The server gave him a look and then cranked out two receipts. He handed one to Suel and the other to Dillon.

As they headed out the door, they both waved goodbye to Bao's mother. She flashed a fake smile and quickly looked the other way. They crossed the street to Flanagan's pub and stepped inside. At the moment, there were only two men in Flanagan's. One was the bartender. "What will it be, gents?"

"Unfortunately, we're just here on some business. An Garda Síochána, Special Branch, wondered if you might have had anyone in here using this credit card," Suel said and handed his receipt from Emerald Gardens to the bartender.

The man looked at the receipt for a brief moment and handed it back. "That's a cash receipt, no card name on it."

"Oh, sorry, that was mine for lunch. Here, the name on one of these two," Suel said, setting the two receipts on the bar.

"Mmm-mmm, I'd be happy with those totals, but that doesn't ring a bell. Most of our business is locals and the occasional tourist. You might try back tonight. Our evening shift comes on at six. I haven't heard anything about a payment being denied. Anytime that happens, there's a message waiting for me."

"We'll try and check back this evening," Suel said, and they left.

"You know I'm thinking about something those two servers said. They seemed pretty adamant that your man had a Dublin accent," Dillon said. "And another thing, the company name on those credit card receipts is ringing a bell, but for the life of me, I can't tell you why."

They stopped in four more pubs and three restaurants over the next few hours and came up empty-handed. No one recognized the image of Jimmy Dugan. The name on the credit card receipt didn't ring any bells. Dillon and Suel passed out business cards at each place.

At 6:30, they were back in Flanagan's. It was a little busier than during their early afternoon visit. Now there were eight people in the place. Two couples at a table and three guys, obviously alone, were seated at the bar.

The bartender was a brown-haired woman. Dillion guessed her age at maybe fifty-five. She was talking to one of the men seated at the bar. Dillon and Suel settled in on stools next to the guy she was talking with.

"What'll it be lads?" she asked as she tossed a couple of drink coasters on the bar in front of them. The coasters featured an image of the bar with the name FLANAGAN'S written in white script across the image.

"Nothing to drink, we're with An Garda Síochána, Special Branch. Wondering if you might remember a couple in here a few nights back," Suel said and handed her a copy of the credit card receipt. "They were across the street at the Emerald Gardens and asked their server to take their picture," he said and slid the copy of the Boston Globe article across the bar.

She picked up the article, looked at it for a moment, and nodded. "Yeah, they were in a few nights back. You remember, Dennis?" she said and handed the copy to the guy next to Suel.

He looked for half a second, nodded, and set the article next to Suel. "Out on the piss, they were. Especially your wan. They were in here twice. Had a couple of drinks the first time then must have gone over to the Gardens. Came back in around half-past nine, ten o'clock. I'd say, at that point, your woman probably couldn't remember her own name. They were here for a couple more drinks, weren't they?"

"Yeah, she's the one who asked Pauly if he wanted to go back to the hotel with them."

"Yeah, that's right. I'm guessing it was her husband that shut that down."

"A hotel?" Dillon said. "Did she mention the name of the place?"

"Riverbank House Hotel," the bartender said and laughed. "I don't think she gave a room number."

"Like I said, she couldn't remember her own name, let alone a room number," the guy said, and that got both of them laughing.

Dillon and Suel crossed the street and entered the Emerald Gardens a little before 7:00. Bao's mother didn't appear very happy with their return. She led them to a table in the main dining room and hurried away. Bao stopped to say hi. They ordered dinner, ate, waited, and eventually left around half-past eight after paying their bill.

"Well, that was a complete waste of time," Suel said as they climbed into the car. "We could have been back in Dublin by now."

"I'm thinking your close friend Bao set us up just so we'd pay for two more meals. I was hoping for something, maybe a free dessert, at least."

"We might as well stop at the Riverbank House Hotel on the way out of town. It's not too far from here," Suel said.

TWENTY-FIVE

illon pulled into the parking lot of the Riverbank House Hotel fifteen minutes later after Suel had them momentarily lost with his bad directions. As they climbed out of the car, Dillon commented on the largely empty parking lot.

"Maybe folks are still out having dinner," Suel said, and they walked to the main entrance.

There was a younger guy standing behind the reception counter. He wore a gray three-piece suit with the hotel logo emblazoned on his breast pocket. He smiled and said, "Good evening, gentlemen."

"Hi ya's," Suel said. "We're with An Garda Síochána, Special Branch."

The smile immediately disappeared from the young man's face.

"We've reason to believe a couple may have rented a room here, two or three nights ago. The man in this picture," he said, placing the copy of the Boston Globe article on the counter. "They may have used the credit card listed on this receipt," he said and placed one of the receipts from the Emerald Gardens on the article.

The young man picked up the receipt and studied it for a moment and then looked at the image on the copy and slowly nodded.

"Yeah, they look familiar. I think they were here a couple nights back. Why, what'd they do?"

"We'd just like to talk to them, get some general information," Suel said.

The young man seemed to think about that and then said, "Hold on for just a moment." He stepped back to a door, knocked as he opened the door, and said, "Hey, Brian. Could you come out here for a second? Some guys from An Garda Síochána have a question."

Brian stepped out of the office a moment later. He wore the same gray suit as the younger man, minus the suit coat. He looked at Dillon and Suel and pasted on a smile. "What seems to be the problem, gentlemen?"

Suel went through the same routine with the copy of the article and the restaurant receipt.

"I'm pretty sure I saw him here a couple of nights ago," the younger man said.

A couple came in the front door and headed toward the reception counter.

"Why don't we step into my office, and I can check our records. My name is Brian, by the way."

"D.I. Suel, An Garda Síochána, Special Branch," Suel said as they headed into the office.

"US Marshal Jack Dillon," Dillon said.

Brian pointed to a pair of chairs in front of his desk. "Please have a seat," Brian said and set the article and the restaurant receipt on his desk. "You said two or three nights ago?"

"That's what we think," Suel said.

Brian began clicking keys on the keyboard. He glanced a couple times at the restaurant receipt, apparently inputting the name from the credit card. A moment later, he said, "Yeah, okay, here we go," and turned his computer screen so it partially faced Dillon and Suel.

"According to this, they stayed with us for two nights. Let me just print a copy for you," he said and pressed a key on his keyboard. A moment later, the printer on the credenza behind him started up and printed off a total of seven sheets. He took the papers, lifted them twice, hitting the bottom of the sheets on his desk, and handed them to Suel. "Anything else I can do for you, gentlemen?"

"I have a question," Dillon said. "Do you have security cameras covering your parking lot?"

"We do. You'd like to check the lot for a vehicle?" Brian asked.

"Be nice to see if you had an image of the vehicle. Maybe we could get a make, model, and license plate number."

"Shouldn't be a problem. What's the time on that room receipt?" he asked.

Suel studied the receipt for a long moment.

"Maybe two lines down on the right side," Brian said.

"Here we go, twelve thirty-seven," Suel read then looked up and smiled.

Brian clicked more keys on the keyboard and eventually brought up an image of the parking lot. It appeared to be a lot fuller than when Suel and Dillon parked fifteen minutes earlier.

"Let's see what we have leaving. I'm starting at noon just in case your man pulled out early." Two vehicles left the lot, neither one driven by Jimmy Dugan. One car entered, and suddenly, there was Dugan walking into the lot and pulling two suitcases behind him.

"That's our guy," Dillon said.

Brian slowed down the speed on the tape. Dugan walked toward a car three rows back in the parking lot. One of the suitcases appeared to be black and had what looked like a length of duct tape on the side, maybe covering a torn section. The other suitcase appeared to be blue or gray with a pattern of large sunflowers all over it. Dugan disappeared from the screen for maybe twenty seconds before walking back onto the screen and disappearing.

Brian sped up the tape as a car entered. Nothing happened for a minute, and then suddenly there was Dugan again, this time walking with a woman. She had black hair and was definitely a different woman than the blonde who held the napkin up in front of her face. She was attractive or could have been. Her arms were crossed, and she stared at the ground in front of her. Dugan walked two or three paces in front of her.

"She look okay to you?" Dillon asked.

"She looks, I don't know, maybe fragile or something," Brian said.

"How about sick or hungover?" Suel said.

"Yeah, that could be," Brian said.

Two minutes later, an A4 Audi came into the picture. Jimmy Dugan was behind the wheel. The woman was nowhere to be seen.

"Where did she go?" Suel asked.

"You think he put her in the trunk?" Dillon said.

"What the hell? Do you mean to tell me he killed her or kidnapped her right in our parking lot?" Brian half-shouted.

"Maybe not," Suel said. "Can you back that image up? I want to see if I can get the license plate number and check out the damage to the front of that car."

Brian backed the tape up until the Audi disappeared. He set the tape in slow motion as the vehicle slowly reappeared.

"Stop it there," Suel said. He wrote down the license number, double-checked it, then read it out loud, and said, "Is that the number you two are seeing?"

"Yes," both Dillon and Brian replied.

Brian continued to run the tape slowly until the Audi disappeared. He ran it for five more minutes, thinking the woman may have driven her car out of the lot, but she never appeared.

"I wish I had more for you guys," Brian said. "We don't have any cameras in our suites. Anything else you can think of?"

Dillon and Suel thought for a long moment and eventually shook their heads.

"Thanks for all you've done for us, Brian," Dillon said and handed him a business card. "Is there a way you could send us a copy of that tape?"

"I don't think that will be a problem. I'd like to check with the company first. I'll email my boss in a minute, but I may not hear back from her until tomorrow morning."

Suel handed him a business card and said, "Tomorrow morning will work. Thank you for your time. Really, you've been a great help."

They chatted for a couple of minutes. Dillon and Suel gave some vague responses to a couple of questions, and they left.

"Interesting," Suel said as Dillon pulled onto the M11 and headed for Dublin. "All in all, it turned out not to be a complete waste of time. Let me just phone in this license plate number. See if we can't get a location or, God forbid, the owner."

He placed a call to a general number and asked to be transferred to someone. Dillon could hear the phone ringing on the other end. A moment later, Suel said, "Yeah, Noel, Paddy Suel. Need you to give me information on this plate number. It's a dark blue or maybe a black Audi A4. Here's the number," he said, reading it from the back of the same envelope he'd written the directions to Emerald Gardens on. "Give me a call in the morning. Thanks in advance, best to Ann," he said and hung up.

"Not in?" Dillon asked.

"Yeah, amazingly, at twenty minutes after ten at night, he's not at his desk. You know, I'm still thinking about how sure those two servers were that this fellow had a Dublin accent."

"I suppose he could have faked it."

"You've been here a couple of years. You think you could fool them."

"Yeah, I see your point, unless he had a couple of phrases. I don't know, maybe he practiced, or took lessons, or something if he wanted to remain undiscovered."

"Okay, sure, good idea. He wants to remain undiscovered, and then he goes out and asks servers in a restaurant and bartenders in a pub to take his picture? It's not adding up. Something doesn't seem right."

"Let's see what we find out on the license plate tomorrow morning."

TWENTY-SIX

Dillon dropped Suel off and drove home. The closer he got to his place, the more he dreaded whatever mess Lucifer undoubtedly had left. The poor guy had been locked inside the house for a good sixteen hours. Who could blame him?

In the past, he could have called Tara, and she'd run over and let Lucifer out two or three times over the course of the day. Just now, he felt that didn't seem to be much of an option, and he hadn't called her.

He pulled into the drive and turned off the car. As he stepped from the car, out of force of habit, he casually glanced over in the direction of Tara's house. There it was, the Mercedes, backed into her drive in front of her car. All the lights appeared to be off in her house.

He silently chastised himself as he unlocked the front door. Two letters lay on the floor after having been dropped through the mail slot. As he picked them up he discovered they were wet and quickly realized Lucifer had left a puddle in front of the door.

Remnants from the wastebasket he neglected to place on the kitchen counter were scattered around the front hall. The wastebasket was on its side in the kitchen and completely empty. Used paper towels, coffee grounds, the Styrofoam container from two pork chops, and another from a slice of fresh salmon were in chewed bits scattered across the kitchen floor. Two deposits, one by the back door and another in front of the stove, served as exclamation points in Lucifer's message to Dillon.

The dog was nowhere to be seen, but then again, given the hour, he was probably asleep upstairs in the bedroom. Dillon spent the next half-hour cleaning the kitchen and the front hall. He tossed the wet mat from the front door outside and then decided, as long as he'd bagged the two deposits in the kitchen, he may as well scoop up the ones outside.

That took another ten minutes, and he knew he'd missed at least one, but it was now approaching 1:30 in the morning, and the porch light didn't extend to the far reaches of his front lawn.

He was tempted for the briefest of moments to drop the deposits on the windshield of the Mercedes but knew he'd immediately be suspected, so he sealed the bag and placed it in his trash bin. He stepped back into the house, locked the door, and on a whim peeked into his sitting room.

Bad idea. Lucifer had torn into the pillow Dillon used when he stretched out on the couch. Small white feathers were scattered from one end of the room to the other. He left the mess for the morning, closed the sitting room door behind him, and headed up to bed.

Lucifer was sound asleep on the bed. No doubt exhausted after messing up the entire house. Two small white feathers were still on his nose. Dillon undressed, tossed his clothes on the chair, and climbed into bed. He was asleep in less than a minute.

He woke with a start and glanced at the digital clock. 3:59. It suddenly came to him, the name on Dugan's credit card, Sterling, Cooper & Partners. It was from the American tv series, Mad Men. He was sure of it. He wrote the information down on the small tablet he kept on the bedside table and settled back to sleep. The alarm woke him in the morning.

Lucifer stretched for a moment and then fell back asleep once Dillon turned the alarm off. Dillon headed into the bathroom. After his shower, he dressed, got the coffee going, and microwaved a bowl of oatmeal.

He woke Lucifer after a half-dozen calls upstairs and enticed him outside with the bribe of a biscuit. He filled the food and water dishes, let him back inside, placed the wastebasket on top of the kitchen counter, and headed for the office.

Suel drove into the parking lot just as Dillon pulled into a parking space and climbed out of his car. Suel stopped behind him and lowered his window.

"I got a call from Noel Reddy."

"The guy you called on the license plate?"

"Yeah, I'm headed to the address now. Interested?"

"Yeah, you think we need backup?"

"We should be okay. It's not too far from here, over by the Croaker."

"But what about Dugan?"

"He won't be an issue. I'm not going to interact with him."

Dillon climbed into the passenger seat, and Suel drove out of the parking lot. They headed across Phibsboro and waited for the light to change at Drumcondra Road. Suel crossed Drumcondra Road, drove three more blocks, and made a left hand turn.

"You sure we don't need any backup? If Dugan is here, he's not going to be too happy about our finding him. He's liable to try anything. I'll make the call, Paddy," Dillon said, and pulled his cellphone from his pocket. "Better that than one of us taking a bullet."

Suel shook his head, smiled, and pulled into the Enterprise Car Rental lot. He pulled into a space against the one-story building with large glass windows.

"What the hell? He works here?"

"No, you lunatic. Haven't you caught on? The car was rented."

"Rented?"

"Yeah, you think I'm going to send the two of us on a death mission to arrest your man Dugan without backup? Come on, let's see what we can find out."

Dillon grabbed the file with the Boston Globe article, and they hurried inside the building. Suel held the door for a middle-aged couple as they left. They were speaking French. The woman carried an Enterprise brochure, and the man held a shiny set of car keys. They headed toward a line of numbered parking places with spotless cars backed into them.

"Fortunately, neither of those two looked like your man Dugan," Suel said and stepped inside.

"Good morning. How can I help you?" the woman behind the counter asked.

Suel smiled but didn't say anything until he was standing at the counter. He held out his ID and said, "We're with An Garda Síochána, Special Branch. We're checking on a car recently rented. An Audi A4." He read the license plate number from a sheet he'd apparently typed up, which made a much better impression than the used envelope he'd originally used to copy down the number.

"An Audi A4? Is there a problem?"

Suel was about to say something when a man seated at a desk behind her said, "I'll deal with this, Shannon. Hi, my name is Devan. How can I help you, gentlemen?"

Suel repeated that they were with An Garda Síochána, showed his ID, and repeated the license plate number. "We believe that the vehicle was rented from this location."

"Yes, it was rented from this facility. It was returned to us yesterday with a good deal of damage. Is this regarding the accident?"

"From what we could tell from a security tape, it looked like a front quarter panel would have to be replaced. The grill and the hood were damaged. We weren't able to speak to the driver," Suel said.

The man nodded. "Your man was pretty vague. At first, he said it happened when the car was parked in a parking lot. Then he said it had been parked on the street. I was waiting for him to tell me he wasn't driving and he'd let a friend borrow it, but he didn't go that route. As a matter of fact, you just missed the car. It went off to the repair shop maybe thirty minutes ago."

"Would you happen to have your man's name and address? We'd like to chat with him," Suel said.

"I do have it. A bit strange, he seemed, I don't know, maybe hesitant when we chatted yesterday. He did say no one was injured and that the accident occurred in a hotel parking lot, which I have a tough time believing. That said, his credit card was accepted. I'll phone him later today with the estimate on the repair bill. No idea what that will be other than fairly substantial. I've got the file at my desk. Hang on a moment." He stepped over to his desk and pulled a file sitting in a rack along the front of his desk.

"Yeah, here we go. A business credit card, maybe that was part of his problem. I'm sure his employer won't be too happy with the repair bill. As I said, I'll have an estimate for the repairs later today, and I'll give him a call. The ahh, credit card was registered to Sterling, Cooper and Partners. Sounds like solicitors, although when I asked him that, he was awfully vague. The gentleman's name is Killian Graham. Here's his phone number along with his address. He just lives over on North Phibsboro Road," he said and turned the file around so they could read the form.

"Would you mind making a copy of that for us?" Dillon asked.

He seemed to think about that for half a moment and then nodded. "Yeah, sure, I can do that. Were you notified of the accident? Hopefully, no one was hurt. But if he was driving under the influence or fled the scene, we'd certainly want to know so we could flag his name from future rentals."

"Unfortunately, we don't have any information on the accident. You said you're going to call him later today?" Suel asked.

"Yes, once I get the damage estimate. That won't be until sometime later this afternoon."

Suel handed him a business card and said, "Would you mind calling me first, Devan? I'd like to offer any assistance we can, just to make sure he doesn't try something to halt payment on the repairs. You know how solicitors can be."

"Unfortunately, I do know. We deal with them almost daily. I'll be happy to call you. Let me make a copy for you," he said and stepped behind his desk to a copy machine. He actually made two copies and handed one to Dillon and another to Suel. "Anything else I can help you with?"

"Maybe, one more detail," Dillon said and pulled the Boston Globe article from the file. "Can you identify this individual?"

Devan looked at the image and said, "Oh, yeah. That's him." He proceeded to read the article for maybe a half-minute. "Jesus Christ, Jimmy Dugan isn't the name he used. I told you, he said his name was Killian Graham, and he had the proper identification. Graham was the name he used to rent the vehicle. And, I could have sworn he was a Dub. This knacker is an American?"

Dillon put the article back in the folder and said, "That's one of the things we're trying to determine. We'd appreciate it if you wouldn't mention this to anyone. When you call this afternoon, we hope to be able to answer any questions."

Devan shook his head and said, "I don't feckin' believe it. What did that article say his name was? Duncan?"

"For now, let's stick with Killian Graham. Thank you for your time, sir. You've been a big help," Suel said, and they headed out the door. As they stepped outside, Dillon gave a look back inside. Devan had the phone up against his ear and was punching in a number.

"Well, what do you think we should do? He's in there, calling someone right now," Dillon said as they headed to the car.

"I think we'd better move before your man phones Graham or Dugan or whatever his name is and spills the beans."

"If he's even at that number anymore," Dillon said.

After they climbed into the car, Suel said, "Let's drive by this address and take a look. On the way there, maybe you could check in with DCI McCabe, bring him up to date on what we know thus far. I'm thinking we get a warrant and go in with a team."

Dillon shook his head and said, "Incredible. So much for covering ourselves in the event of bogus pictures. By the way, the name on that credit card, Sterling, Cooper and Partners…"

"Yeah, what about it?" Suel said as he pulled out of the Enterprise lot and headed back the way they'd come.

"It's from an American TV series called Mad Men. Ring any Bells?"

Suel seemed to think for a moment and shook his head.

"The series was popular in the states a few years back. It's about an advertising agency in New York. The series won a bunch of awards. Anyway, Sterling, Cooper and Partners was the name of the agency. I think the last season was five or maybe six years ago."

"And that's the name on the credit card? What? Is that some kind of coincidence?"

"My guess is no. That said, everyone we've talked to who debited the card for payment seems to have been paid. There's no report of any credit card scam."

"So what do you think?"

"I think it could be one more thing that may confirm that this really is Jimmy Dugan. Bogus name on the credit card and apparently believable identification," Dillon said.

"And then he asks bartenders and waiters to take his picture, and it ends up in a newspaper? It doesn't make any damn sense."

"Yeah, there is that," Dillon said and pulled out his cellphone. "Let me just call McCabe and mess up his day."

TWENTY-SEVEN

McCabe answered on the second ring. "D.C.I. MCabe."

"Good morning, sir. Jack Dillon, here."

"Where are you two? Please don't tell me you're still down in Wexford."

"No sir, we were back late last night— interesting interviews with a number of people. We just finished talking with a gentleman at Enterprise Car Rental. Seems your man rented a vehicle to an individual by the name of Killian Graham." Dillon went on to fill McCabe in on the details, as far as they knew them.

"And you're on the way to that address now?" McCabe said.

Dillon could hear a keyboard clicking in the background.

"Only as a drive-by, sir. We're thinking we should have back up and a warrant before we go any further."

"I've got that building on North Phibsboro Road up on my computer now. It's a two-story structure, just down from North Circular Road. Hold on a minute, here. Okay, yeah, there's a coffee takeout directly across the street called Kennedy's."

"I know the place, been there a few times."

"Are you driving?"

"No sir, Suel's driving."

"Alright, good. Park on Phibsboro Road and watch the front of your man's building from inside the coffee shop. I'll phone you with more details. This is going to take a bit to get a warrant. Give me the information you have, and I'll write it down."

Dillon spelled out Graham's name. He read off the address and phone number as well as the credit card details from the sheet Devan, at Enterprise Car Rental, gave him.

"Very well, I'll be back to you as soon as we have something. You are not to attempt to enter that building. If this individual should happen to appear, follow at a distance but do not interact. Presume he's armed," McCabe said.

"Yes, sir."

"One other bit. We received more photos yesterday from the American embassy. I'll have someone send them to you shortly. Anything else?"

"No, sir."

"Very well. I'll get back to you," McCabe said and disconnected.

"What are we doing," Suel said.

"Cooling our heels in Kennedy's coffee shop. It's directly across from where this Graham or Dugan or whoever he is, lives. If he leaves, we're to follow but not engage. McCabe's going to be getting a warrant, and he'll be in touch when he has more information. Oh, and apparently, they received more photos via the American embassy."

"I wonder if they may be the photos your man Tommy took at the Emerald Gardens the other night."

"And maybe that the woman bartender at Flanagan's took."

"All right," Suel said. A couple of minutes later, he took a left off North Circular Road and headed down North Phibsboro Road. Kennedy's Coffee was almost immediately on the left-hand side and directly across from the building Killian Graham had listed as his address.

Suel drove past Graham's building, a two-story brick structure. The first floor was retail. There was a hairdressers, a massage parlor, a nail and waxing place, and at the end of the building, a Chinese take-out. Suel pulled in front of McGowan's pub and waited for a bus to pass. He made a U-turn and pulled into a parking place maybe twenty feet from Kennedy's.

They stepped into the coffee shop and took a table at the front window. Maybe half the tables in the place were filled. They placed their orders. Dillon got a coffee and a pastry. Suel ordered a tea. The server brought everything over a couple of minutes later.

"Looks awfully quiet," Suel said, staring out the window.

"Hopefully, if he goes anywhere, we'll spot him and be able to follow," Dillon said and took a bite of his ginger roll covered in white frosting.

"Are you going to share?" Suel asked.

"I wasn't thinking of it," Dillon said just as his phone rang.

"McCabe?" Suel asked.

Dillon glanced at his screen and shook his head. "Hello, Myra," he said and turned away from the window.

Suel signaled he'd watch, and Dillon walked toward a quiet corner at the back of the shop. "Any news on the girls?"

"Yes, unfortunately. There was another phone message waiting for me this morning when I arrived. It came through last night just after midnight."

"And what did it say?"

"It was a husky voice, a woman. I'm pretty sure she was attempting to disguise her voice. She said the girls were returning on a Ryan Air flight tomorrow evening. The flight was departing from Lille, France, arriving in Dublin at 8:45."

"So they're okay?"

"Well, not exactly. She said they would be attempting to smuggle drugs."

"They're smuggling drugs?

That's what she said."

"No indication how she got this information? No name or a way to contact the caller?"

"No, nothing like that. I listened to the message and haven't touched my phone since. Thought you should know."

"What do you think about the call?"

"My first thought is it's bogus. Someone trying to get the girls in trouble. That said, it could be legitimate. I just don't know."

"Drugs, you could be talking a pretty good chunk of change. Strange she wouldn't have called the Garda. You have the flight numbers?"

"Yes, and the times."

"Go ahead and give those to me again," Dillon said as he took his notebook out of his pocket. He wrote down the flight information and added the girls' names. "Myra, do you have the girls' passport numbers?"

"Not in front of me, but I can get them."

"Text them to me when you get them. I'll send them to passport control out at the airport. This is sounding a little fishy. I'm thinking, as you suggested, this is someone trying to get the girls in trouble. That said, I think we better play it safe. I'm involved in something at the moment, but I'd like to be at the airport when they land tomorrow. Better safe than sorry," Dillon said.

"I'm sorry to interrupt whatever you're involved in."

"Not a problem, Myra. I appreciate your call. Text me those passport numbers if you would please. If anything else develops, let me know. Oh, and one more thing. Please hang on to that phone message. I'd like to listen to it."

"I'll forward it to you in just a bit. Stay safe in whatever you're doing and sorry to interrupt."

"Glad you called, Myra. Keep me posted."

"Oh, believe me, I will. Thanks for taking the time," she said and disconnected.

Dillon headed back to their table at the window. Suel was focused on the building across the street. The plate with Dillon's ginger roll was empty.

"Anything?" Dillon asked.

"No, I thought there was something, but it turned out to be a woman just going into the hairdressers."

"Did she stop in here first and eat my ginger roll?"

Suel smiled and said, "I couldn't resist. Relax, I ordered you another one."

Just as he finished saying that, the server arrived with another ginger roll covered in creamy white frosting. She looked at Suel and Dillon, not quite sure where to set the plate.

Dillon raised his hand and said, "That's for me. I need the sweetening."

She smiled and set the plate down in front of him.

They ordered another tea and coffee, sat for over an hour, and still nothing happened. Fortunately, Kennedy's still had two open tables, but the early lunch crowd was beginning to arrive. The couple at the table next to them had just ordered ham sandwiches.

"You think we should check in with McCabe again?" Dillon asked.

"We've nothing to tell him, other than the ginger rolls are very good. He's probably juggling a half-dozen different problems. No point in calling if we've nothing to report," Suel said.

They waited for another thirty minutes, and Dillon pulled out his phone.

"Don't call McCabe," Suel said.

"Not to worry, but McCabe was going to have someone send us that new batch of photos that arrived yesterday. Let me check with Eric. Maybe we can get him to send them to us."

"Bergman at the embassy?" Suel asked.

Dillon nodded and a moment later left a message, "Hi Eric, Jack Dillon here. I'm actually on a bit of a stakeout. Heard a rumor some more images of Jimmy Dugan arrived in Special Branch. Text them to me if you're able. Thanks," he said and disconnected.

They ordered pot pies for lunch, and still, nothing happened across the street. They ate the pot pies in silence. Dillon bussed their dishes back to the counter and handed them to the woman.

"Can I get youse anything else?" she asked.

"Not at the moment. Sorry we're taking so long. We're supposed to meet a friend here, but he keeps getting delayed."

She smiled and nodded as if what she'd just been told made sense. Dillon sat down, and a few minutes later, his phone signaled a text coming through.

"McCabe?" Suel asked.

Dillon shook his head. "Eric from the Embassy. Hmm-mmm," he said, scrolling over the three images in the text message. Jimmy Duggan and a gorgeous black-haired woman.

"Take a look at these. Is that the same woman we saw following Dugan into the hotel parking lot on the hotel tape?" he asked and handed his phone to Suel.

Suel swiped his finger across the screen, bringing up the images. He studied the first two and spent a long moment examining the final one, Dugan and the woman standing at a bar. It looked like it could be Flanagan's. The woman had undone most of the buttons on her blouse and was exposing herself. The description from the bartender and the guy at the bar in Flanagan's the other night seemed to fit. She appeared so intoxicated she couldn't have remembered her own name.

"They both look like they've had too much to drink. I wonder if that isn't what happened to the Audi. Your man was too far gone to see where he was going. Might be wise to call down to Wexford and ask if there's a hit and run or worse, someone lying in the morgue."

"Maybe give them a call," Dillon said.

TWENTY-EIGHT

Jimmy Dugan slid out of bed and tiptoed down the hall to his bathroom. He shaved and hit the shower. Like every morning, he had his clothes already laid out in his bathroom. He dressed in his pin-striped trousers and white shirt and headed into the kitchen. The coffee was on. He filled a mug and headed into his office. It was just after seven, and Sarah wouldn't be up for another three hours.

Nothing against her, she'd put up with a lot over the past years, but he enjoyed his time alone in the office. He turned on his computer and scanned his email messages. Once upon a time, he would have had thirty or forty waiting for him first thing every morning. Today there were two, one from a political fundraiser that he deleted immediately and another from a restaurant in his old stomping grounds on the south side of Boston.

He read the email, an ad for a cabbage and ground beef hot dish. Jimmy used to be in that restaurant at least once a week until his last arrest. It quickly became obvious he had to leave the old neighborhood, and about eight years ago, the restaurant had passed to the next generation. Now, it was too trendy for the likes of Jimmy, not that he could ever go back anyway.

He opened the door to the balcony and, for a moment, relished the morning sunlight warming his bones. By the time Sarah was up, it would be too hot and humid to step outside. It was nice now, but he missed the sounds of Boston traffic, the cars, the horns, the buses, and trucks. He longed for the smell of exhaust and the sound of someone bitching at another driver. He missed home, but he knew if he ever went back, the bastards would have him locked up within twenty-four hours, and he'd never get out.

He closed the balcony door and settled in behind his desk. There was nothing of interest to look at online. He clicked on the Boston Globe site, brought up the morning paper, and there he was, just below the fold on the front page. The headline read, 'Jimmy Dugan's Playing With Us.' He read the article three separate times and felt his blood pressure rise each time he read it. Among other things the damn Globe listed the name on his credit card, Sterling, Cooper and Partners. As if that wasn't bad enough, they went on to explain he'd taken the name from the Mad Men series. He shook two blood pressure pills from the prescription bottle on his desk, tossed them in his mouth, and washed them down with coffee.

How in the hell did this happen? The article suggested it was all a ploy, maybe fake pictures with a Jimmy Dugan lookalike? There was a mugshot from his last arrest twelve years ago, along with a picture of the couple in a restaurant and another of them in a bar. The drunken woman had her blouse pulled open. She was well-endowed and for probably the first time in his life, he wasn't impressed.

For Christ's sake, he'd be the laughingstock of everyone in the old neighborhood. He couldn't let this happen. They find this idiot Killian Graham, and it wouldn't be a huge leap to track things back here to sunny Florida.

He shook his head. It had been a good idea, a damn good idea, but this idiot at the Globe just wrecked the entire deal. Okay, fair enough, if that's the way they wanted it. The first thing he had to do was cancel the credit card. The second was to get hold of someone who could handle this properly.

He took out a burner phone and dialed a number. It was a nine-minute phone call to the bank to cancel the credit card. Once that was done, he set that burner on his desk and pulled out the burner phone where idiot Killian Graham had sent the last batch of images. They'd both have to be destroyed. Freddy could handle that. He placed a call to Freddy and ended up leaving a message.

"Freddy, call me when you get this. A little project for you. Nothing difficult. Call me, damn it."

He placed his next call, hoping the number was still good. The recording recited the number he had dialed and told him to leave a message.

"Yeah, Sloane. A voice from the past. They ever get you for what you did to that redhead? Call me at this number. It's a burner."

There, if Sloane O'Kelly got the message, the mention of the redhead would be all he'd need to hear to know the call was legitimate. If he didn't call back in twenty-four hours, Jimmy would have to find someone else. Damn it, and things had been going so well.

He heard a noise out in the hallway. Sarah was up early. He'd better say good morning, or she'd be coming in to find out what he was up to. He headed out to the kitchen.

She'd just turned on the kettle for her morning tea. She was in her blue silk kimono, the one with the floral pattern that hung down to her knees. There once was a day, now distant and seemingly centuries ago, when she would have been wearing a smile and maybe some lipstick. This morning, instead of asking if he'd like to go back to bed, she asked, "How'd you sleep?"

"Perfectly," he said since she hadn't woken him in the middle of the night in at least a decade. "How about you?"

"The usual, I was up reading until a little after one. Finally fell asleep sometime after three, I think."

God, but he longed for the old days. "Call me when breakfast is ready. I'll be in my office."

"I'm going to shower first. It'll be closer to ten," she said as he wandered back to his office, hoping the phone would ring. The morning continued to drag. He placed two more calls to Freddy by lunchtime. He'd eaten lunch, a damn salad and an open-faced sandwich with paper-thin slices of turkey. He was back in his desk chair, napping, when one of the burner phones rang.

"Where in the hell you been?" was how Jimmy answered.

"I had a doctor's appointment and did some grocery shopping. What's the hurry?" Freddy said.

"I got a burner I want you to get rid of for me."

"So pull it apart and dump it down the bin in your building."

Jimmy closed his eyes and counted to five. "Freddy, get your ass over here and get this damn thing. I'm going to be shutting things down over in Ireland."

"Shutting it down? But boss, you liked what the guy was doing."

"Yeah, well, he got a little carried away, and I read a newspaper article this morning. They're getting a little too close for comfort. So I'm shutting it down."

"You sure you want to do that. I mean, you really liked—"

"Yeah, I'm sure. I already canceled the credit card. I'll have to think of something else to keep them away. So get over here and get rid of this burner for me."

"Okay, on my way," Freddy said and hung up the phone.

"Hey, Lady," he called, and a moment later, a little white dog stepped around the corner. "Let's go for a walk. Then daddy's got some business he's gotta do."

He clipped a leash onto the dog's collar and headed out the door.

TWENTY-NINE

Killian Graham was finishing a late breakfast on the couch while watching another episode of Love, Death & Robots on Netflix. As enjoyable as drunken Riona had been, it was nice to have some peace and quiet for a day. He checked his phone for a text message from the American. Fortunately, there wasn't one. He was dreading the call from Enterprise Car Rental with the repair bill cost, but what could he do? Hopefully, the American wouldn't care. That hope caused Killian to resume his internal debate about whether or not to text him the cost, and maybe he wouldn't notice.

He had a twenty euro note in his pocket, and he thought it might be a good idea to walk up to Paddy Power and place a bet. With a little luck, he could pick up some pocket change if he won his bet, and once he won, he just might be in the mood for some entertainment.

As he dressed, he debated who he could call. Emma was always available, and she'd be happy meeting in a pub and drinking a pint instead of expecting to be taken out to dinner. Best to see what was available for an easy score up at the shop before he made the call.

Dillon and Suel had finished their lunches and taken turns reading the paper. There was still no Killian Graham activity. The lunch crowd had eaten and departed almost an hour ago, and they were back to being just one of three tables occupied in Kennedy's.

One of the tables was a guy on his computer, and Dillon was just thinking *it would have been a good idea to have brought his laptop* when Suel suddenly said, "Well, it's about fecking time," as Killian Graham stepped out of the building. He glanced up at the sun for a second and then wandered up the street. He was wearing jeans and a light blue Dublin jersey.

"Here we go, finally," Dillon said as they headed out the door.

"Thank you," the woman behind the counter called.

"I'll cross the street and follow. You stay on this side," Dillon said and crossed the street, not waiting for a reply.

He walked at the same pace as Graham and maybe fifty feet behind. Suel had sped up a bit and was almost even with Graham but across the street. Graham didn't appear to be in any particular hurry, and based on the quick look they had, the individual was indeed Killian Graham.

He arrived at the corner with North Circular Road and took a left, disappearing around the corner. Dillon hurried to the corner then stepped to the curb, appearing to wait for the light to change so he could cross. Graham continued to stroll down the street, and after a brief moment, Dillon headed in the same direction.

Suel hurried across the intersection, not waiting for the light to change. A woman slowed for him and honked as the light turned yellow. Suel smiled, waved, and continued on his parallel route. Three doors later, Graham stepped into the Paddy Power betting shop.

Dillon walked past and casually glanced in the front window. Unfortunately, it was covered with a poster announcing the Dublin versus Kerry hurling match next Saturday, and he couldn't see inside. He walked a little further and took up residence in a glass-covered bus stop. Suel leaned against the front of a pub directly across the street from the betting shop.

They waited for a good twenty minutes before Graham stepped out of the betting shop and headed back to his apartment. They followed and walked a short distance beyond the building until they were out of the apartment's line of sight.

"What do you think we should do?" Suel asked.

"I hate to return to Kennedy's," Dillon said. "If we didn't draw attention before, we certainly will going back in there. What if you settle in the car and I stand on the far corner? That way, if he heads out on foot, we'll have him covered either way."

"That'll work, but before we do that, maybe go behind the building. If there are cars parked back there, take down the license numbers and phone them in. If he pulls out of here in a car, we have no way to know it's him until it's too late."

Dillon headed for the parking area behind the hairdressers. It was a small lot with a half-dozen vehicles parked in it. He jotted down the license numbers and hurried back to the street. Suel was already seated in his car. Dillon gave him a wave as he headed up to the corner.

He phoned in the license numbers and waited while the officer on the other end input them. They got a hit on the fourth vehicle. Killian Graham was listed as the owner of a black 2007 Peugeot. He texted the license number along with the vehicle description back to Suel.

Dillon was leaning against the corner building, watching Graham's place. He could see Suel's car, but he couldn't make out Suel seated behind the wheel. Maybe ten minutes later, his phone signaled a text message coming through. The text was from Myra Harrison with Gretchen Malden and Mary Ellen Schneider's passport numbers. Dillon forwarded the text to his contact with the Dublin airport police, Brendan Kane, and then followed up with a phone call.

"Dillon?" was how Kane answered the phone call.

"Hi Brendan, I just sent you a text message."

"Yeah, I was looking at it when your call came through. You suspect they're bringing in cocaine?"

"Well, that's the general information we have, but it's sketchy at best." He went on to tell Kane his suspicions regarding the caller then finished up with, "I'd like to be there to meet the flight and listen in on any interaction you may have."

"Not a problem. Coming in from France, it wouldn't be uncommon for the flight to arrive early. At that hour of the day, there won't be much of a line for non-EU passports, if at all. Maybe plan on being here around 8:15. We'll bring them into separate rooms. Our female officers will conduct a search, and any checked luggage will be pulled."

"Hopefully, this is all a stunt by some jackass but check them thoroughly. I'm going to look into an individual on this end. With any luck, I'll see you tomorrow night, Brendan."

"I'll look forward to that. Thanks for the text and the update," Kane said and disconnected.

THIRTY

It was another hour before Dillon's phone rang. DCI McCabe was finally calling back. "Yes, sir," was how Dillon answered.

"Sorry for the insufferable delay, Dillon. God save me. Anything happening on your end?"

Dillon gave him an update, which consisted of Graham walking to the Paddy Power shop and returning to his apartment twenty minutes later. He finished by reading McCabe the license number on Graham's 2007 Peugeot.

"Very well, a team is on the way armed with a warrant. I want you and Suel to hold your positions and follow them in. You are not to lead. Once Graham is in your custody, transport him down here, and we'll begin our interrogation. I've assembled files for the two of you. Any questions?"

"No, sir."

"I've issued instructions that Graham is to be considered armed and dangerous. Remember that, and it might serve to remind DI Suel of that as well. Good luck and wait for the team to arrive," McCabe said and disconnected.

Dillon called Suel to give him the update.

"I got off the line with McCabe not five minutes ago," Suel said. "He told me he was going to call you."

"Well, I'm supposed to tell you that we're to hold our positions and follow the team in," Dillon said.

"That's exactly what he told me to tell you," Suel said.

"Good, then we both got the message," Dillon said just as an unmarked black van turned the corner and headed down the street. "The van just passed me. I'm coming your way," Dillon said.

"Not too fast. It's going to take them a minute to get situated," Suel said.

The van had already pulled to the curb, and Dillon began walking toward it. No one stepped out for the better part of a minute when suddenly the back door flew open, and six men dressed all in black jumped out the back. The first two disappeared along the side of the building, and Dillon figured they were probably headed into the back parking lot just in case Graham tried to make it to his car.

The remaining four men gathered around the front door leading into the apartments. As Dillon and Suel drew near, one of the men swung a battering ram that burst the door open, and all four disappeared inside. Dillon strained his ears for the sound of gunshots but fortunately didn't hear any. Suel joined him, and with pistols drawn, they headed up a steep set of stairs.

They heard a large boom followed by shouting coming from off to the left of the top of the stairs. By the time they made their way to the top of the stairs, all they saw was a door to the left that had been battered open. An older man at the opposite end of the hall stepped outside his apartment just long enough to see Dillon and Suel with weapons drawn before he stepped back inside.

They stepped into the small apartment. The tv was playing a cartoon of some sort. Two officers stood in front of a ratty-looking couch with yellowed sponge stuffing peeking out of a torn cushion. Lying on the couch was Killian Graham or Jimmy Dugan, whichever name he was using. He was wearing a red and black plaid Terri-cloth robe over his Dublin jersey, a recently added set of handcuffs, and a very surprised look on his face. Dillon and Suel didn't see a weapon anywhere.

"Why won't you lot tell me what in God's name you're doing here?" Graham said.

The apartment was small. Tiny might be a better description. The kitchen area was at one end of the sitting room. Along with a sink full of dirty dishes, there was a two-burner stove, a small refrigerator, and a toaster that took up almost half of the two-foot counter space.

The bedroom had a small double bed with a pair of blue jeans tossed on it. The chest of drawers looked like something Ikea would reject. There was only room for one officer in the bedroom, and he was going through a small rack of hanging clothes. There wasn't a closet in the bedroom. Another officer was in the bathroom, checking the drawers in the small vanity beneath the sink. Dillon stepped back into the sitting room and glanced out the front window. The two officers that had run around to the back of the building were seated in the back door of the van, drinking what was probably tea from a thermos.

"Will one of youse please tell me what the feck you're doing here. I haven't done anything wrong."

"You see any point in staying here?" Dillon asked Suel.

"No, let's transport him back to the station. They'll want to let him sit for an hour or two in an interrogation room. Give him a chance to think about the trouble he's in."

"I don't know," Dillon said. "For a guy with a record like Dugan's, he sure isn't what I expected."

"Yeah, a bit strange that. By the way, he sounds like a real Dub. You'd never guess he was an American."

One of the officers stepped over to them and lowered his voice. "You're going to transport him?"

"Yeah, anything you need from him or us?"

The officer shook his head. "No, I have to tell you, he was beyond shocked when we burst into the place. This muppet is supposed to be some sort of crime boss in the states? We called him by his name, Dugan, and he told us we had the wrong place. We haven't done a complete search yet, but so far, we haven't come across anything suggesting a weapon. He was in here watching a cartoon for God's sake."

"Well, he's definitely the fellow in the pictures. He's the same person the American press wrote about. His record, among other things, is nineteen murders. Those are the ones we know about," Dillon said.

"Very strange," the officer said and shook his head. "Yeah, I suppose you can go ahead and get him out of here. I'd tell you to send those two louts outside back up here, but there isn't room for them. That's another thing. He's a big-time criminal in the states, and he's living here? In this place?"

"He's been keeping a low profile," Dillon said, realizing just how stupid that sounded.

"You can keep a low profile in a suite overlooking a nude beach in Spain," the officer said.

"Can someone please tell me what in the hell is going on here?" Graham asked again.

"Let's get him out of here," Suel said. He faced Graham and said, "Mr. Graham, or Mr. Dugan, or whatever name you're going by at the moment, we're placing you under arrest. You are not obliged to say anything unless you wish to do so, but whatever you say will be taken down in writing and may be given in evidence. Now, if you'd come with us please," Suel said as he placed a hand on Graham's arm and pulled him to his feet.

"What the hell is wrong with you people? Who the hell is this Dugan character you keep talking about? You're making a big mistake. Let me just tell you," he said and seemed to be raising his voice with every step as they led him to the door. "I am going to sue your asses off. Don't say I didn't warn you."

"If you'd come this way, Mr. Graham," Dillon said and directed Graham toward the door leading out of the apartment.

"Can I at least put on my jeans and some shoes?" Graham said.

Suel looked at Dillon, who nodded, and they steered Graham toward the bedroom. The officer in the bedroom had just poured the contents of a dresser drawer onto the bed.

Graham looked at Suel and Dillon and said, "What in the hell is wrong with you people? Honest to God. I tell you what," he said to the officer who had just emptied the dresser drawer. "You find any money, you gotta split it with me."

"If you'd please sit down, sir," Dillon said and gently pushed Graham onto the bed. He picked up the blue jeans and handed them to Graham. It took some time since he was handcuffed, but Graham was eventually able to pull on the jeans. Using his foot, Dillon slid a pair of shoes over in front of Graham, who slipped them on. He wasn't wearing socks.

They led him out to Suel's car, still wearing the plaid Terri-cloth robe, and opened the rear door for him.

"You can't be serious. This is your car? Are you two even cops?" Graham asked. He didn't seem to be kidding.

Thankfully, the ride to the station was uneventful. Suel pulled up to the rear door in the parking lot. Dillon hopped out and opened the car door for Graham. They waited for a couple of minutes until Suel joined them then hurried inside the station. They stepped off the elevator on the fourth floor and led Graham down a hall and into the interrogation area. McCabe had made arrangements, and they brought Graham into interrogation room three. Suel pulled out the chair for Graham, and he sat down, still handcuffed and wearing the bathrobe. "Make yourself comfortable," Suel said, and they headed out of the room.

"I'd like to speak to a solicitor, please. I'm going to sue your ass," Graham said, just before they closed the door, leaving him in the room.

"What do you think?" Dillon asked Suel.

"I'm thinking this isn't adding up. If your man is playing us, he's giving the best performance I've ever seen."

THIRTY-ONE

Not for the first time, Jimmy Dugan looked out the door to the balcony and studied the parking lot below. Where in the hell was Freddy? It was a ten-minute drive over here, and they'd talked almost an hour ago. He was ready to call him again when he spotted Freddy pulling into the parking lot. He was hard to miss driving around town in his orange Dodge Viper. The damn thing was supposed to look like a sports car. Instead, given the stupid headlights, it looked like a scrawny cat on the prowl.

Jimmy smiled as Freddy pulled into an empty parking space, purposely centering the vehicle on the line separating two parking places. Freddy's thought process was, that way, no one would park too close to his car. The idea had failed more than once.

Now came the fun part, watching Freddy attempt to climb out of the vehicle. The driver's door opened, and Freddy's legs eventually swung out and onto the pavement. Jimmy could almost hear him groaning as he inched his fat ass to the edge of the seat. He attempted to thrust himself forward two, three, and finally, on the fourth attempt, got halfway out of the vehicle. With one hand on the driver's seat and the other on the steering wheel, he proceeded to inch his way up until he was standing red-faced in the parking lot with a heaving chest.

While Jimmy chuckled, Freddy glanced around, wiped the sweat from his forehead, and then turned and leaned into the driver's seat for a quick moment. *Oh no,* thought Jimmy. *Don't tell me he brought the damn dog.*

Freddy stood and stepped away from the car, carrying his little white dog. He gave the driver's door a hip check and headed into the building. Jimmy swore and hurried out of his office to the intercom. Sarah was in the living room, watching some ridiculous cooking show. The intercom buzzed and then buzzed again twenty seconds later.

"Aren't you going to answer that?" Sarah said, not taking her eyes off the television.

"Yeah, relax, I got it."

It buzzed again, and she looked over at Jimmy.

"Relax, I got this. Hello?"

"Yeah, Jimmy, it's me, Freddy."

"About time. Get up here," Jimmy said and pressed the button to unlock the door.

"Why did you make him wait?" Sarah asked.

"Just stick to your show."

Freddy knocked on the door a couple of minutes later.

"What took you?" Jimmy asked as he opened the door.

"I had to wait for some broad with a walker to get in the elevator. She took her time gettin' on and took even longer gettin' off. Hi Sarah, how's it going?"

"Fine, Freddy. Oh, look who you brought over. Bring her over and let me see her."

"We got shit to do," Jimmy said.

"So go do it. Freddy, let me hold her. You go ahead with Captain Crabby there and attend to whatever is so important."

As Freddy handed the dog to Sarah, it proceeded to lick her face.

"Oh, Jesus, come on back to the office," Jimmy said and headed down the hall. Freddy dutifully followed. Once in the office, Freddy closed the door behind him and then settled into a chair in front of the desk.

Jimmy sat down and pushed the two burner phones across the desk. "Get rid of these damn things. Pull the batteries and the SIM cards out, toss them in different bins. Then smash the phones and place them in different bins."

"Jimmy, I know all this shit. Consider it done. So what happened with this Irish guy, what's his name, Killer Grim?"

"Killian Graham is his name. What happened is this piece of shit at the Boston Globe wrote an article and ran three pictures of me. Well, actually, one was my mug-shot from 2002, and the other ones were this idiot Graham and some bimbo. That ain't the problem, exactly.

The problem is, in the article they ask the question, 'Are these really pictures of Jimmy Dugan?."

"Of course it is. Who in the hell did he think the mug shot was? Dumb bastard didn't check with the cops? They would have—"

"Freddy, the mugshot ain't the problem. The problem is the two pictures of Graham and the woman. One of 'em, she's got her blouse pulled open, and she's showing off her hooters."

"So since when didn't you want to be seen with a pair of—"

"Will you just listen? The article said it's strange behavior for a guy trying to keep a low profile. And damn it, he's right. It was one thing to have a picture in a restaurant. Hell, they just look like someone took it on the sly. But this one, it ain't what I'd be doing while trying to stay under the radar at the same time."

"You gonna tell this Graham guy in Ireland to knock it off?"

"Nah, I don't even want to contact him. Cops take a look and maybe ask him a couple of questions. It can't be good. He don't know my name, and he don't know where I live. He thinks I run a tour or travel company, and that's the way I wanna keep it. It was good while it lasted, but now's the time to get out while I can. The right person gets hold of this, it could be the beginning of the end. So anyway, ditch these burners and do it right away."

"Got it. Anything else you need?"

"Yeah, don't forget your dog on the way out. Sarah hangs on to him much longer, she won't give him back."

"It's her."

"What?"

"It ain't a him. It's a her, a girl dog."

"Ya mean a female?"

"Yeah, that's what I just said."

"Go on, get outta here. And, Freddy, take it easy and be careful."

"You too, Jimmy. You be careful, too."

Jimmy watched out the balcony door and laughed as Freddy struggled to get back into his car and eventually drive away.

THIRTY-TWO

Dillon and Suel stood in the dark behind the tinted glass window with DCI McCabe staring at Killian Graham sitting in the interrogation room. He'd been in there for over an hour, still handcuffed and wearing the red and black bathrobe.

"He doesn't appear to be very nervous," Dillon said.

"Just pissed off," Suel said.

McCabe handed Dillon the file and said, "DNA and the records we checked prove beyond any doubt that he is indeed Killian Graham. Other than three days in Paris eighteen months ago and a one day trip to London for a rugby match three years prior to that, he has never left Ireland. He's certainly never been to the US. That said, he is involved in some way, shape, or form with this Dugan character, and I want you to find out how."

Dillon and Suel left the room and stepped into the interrogation room.

"What, you two again? I told the likes of youse before, I ain't whoever it is you're looking for. I intend to sue the hell out of your worthless ass. So just keep wasting my time because you're going to have to pay me that much more."

"Tell me, Killian. How'd you ever meet up with Jimmy Dugan?" Dillon asked.

"Who?" Graham got a look on his face that suggested he didn't know who Dillon was talking about.

"Jimmy Dugan. He's a somewhat famous American. You meet him in pub or a restaurant?"

"I can honestly say, I have no idea what yer talking about. Who in the hell is this Jimmy Dugan?"

"This is him right here."

Dillon said and pulled out the mugshot of Dugan.

Graham glanced down and then did a double-take and stared at the photo. "This some game you lot are playing? This says Boston Police. I ain't never been to the states, so whoever put this together made a big mistake. I don't know what your game is, but it ain't working."

Dillon gave Suel a look. Suel pulled out the article with the picture of Graham and Ciara at the Emerald Gardens. Ciara had the linen napkin held up in front of her face. "Are you telling us this isn't you? Are you suggesting we made a mistake?"

Graham's eyes grew wide, and he stared at the copy of the article for a long moment, as he read the copy. "This says Jimmy Dugan here. But that's me and Ciara. We was down to Wexford. How did this—"

"We know it's you, Killian. You're posing as Jimmy Dugan. I think you probably know that, but just in case, let me fill you in. He's one bad feck. Responsible for an awful lot of crime. What is it, Marshal, nineteen murders in the US?"

"Those are just the ones we know about, so far," Dillon said. "He's going away to prison for the rest of his life except that they might just waive that and put him to death. We do that in the states, you know, put bad operators to death."

"Now you lot, just wait a damn minute. I don't know this, this, Dugan person. He's not a mate. I've never met him or anyone like him, swear to God."

"You sure, Killian? I mean, just for starters, you're a carbon copy of him. And if you never met him, I guess the only question I have is— just how in the bloody hell did this picture end up in the bleedin' Boston newspaper?" Dillon shouted. "You and your love interest for the night, Ciara. You're looking at some serious time behind bars Killian. It could even end up to be for the rest of your damn life."

Graham's eyes grew wide, and he said, "I, I don't know how this picture got in the Boston newspaper. I've never been to Boston. I told you I've never even been to the states, honest."

"Then how did they get these pictures? Did you send them to Wendell Murphy at the Boston Globe?" Dillon asked and pointed to Murphy's name just below the headline.

Graham shook his head and said, "No, no, honest. Look, every month or so, I send photos to a guy who contacted me a while back. I don't know his name, okay.

God, if I did, believe me, I'd tell youse. I think he runs a travel agency or a tour company or something. He asked me to go out to dinner with a woman, any woman, and have our picture taken. I just send him pictures, end of story. Okay? The guy deposits two hundred euros in my bank account every month. He pays for the dinners, he pays for the hotel, never questions me. The other day I rented a car to impress this woman I took down to Wexford, and he paid for the car. All he wants me to do is take a woman to dinner, stay in a nice hotel, and have my picture taken. That's it."

"How does he pay for the dinners, the hotels, and the car?" Suel asked.

"How? He gave me a Visa card. It's made out to his company, I think. It's in my wallet, which by the way, your lot took from my apartment. Honest, you gotta believe me. I don't know who this guy is. I never met him. When I get instructions from him, it's always in a text message. The pictures are taken on my cellphone, usually by a server or the bartender. Once in a while, someone at another table takes our picture. At the end of the night or the next morning, I send the pictures to him. He always has me text them to him, always to a different phone number."

"And none of this struck you as strange?"

"You kidding? Of course, it's strange. But I get two hundred euro every month and a couple of nights in a fancy hotel. I eat in great restaurants with beautiful women who are more than happy to show their gratitude. I mean, what would you lot do?"

Both Suel and Dillon had to admit that Graham had a point.

"Pardon us for a minute, Mr. Graham. While we're out of the room, you might want to think about what else you can tell us," Dillon said as he and Suel stood and walked out of the room. They joined DCI McCabe watching through the tinted glass in the room next door. "What do you think, sir?" Dillon asked as they entered the room.

McCabe shook his head. "It's so strange I fear it's credible. Clearly, he's not this American Dugan, although he does look like the man. We've got records going back to his primary school days. He is who he says he is. And, unfortunately, his argument about receiving two hundred euros every month and a couple of nights at a five-star hotel with a woman stupid enough to put up with him for forty-eight hours is credible."

"You want us to turn him loose?" Suel asked.

"Yes, in a manner of speaking. Take him under your wing. Let's maintain a positive contact with him. Tell him, next time he's asked to have his picture taken, we would appreciate a phone call. In the meantime, we'll work with his bank to see if we can trace where the monthly deposits are coming from and let's track that credit card as well."

Dillon and Suel stepped back into the interrogation room. Graham eyed them but didn't say anything. Dillon sat down opposite Graham. Suel stood, leaning against the wall just behind Dillon.

"Mr. Graham, we're going to take you home and let you get on with your life for the time being. I think it might be wise if you remained in touch. Should you receive a request to stay at a hotel or go out to dinner, it would probably be a good idea to contact us immediately. There's no telling what Jimmy Dugan has in mind."

Dillon waited for a response, maybe another lawsuit threat, but Graham simply nodded and looked relieved. "We'll collect your wallet and cellphone on the way out." Dillon nodded. Suel stepped over and removed the handcuffs from Graham's wrists.

They collected his cellphone, wallet, car keys, and a few other items on the way out of the station and climbed back into Suel's car. The closer they got to Graham's apartment, the more back to normal he became.

"Look, I know you're doing your job. But for the love of God. Wouldn't you do a little more research before you breakdown someone's door and arrest them? What about just stopping by for a chat, and we could have sorted things out. Fair warning, lads. My first call the moment I step into my place will be to a solicitor, and we'll be coming after youse. This was nothing but abuse."

Neither Dillon nor Suel responded.

"I might just call RTE after the solicitor. I'm thinking they'd love a story like this. A lad just watching the telly in the supposed privacy of his home when suddenly the door gets battered in. By the way, who's going to pay for the damage?"

"Have your landlord contact An Garda Síochána," Suel said. Dillon glanced over and saw the jaw muscles flexing as Suel ground his teeth.

They pulled to the curb a few minutes later. Dillon hopped out of the passenger seat and opened the door for Graham, still ranting. "I mean, it beggars all belief. Whatever happened to the rights of a citizen? And you know what else? I—"

Dillon pulled out a business card and handed it to Graham. "Mr. Graham, if you hear anything from Jimmy Dugan, it would be best to give us a call. This is an on-going investigation, and it would be a shame to appear to be withholding information. Thank you for your patience, sir," Dillon said and hurried back into the passenger seat. Suel accelerated before the door was closed.

"What a bleeding disaster," Suel said.

"I fear we haven't heard the end of it," Dillon said.

"Would they not have checked things out before issuing the warrant and sending the team in? For that matter, what that plonker Graham said is right. Why didn't they just knock on the door instead of banging it open?" Suel just shook his head.

THIRTY-THREE

Jimmy Dugan was shredding receipts when the burner phone in his desk drawer signaled a call coming through. He opened the drawer. There was only one burner in there, and he had used it to call Sloane O'Kelly. He let it ring three times before he picked it up, pressed the screen, and said, "Yeah?"

"Is this the voice from my past?" O'Kelly said and chuckled.

"Great to hear from you, Sloane. It's been too long."

"Funny you mentioned the redhead. What was the name of that place behind your Key West house?"

"The Silver Palms Inn."

"Yeah, that's it. You in Key West now?"

"No, I hang on to that just in case, but things have been nice and quiet."

"Good job of laying low, Jimmy. This wouldn't happen to be regarding those two articles in the Globe, would it?"

"In a manner of speaking but not what you might think."

"Good, I was going to caution you. Murphy, the newspaper douche, is pretty much untouchable after writing them articles. You could do something, but it would only intensify an investigation. I gotta tell you, word on the street was you passed on. Hell of a good job keeping out of sight. A shame those two articles ruined that."

"Yeah, I need to sort that out. You interested in taking a little trip?"

"Depends on where."

"Ireland."

"That's where you are? You mean those pictures in the articles were legit?"

"That's where I'd like your services performed," Dugan said, sidestepping the question on his location.

"Yeah, I can go over there, I guess. I'd need a contact for equipment once I arrive. All the security and scanners and shit, you're just asking for trouble trying to sneak a weapon on board a plane."

"I don't have a contact over there. Can you go back to basics? Make this more of a hands-on experience?"

"Yeah, I guess I can. It'll increase the cost. I can use a knife or a hammer, hell, or even a necktie."

Dugan chuckled at that last line. "I'll leave that part up to you."

"I'll need half upfront, Jimmy. No offense, but them newspaper articles, they stirred the pot. Suddenly, the cops dusted off the files, and they're taking another look. Word on the street is the feds are interested, too. If you haven't done so, you might just want to cut all ties to whoever this is."

"Already done that," Dugan said. "I'll send you the information, and then I'm gonna ditch this phone. I'll call you in twenty-four hours."

"Give me two days. Is this person in Dublin?"

"He is."

"I'll book a flight, and as soon as we hang up, I'll send you account information. Ten now, ten on completion. Nice hearing your voice, Jimmy."

"Likewise, send me the info," Dugan said and disconnected. "Shit," he said to his empty office. *Twenty grand to shut this down, times had definitely changed.*

Sloane O'Kelly went online and pulled up the numbers for his offshore account. He punched them into his text message, double-checked to make sure they were correct, and then pushed 'send.'

Dugan's burner phone vibrated on his desk. He opened the text message and wrote down the account number. It took fifteen minutes, but he was able to send the funds and received a reply that the deposit had been made.

He debated calling Freddy back to get rid of the burner but just as quickly decided he should deal with it himself. He turned the phone off, stuffed it in his pocket, and headed out the door.

Sarah was napping on the couch. He left without waking her. He climbed in the car and drove down to the pier. There was a half-full parking lot in front of the pier. He parked and sat in the car for a couple of minutes while he disassembled the burner phone. Once that was accomplished, he locked the car and strolled onto the pier. He placed the phone battery in a waste bin. He dropped the SIM card in a bin next to a food stand when he ordered a strawberry shake. He sucked on the straw as he headed toward the end of the pier, tossing the halves of the burner in two different trash bins.

He stood for five minutes watching two fat guys fishing off the end of the pier. They seemed more asleep than awake, and he eventually wandered back to his car. On the way home, he stopped at Digital World and purchased five phones at $19.99 each. He paid cash for the phones and headed home.

Sarah was in the kitchen, working on whatever was on tap for dinner. He shouted a hello, headed into his office, and placed the bag with the phones in his desk drawer. He headed back into the kitchen, gave Sarah a kiss, and sat down at the kitchen counter.

THIRTY-FOUR

uel pulled in front of the station, dropped Dillon off, and left after giving the excuse he had to meet someone. Dillon went in the main entrance, walked through the building and out the rear door into the parking lot.

He picked up a bottle of wine at a shop on the way home. When he pulled into his drive, there was no Mercedes parked in front of Tara's car. He felt relieved about that and headed into the house.

Lucifer met him at the front door and hurried outside. Dillon went into the kitchen, set the wine bottle on the counter, and grabbed a biscuit from the cookie jar. Lucifer was sniffing around the front garden when Dillon called him and tossed the biscuit. He turned on the oven, pulled a TV dinner from the refrigerator, and opened the wine bottle.

Ten minutes later, Lucifer was scratching at the door, and Dillon let him inside. They settled down on the couch, Lucifer with another biscuit he inhaled in two bites and Dillon with the TV dinner and glass of wine. They went for their evening walk and were both in bed just after ten. Dillon slept through the night until the alarm went off.

He was dressed and finishing breakfast when he heard Lucifer come down the stairs. He let him outside and was in the process of filling his water dish when his phone rang. The number was listed as unknown, but he answered anyway.

"Hello?"

"Is this Marshal Dillon?" The voice sounded familiar, but Dillon couldn't place it.

"It is."

"Killian Graham, Marshal. I just got off the line with Enterprise Rental."

"Oh," Dillon said and wondered if Graham had spoken with Devan at Enterprise.

"Yeah, guess what? Apparently, the Visa card I had from Sterling, Cooper and Partners has been canceled."

"Really! Did they say when it had been canceled?"

"It must have been yesterday because it worked when I checked out of the Riverbank House Hotel two days ago, and it worked when I returned the car. They only found out about it when they tried to run the repair bill through."

"What was the repair charge?"

"God, the bill is sixty-three hundred euros. I know they're overcharging me, but what can I do?"

"Sounds like you're going to have to pay the bill. Can't you work out some payment arrangement?"

"I can't believe this Dugan guy is screwing me like this. By the way, I Googled that worthless knacker. If I'd known this was who I was dealing with, I don't think I would have done it."

Yeah, except it was such a good deal you couldn't say no, Dillon thought. "Did you see the pictures of him?" Dillon asked.

"See 'em, you kidding? I studied each and every one of them. I didn't count em, but there must be a couple hundred on Google Images. I checked 'em all. I gotta say, you lot were right, he looks like me. A lot like me."

"Yeah, and that's why he wanted the pictures of you out on the town enjoying yourself."

"Okay, okay, I get that. But I didn't know who he was at the time. I mean, if you had seen me in one of them high-class restaurants, would you have thought I was this Jimmy Dugan shite."

"To be honest, I knew his name, but I didn't know what he looked like."

"Yeah, see, and you're the law. So how was someone like me supposed to know?"

"Yeah, I get your point."

"Well, here's the deal. If you could maybe find a way to help me on this repair bill for the rental car, maybe I could call off the solicitors on suing you and your mates."

"Mmm, interesting, what'd you say the bill was?"

"Sixty-three hundred euros."

"Tell you what, Mr. Graham, let me check into it. I can't promise anything but let me see."

"Maybe you could call this guy back at the car rental place, tell him you're looking into it?"

"Let me check with the powers that be, first. This is above my pay grade," Dillon said.

"You'll call me right back?"

"It's going to take longer than a couple of minutes. I'll call Enterprise and tell them we spoke, ask them to give you some time. I'll get back to you as soon as I can, okay?"

"Yeah, okay, but the sooner, the better," Graham said and disconnected.

Dillon let Lucifer in the house and headed to the office. He was in before Suel. McCabe was in, but he had two guys in his office. Dillon cleared two mugs and plates from his desk, poured himself a coffee that wasn't half bad, and settled in at his desk. He phoned Myra Harrison at DCU, intending to leave a message, but surprisingly, she answered.

"Hi Jack, did you find anything out?"

"Only what you told me, Myra. Are you going to be there for a bit?"

"I'm here all day."

"Would you mind if I came over? I'd like to listen to that phone message and see where it came from."

"Sure, anytime, as I said, I'm here all day."

"I'll be over in the next half-hour."

"Come straight back to my office. No one is at the front desk until nine."

"See you shortly," Dillon said and headed out to his car. He pulled into the lot at DCU fifteen minutes later. He made a mental note of all the half-awake students seemingly wandering aimlessly at this hour of the morning. He entered Myra's building and headed back to her office.

She was seated at her desk as he knocked on the doorframe.

"Oh, wow. That was fast," she said. "Grab a chair."

They chatted for a couple of minutes, and then Myra brought up the phone message and put it on speaker. Dillon listened to it three times.

"Well, definitely someone was attempting to disguise their voice. Any idea who?"

Myra shook her head.

"Send a copy of that to my cellphone, please," Dillon said.

Myra nodded and punched in his number. His cell signaled a text message coming in a moment later.

"Whoever made that call, they're in a small world. No offense, but contacting you instead of An Garda Síochána suggests to me it's probably someone here at DCU who has an ax to grind. The information is correct. The girls are due in tonight. I'll be out there with the airport police. They're going to take them into a private area, search them and their luggage and then hopefully send them on their way. In fact, if everything is okay, and I'm pretty sure it will be, I'll give them a lift to campus."

"So you're not expecting a problem at the airport?"

"No, in fact, just the opposite. Still, the phone calls having been made, we have to react. Like I said, if someone wanted to have them caught, arrested, whatever, they would have contacted the Garda. They didn't do that. Instead they called you anonymously. Are you aware of any problems the girls may have had with someone?"

She shook her head. "No, nothing. I checked, and they're current with all their classwork. Both of them doing well as a matter of fact."

"You get another phone call or hear anything, please let me know," Dillon said. "I'll leave a message for you once we've dealt with their arrival."

"Thank you. I'd appreciate that."

Dillon left Myra's office and headed over to the building where Shannon O'Leary and the girls lived. He punched in the room number, 206, followed by the pound sign but didn't get a reply. He waited a couple of minutes and phoned again but still didn't get an answer, so he left.

Back in the Special Branch office, there weren't any dirty dishes on Dillon's desk. He hurried into the break room, poured a mug of coffee, and knocked on McCabe's door.

"Enter," said McCabe, never looking up. He finished writing then smiled and said, "Good morning, Dillon. What can I do for you?"

"Just an update on the Jimmy Dugan, Killian Graham situation, and the latest on the two girls from DCU," Dillon said. He proceeded to bring McCabe up to date on Killian Graham and the canceled credit card.

"Interesting, do you think that's because of the cost of repair, or do you think these two articles in the Boston Globe have Dugan suddenly cutting ties?"

"Difficult to say. My first thought is, if the repair cost was an issue, Graham would have been informed one way or another, a text message, an irate call, something. To just cancel the card after all the times Graham has used it seems a bit strange."

McCabe nodded and said, "The girls in Paris?"

"They're supposedly on a flight arriving this evening. They'll be taken aside and searched. I could be wrong, but I think this is someone with a personal ax to grind. If this was legit, why would you call a school administrator? You'd call An Garda Síochána or airport security but not the school."

"Although, if the airport police were contacted, that could end up with having everyone searched on all incoming flights. You'll be at the airport this evening?" McCabe asked.

"Yes, I don't expect anything, but I'd like to be there just to be sure."

"Very well, keep me advised," McCabe said. "Anything else?"

"No, sir. D.I. Suel is chasing down some information on the Russian women and the Stiles street address but nothing concrete thus far."

"I'll leave you to it," McCabe said and flashed a smile dismissing Dillon.

THIRTY-FIVE

Once back at his desk, Dillon phoned Devan at Enterprise Car Rental. "Oh, yes, Marshal Dillon. What's the news?"

"None really. I believe Killian Graham phoned you regarding his credit card being canceled."

"He did, told me his employer was not happy."

"His employer? That's the term he used?"

"Well, no, not exactly. That's more a case of me sensing what was going on."

"We're going to be involved on this end, see if we might be able to help Mr. Graham."

"I wonder, should I just change that invoice to An Garda Síochána?"

"Ahh, no, at least not yet. If I could ask for a few days patience until we have things sorted out on this end. You can imagine the red tape we're climbing through."

"Preaching to the choir. I'll take care of things on this end. If I could hear from you, oh, say in the next two or three days, that would work."

Two or three days? thought Dillon. *He was guessing weeks if not months.* "That should work just fine," he said and disconnected.

He worked through the day, seemingly not making any headway. He drove home early to give Lucifer an early evening walk before heading out to the airport. On their way up to the green to chase the tennis ball, Dillon couldn't help but notice the black Mercedes backed in front of Tara's car and felt his blood pressure rise.

Whoever he was, Tara was giving him a lot more attention than Dillon had ever received. So be it. He tossed the ball for the better part of a half-hour before Lucifer called it quits and stretched out on the grass.

They headed home. Dillon debated pouring a handful of sand in the Mercedes gas tank before he quickly decided against it. He was out at the airport well before eight and made his way to Brendan Kane's office.

"Oh, Dillon, perfect timing. That Ryan Air flight is due in from Lille in fifteen minutes. It's landing at Terminal One. Let's head over to security there and watch the girls coming in. You said they're traveling on American passports?"

"Yes, that's my understanding."

"We've got those two numbers flagged. The agent will hold them, and two officers will escort them to a room to be searched. Once that's done, we'll search any checked luggage."

"You think they'll have some?"

"Checked luggage? It's an additional cost with Ryan Air. They're flying out of Lille instead of Paris to save money, so it's doubtful. We'll see. Let's walk over to Terminal One, and we can watch the proceedings."

Terminal One in Dublin Airport was the original airport building, updated and modified a few hundred times. It was used largely for flights to and from the UK, France, and Germany. It was a good ten minute walk by the time they were in the security area watching the passport control area on monitors. Another fifteen minutes passed before passengers began arriving in passport control from the Ryan Air flight. Almost all of them were traveling on EU Passports.

Another ten minutes passed before two young women, a blonde and a brunette made their way through the sectioned lanes leading to the one officer checking non EU passports.

"Screen five," Kane said, and the monitor suddenly switched to a larger screen mounted on the wall. A red light suddenly began to flash on the screen as the officer checking the passports slowly paged through the first woman's passport. Two officers suddenly appeared and escorted both women toward a distant door.

"The blonde is Gretchen Malden. Mary Ellen Schneider has the darker hair. It'll be a couple of minutes while they search them. Let's go down there. We can wait in the interrogation room, and they'll be brought in," Kane said.

They took an elevator up to the first floor, walked through the baggage claim area, and took a staircase up to a series of rooms. Based on the doors, three of the rooms were interrogation rooms. Kane held open the door to interrogation room two, and Dillon stepped in.

The room was carpeted and had gray walls and the standard tinted glass on one wall. A darkened room for observation was on the other side. It was another twenty minutes before the girls were led into the room. The fact that they were both entering the room, together, with their carry-on luggage, suggested no illegal substance had been found.

"Good, nothing was found," Kane whispered to Dillon. He pressed a button to begin recording.

The girls had obviously been crying, and Kane handed them a box of tissues as they sat down. "Please have a seat, ladies. I'm DCI Brendan Kane with An Garda Síochána. This is Marshal Dillon with the US Marshal's Service currently assigned to us."

"We didn't do anything," Gretchen said and began sobbing. Mary Ellen wrapped her arm around her.

"We know that, and we want to thank you for cooperating with us. You're both okay. You're not in any trouble. We have a couple of questions, and then you'll be free to go. Marshal," Kane said as he turned toward Dillon.

Dillon cleared his throat. "Here's what's happened, ladies. Someone called the offices at DCU and reported you two. We're pretty sure it was a woman. She said you would each be transporting drugs from France. She named you specifically and provided your flight information."

"Shannon O'Leary," both women said.

"That bitch," Gretchen said. "She's pissed off because her boyfriend dumped her and came with me."

"Who can blame the poor guy? She treated him like absolute shit," Mary Ellen said.

"She had your flight information?" Dillon said.

"She could have copied it down. We printed it off, and it was lying around in our rooms. Her boyfriend dumped her about a month ago. I knew who he was but just to say hi and, you know, talk a little. I didn't have a relationship with him or anything. After he dumped her, we talked a little bit. We had lunch together."

"That party at the French guy's apartment," Mary Ellen said.

"Yeah, a party, about three weeks ago. Umm, wine, and beer. Lots of beer, and we maybe started seeing each other."

"He and his brother came with us to France. None of us had ever been there, and we had the best time," Mary Ellen said.

"Yeah, really fun. I mean, Paris, come on."

"So they were on the flight with you?"

Both girls nodded.

"They're Irish?" Kane asked.

The girls nodded.

"What are their names?"

"Eamon and Michael McGinty," Gretchen said. "In fact, they're probably waiting for us. We're sharing a taxi back to DCU."

"I'll get someone to let them know you'll be out in just a minute," Brendan said and hurried out the door.

Kane didn't return, and Dillon kept talking and asking questions for the next half hour. Finally, the door opened, and another agent stepped in. "Marshal Dillon, if I could see you for a moment."

"Ladies, if you'll excuse me," Dillon said and stepped outside. "What's up?" he asked as they stood out in the hallway.

"Those two traveling with the women, they were each carrying a brick of cocaine."

"You gotta be kidding me."

"I wish I was, sir. They're in rooms one and three."

"Is Brendan Kane in one of the rooms?"

"He's in room three."

"Can I get into the observation room and watch for a minute?"

"Yes, one of the officers is in there. I'll let you in."

Dillon stepped into the small, dark room, nodded at the officer in the black sweater, and said, "They were carrying a kilo of cocaine?"

"Both of them, so a total of two kilos."

"Jesus Christ. Has he said the two women were involved?"

"No, just the opposite, and Kane's been pushing him pretty hard. He says the girls didn't know anything about it."

"I'll be telling you again. They knew shite all about it. We thought we'd get through. Youse would be on the lookout for your wans. It's the only reason we brought them along."

"And why would we be on the lookout for the two women?"

The guy shook his head. "My girlfriend was supposed to make a call. Tell youse they were trying to smuggle it in. We figured you'd be so busy tracking them you'd let the likes of us through."

"So you're telling me the two American women had nothing to do with this."

"You kidding, they were too busy looking at the bleeding apple tower and the lot to get into our business."

"One of them referred to you as her boyfriend."

"That'd be Gretchen, the blonde. Nice enough but not my type."

"You're still with Shannon, are you?"

He shook his head. "Jaysus, don't tell me you already picked her up. She said she'd never get caught."

"She got caught," Kane said then stood and left the room.

Dillon hurried out of the observation room door. "You hear that shite?" Kane asked as Dillon stepped into the hall.

"Yeah, what are you going to do?"

"I think we'll send someone to pick her up. She's the roommate of one of the women?"

"She's the roommate of both of them."

"Okay, we'll pick her up. She and the lads will be under arrest. You know, they almost pulled it off."

"How did they get it through security?"

"In cans of coffee. It's why they flew through Lille. They don't have all the technology, and a flight at 8:00, one of the last ones through. Everyone's anxious to get home from work. You know the drill."

Dillon nodded. He did know the drill. Right now, he was anxious to get home. Unfortunately, he had some unpleasant business to attend to.

"I'm going to go in and update the two Americans. Let me know when their roommate has been arrested, and then I'll get them back to DCU."

Kane nodded and headed down the hall. Dillon went back to the interrogation room with the two Americans.

"Is everything all right?" Gretchen asked as he sat down.

"There's been a bit of a change," Dillon said and pulled out his cellphone. He clicked on the copy of the call sent to Myra Harrison at DCU. "I'd like you to listen to this phone message that was left at DCU," Dillon said. He placed his cell on the table and then touched the screen. The girls listened to the husky voice leaving the short message.

Gretchen shook her head, and when the message was finished, she said, "What a stupid bitch. That's definitely Shannon O'Leary."

"You're sure?"

They both nodded, and Mary Ellen said, "It would be just like her to try to disguise her voice like that. She'd think it was pure genius, but of course, it doesn't work."

Dillon went on to update them on the arrests of the McGinty brothers.

"So you're telling us we were being played by Eamon and Michael, and it was all Shannon's plan?"

"Looks that way, at least that's what they're telling us."

"That bitch is so dead. Wait till we see her."

"That may be a while. She being arrested as we speak."

"Better lock her up for her own protection," Gretchen said.

Kane popped his head in the room about an hour later. Dillon was in the process of learning more than he ever thought possible about the postgraduate program in International Studies. "All clear, Marshal," Kane said.

"Ladies, let's get you home."

"Shannon isn't there?"

"It sounds like Shannon will be living under the trusted care of the state for some time."

"However long it will be, it won't be long enough," Gretchen said. "I just want to get back to our room, take a hot shower, and wash Eamon off of me."

"Save some hot water for me," Mary Ellen said.

They picked up their small suitcases and followed Dillon out the door. They tossed the suitcases in the backseat. Mary Ellen climbed in next to the suitcases.

Gretchen took the front passenger seat. Neither woman spoke for a couple of minutes, and then they carried on a conversation as if Dillon wasn't in the car.

They discussed who they would call first. Agreed not to tell their parents. They decided they would go to student housing first thing in the morning and request a new room. They went on and on. Dillon pulled up in front of their residence and offered to go up to their room with them and check it out, but they would have none of it.

They climbed out of the car, grabbed their suitcases, and hurried into the postgraduate residence. Dillon looked at the dashboard clock. It was almost midnight.

He drove home and pulled into his drive. He glanced over at Tara's, and sure enough, the black Mercedes was still backed in front of Tara's car. He was too tired to care.

He stepped inside, prepared to have to deal with a mess, but the place was reasonably clean. He got the coffee ready for the morning and quietly headed upstairs. Lucifer was asleep on the bed. Dillon undressed, climbed into bed, and was sound asleep within a minute.

THIRTY-SIX

At half-past seven, Dillon was at his desk drinking his second cup of coffee, enjoying the peace and quiet. He sent a text message to Myra Harrison, asking her to call him when she had a moment. He mentioned that Gretchen Malden and Mary Ellen Schneider were safe and sound back in their dorm room as of last night. He didn't mention anything about Shannon O'Leary or the McGinty brothers.

Suel wasn't in yet. He sent Brendan Kane an email asking him to call when he had a moment just to update him. He called Eric Bergman at the US embassy to see if there were any updates on Jimmy Dugan and ended up leaving a message.

Suel arrived maybe fifteen minutes later. He turned on his computer, arranged some things at his desk, and on his way to the break room, asked Dillon if he wanted any more coffee. Dillon followed him into the break room and refilled his mug.

"How was your night?" Suel asked once he put the kettle on to boil.

"Interesting," Dillon replied and went on to tell him about the foiled smuggling operation and the two American students.

Suel just shook his head and said, "Lord, save us. I found something of interest. You were going to investigate the property on Stiles Road."

"I was, and then we were onto Killian Graham, and it got pushed to the side."

"Right, so as usual, I got tired of waiting and did my own investigation."

"And exactly what did you find out?" Dillon asked.

The place is owned by an Irish Corporation named…"

"Named Estate Investments. Yeah, I know," said Dillon.

"Ahh, but did you happen to look into Estate Investments to see who owned that?"

"No, I never got that far. Who is it?"

"Two people, actually."

"Okay, are you planning to tell me?"

"How about Nora and Bertie Scallen?" Suel said. "It's a corporation they formed thirteen years ago. Turns out they own a number of properties, two of which are the one on Stiles Road and another at 44 Reginald Street."

"So they own both the places Billy the Butler told you about, interesting. Any news from him?"

"No, which is a bit strange. I've two calls into him. You'd think he'd be sleeping out by the door to the station, hoping we'd put in a good word for him."

"Anyone you can contact who may have seen him?"

"I've a call into a woman he's sometimes with."

Dillon's cell phone rang, and he pulled it from his pocket. Myra Harrison from DCU. "I gotta take this," he said and walked back to his desk. "Hi, Myra. Thanks for calling."

"My pleasure. The girls are safe and sound, and everything went okay?"

"Not exactly," Dillon told her the story about the McGinty brothers and Shannon O'Leary. "I'm afraid at this point it looks like Shannon is, or maybe was, the brains behind this escapade."

"Oh, God. You have got to be kidding me."

"Believe me, I wish I was. When I dropped them off last night, the girls said they were going to request a new room. I don't know if that would go through you or someone else, but I thought I should give you a heads-up. Understandably, they were pretty wound up last night. I think they were both led to believe that the boys had an interest in them when, in fact, they were just being used as a distraction to get through airport security."

"And Shannon O'Leary is under arrest?"

"That's my understanding, at least for now, but I suspect she'll be released sometime in the next forty-eight hours. Her court date may not be for another six months."

"Oh, major headache," said Myra. "Well, okay. Glad you were there, and thanks for bringing them back here last night."

"I felt it was the least I could do. I think if they ever see Shannon, there's liable to be a real problem. They were not what you'd call happy."

"Can't say as I blame them. Okay, thanks for the update. I'll keep you posted. We'd better get on the stick and find them a new room. Talk to you later," Myra said and disconnected.

Dillon hadn't set his phone down when Eric Bergman called.

"Hi, Eric," was how Dillon answered.

"Hi, Jack. Sorry it took so long to get back to you. Things have been crazy here. Three Senators on the way to an EU meeting stopped off for a free meal and to taste the whiskey."

"Don't get me started on politicians," Dillon said. He went on to give Bergman an update on Killian Graham and the credit card from Sterling, Cooper and Partners being canceled.

"And he's claiming he had no personal dealings or knowledge of Jimmy Dugan?"

"That's correct, and to be honest, what he says matches all the investigating we've done to date. We never found anything identifying Dugan as the person requesting the images. There were no obvious ties to Dugan on the credit card. Graham has never been to the US. He's only been out of Ireland twice. Once to Paris for a couple of days maybe a year or two ago. That trip was paid for with the credit card. He traveled once to London for a rugby match, same day over and back maybe four years ago."

"So it sounds like he isn't under investigation at this stage."

"No, in fact, he did some damage to a rental car and contacted me this morning because the credit card was canceled yesterday, and now he's out a little more than six grand. Anymore on your end with pictures or articles in a newspaper?"

"Nothing, all quiet on that end. I'm more than happy to turn the Jimmy Dugan investigation over to you guys."

"Yeah, such as it is. Thanks for the call, Eric. Anything changes, I'll be in touch."

"Thanks, I'm glad to hear the girls were cleared. I was not looking forward to them being charged."

THIRTY-SEVEN

Jimmy Dugan was sitting at his desk, drinking his second cup of coffee. He was going through the recent images from Killian Graham. It looked like a fun evening, and Jimmy imagined himself with the woman holding her blouse open in the bar. He missed that kind of activity. It had been far too long, spending years essentially living under house arrest.

A phone vibrated in his desk drawer, and he pulled it out. Sloane O'Kelly. "Good morning," Dugan said.

"How you holding up?" O'Kelly asked.

"I'll be doing a lot better once this potential problem is put to rest in Dublin."

"I'm heading over tonight. The flight lands at 6:30 Dublin time. That's 6:30 in the damn morning. I need you to send me this dude's address and phone number."

"Phone number? What, you're planning to call him?"

"No. I'm planning to cover all my bases. Just in the event I need to have him meet me somewhere. It's just nice to have the option. I'm hoping I don't have to contact him, and if I do, it'll be on a burner I'll get over there."

"Just to let you know, Sloane, I've canceled all communication with him. He has no way to contact me. I canceled the credit card I gave him. Bastard smashed up a rental car and expected me to pay for it. No way, man."

"You know what might work. What about you contacting him, tell him you're sending someone over with a new credit card, or better yet, tell him you're sending me over with cash to cover him for three or four months. Get him relaxed. Have him thinking there's a nice chunk of change coming his way. I'll find a place he can meet me. In a park or on a damn mountain or someplace."

"Why not set up the meeting at his place? Private, quiet, no one around, and you can be nice and gentle and break his neck."

O'Kelly thought about that for a moment and liked the sound of it. "I'll give you a call once I land. As much as I'd like to head back tomorrow night, I'm thinking that might draw attention. I booked a hotel and I'm staying two nights. I want to get out of there as fast as possible. Staying two nights will make it look like I'm not running. We'll talk tomorrow. I'll call you around 7:00 tomorrow morning your time. Okay?"

"Yeah, I should be up."

"Make sure you're up, man. And remember, time over in Dublin is five hours ahead of you."

"I got it," Dugan said and wrote down '5 hrs' on his calendar. "All right, I got it down, and… Hello? Hello? Sloane, are you there?"

THIRTY-EIGHT

Freddy slowly came awake. He was attired in his boxer shorts, t-shirt, and one black sock. His neck, back, and hips were killing him. His mouth was dry, and his tongue felt twice its size. He slowly sat up on the couch and groaned as the pounding in his head increased. He eventually looked around. At least the scene was familiar, his den. Apparently, he'd made it home okay. He'd lost count of the drinks everyone was buying him at the social club. From the looks of things in the den, he didn't stop drinking once he came home. There was an almost empty bottle of Maker's Mark bourbon on the coffee table next to the empty glass.

Two empty plates with pizza crusts and a wine glass rested at the opposite end of the coffee table. The wine glass had traces of lipstick on it. He tried to retrace his steps last night, but his mind was awfully foggy.

He'd been at the social club, meeting up with some pals. They'd been sharing stories, and he'd pulled Jimmy's burner phone out. The one with the picture of the woman pulling her blouse open. He may have embellished the story a little, suggesting the woman had been with him. That's when they started buying him drinks. So who in the hell was here drinking wine and eating pizza last night?

And Jimmy's burner phone, he'd better get rid of that damn thing. He was supposed to have done that yesterday. He grabbed his trousers from the floor and checked the pockets, no phone. Come to think of it, his wallet wasn't in his trousers either. He stood, took a second or two to steady himself, and hurried out to the kitchen.

A pizza delivery box was on the counter next to a half-empty wine bottle. He lifted the box to see if Jimmy's burner phone was underneath. Unfortunately, it wasn't. He hurried into the bathroom, but it wasn't there. As he glanced in the mirror, he noticed the lipstick smudges on his face. It was the same thing in the bedroom, no phone, although all the dresser drawers were partially open, and the top two had been dumped out on the bed. Someone rifled through his dresser drawers?

His jewelry box was missing from on top of the dresser. He tore open the closet door, pushed the hanging shirts to the side, and stared at the open safe, now empty. He'd been robbed.

He ran into the living room, swearing a blue streak as he went. He looked out the window and stared three stories down at the empty parking place where he always parked his orange Dodge Viper. What the hell?

THIRTY-NINE

illon was about to head to the break room for some lunch when his desk phone rang. "Marshal Dillon," was how he answered.

"Yes, Marshal, this is Emily down in tech. We've received some activity on one of the cellphone numbers you requested we track."

Dillon had to think back, cellphone numbers, and then he remembered the numbers they'd taken from Killian Graham's phone the other day. "The cellphone you're tracking was in the US. Is it still there or over here?"

"It's still in the US, sir. The state of Florida, actually."

"Could I come down there and see this?"

"I suppose you could, sir. Rather boring, I'm afraid. Nothing really to see other than a screen with locations."

"I'll be right down. You said your name is Emily?"

"Yes, sir. I'll meet you at the door."

"I'm on my way. Give me five minutes," Dillon said and hung up. He headed out the door, waited a couple of minutes for the elevator, and took it down to the first floor. The tech lab was at the end of a labyrinth of criss-crossing hallways and dead ends. Fortunately, the path he wanted was marked on the floor with red tape.

The door was about a thousand times more secure than the door to the Special Branch office. It was steel with a window of two-inch thick bulletproof glass. Dillon ran his ID card over the keypad, but nothing happened. The door opened a moment later, and a dark-haired young woman in a white lab coat said, "Marshal Dillon?"

"Yes, Emily?"

She smiled, nodded, and said, "Come on in. You've been down here before?"

"Yeah, a number of times and always came out with the idea that I was dumber than everyone in here."

She laughed at that and said, "Oh, I don't know. I could tell you stories. Let's go back to my workbench."

"You said you were tracking the cellphone in Florida?" Dillon asked as they wove their way around desks, tables, and file cabinets.

"Yes, interestingly, it apparently doesn't have the typical security apparatus most phones have."

"Meaning it's more secure?"

"No, on the contrary, less secure. Quite a bit less."

"That would suggest it's a burner phone. Cheap, used for a call or two, and then discarded."

"Based on what I've come up with, this phone would fit that description. Okay, here we are," she said, standing in front of a counter with four different laptops.

Only one appeared to be on at the moment. The screen was filled with lines of computer code.

"I guess I expected a map or a street or something. Maybe pictures of a house."

"I can get you that," she said and pressed a button on another laptop. The screen immediately lit up, and she typed in some lines of code from the screen Dillon was looking at. Her fingers were a blur as she typed in the code. An image suddenly appeared of a one-story white structure that looked like it could have been in Mexico or maybe Spain. A wall maybe three feet high covered by a vine and an archway led into a small patio. A total of six doors were along three sides of the patio. Each one apparently led into an apartment.

"That's not a live image on the screen," Emily said. "You're looking at the Google Maps image."

"But that is where the cell phone is located, right?"

"At this time. It's in unit three," she pointed at a door at the left-hand corner of the patio. A flower box with what looked like pansies rested below the window next to the door.

Dillon wrote down the address that appeared in the upper left-hand corner of the screen. "Ponce De Leon Avenue in Venice, Florida. Can you keep an eye on this phone for me? Let me know if it moves."

"I certainly can, sir. I have to warn you, based on your description of it being used for a call or two and then discarded, this could disappear at any moment."

"Yeah, I get that. But at least we have an address. That's a start."

"Good, I have this set to record, so if it travels, we'll have a record of addresses. Not that it will mean much. It could just be grocery stores or a petrol station, but you'll have the address," she said and smiled.

"Let's talk at the end of the day and see if anything has changed," Dillon said. "Thanks again for the call."

Emily walked him to the door, and they said goodbye again. Dillon hurried back up to his desk and placed a call to Eric Bergman at the American embassy.

Bergman answered on the third ring, "Hi Jack, what's up."

Dillon explained the phone numbers they'd gotten from Killian Graham's phone and how one of them appeared to be in service. "Eric, there's an awfully good chance this is a burner phone, so it could disappear from the grid at any moment. That said, it happens to be live now. Is there a way you could contact the powers that be and let them know about this?"

"I can try," Bergman said.

"Please, do. I've got a couple of contacts over there I can call, too."

"You know who we should call," Bergman said, "the guy who wrote the articles on Dugan."

"Wendell Murphy, I was planning to call him first."

"You're pretty sure Dugan placed a call using this phone, right?"

"Yeah, a couple of days ago, and I see your point," Dillon said. "If nothing else, this may suggest a general location. A lot better than saying Duggan is somewhere in the US. If they could narrow it down to Florida or, God forbid, this town of Venice, that would be a huge improvement."

"Yeah, exactly," said Bergman. "I'll call a couple of folks. You're going to call the Boston Globe?"

"Wendell Murphy is the reporter who wrote the articles. Let me know if anyone you talk to seems interested," Dillon said, and they disconnected.

He pulled the file with the copy of the Boston Globe article. There was a number listed to contact reporters. Dillon punched it in and then listened to the recording. He listened to three more recordings before he got to what he hoped was Wendell Murphy's number. The phone rang four times, and Dillon promised himself he would hang up if he got another recording. "Wendell Murphy," a man said and then a moment later, "Hello. Hello?"

"Hi, Mr. Murphy. My name is Jack Dillon. I'm a US Marshal attached to An Garda Síochána over in Dublin, Ireland."

"You're calling me from Dublin?" Murphy asked.

"Yes. Long story short, the American embassy received copies of your articles regarding Jimmy Dugan and his apparent appearance over here." Dillon went on to explain their investigation, interviewing Killian Graham, and among other things taking down the phone numbers used to send him instructions. The same numbers Graham sent back the images to, of him living the good life for a couple of nights.

"I'd be interested in chatting with Mr. Graham," Murphy said.

"I'll run that by him. Is this the number where he would reach you?"

"No, by the way, thanks for your patience waiting to have the phone finally ring at my desk. It a charmingly archaic system we have," he said and laughed. He gave Dillon the number to his cellphone.

Dillon gave his cell phone number to Murphy and then went on to explain the tracking of the suspected burner phone in Florida.

"I would love to get that number from you," Murphy said.

"I think it best if we leave that alone. That said, I'm wondering if you might know of someone I could call. Maybe someone on an investigative force in Boston or the local FBI office. It would seem—"

"I do know someone. He's a field agent in the Boston office. Our connection is or maybe was, that we would both receive these photos supposedly of Dugan living the life in Ireland. Now, if what you say is correct, the credit card being canceled, no contact, maybe that's finished. But let me give you his number. Give him a call and please mention my name. We had lunch a week or two back over this very subject."

Murphy gave him Kevin Byrne's name and number. They chatted for another minute or two and hung up.

FORTY

After speaking with Wendell Murphy, Dillon headed into the break room for a fresh coffee. Suel walked in just as Dillon was going back to his desk.

"You working something?" Suel asked.

"Contacting an FBI agent back in the states. I got a location on one of the burner phone numbers we got from Killian Graham."

"Somewhere in Boston?"

"No, as a matter of fact, it's down in Florida, on the Gulf coast. A town called Venice. At first glance, it looks like the perfect place to keep a low profile. Quiet, a lot of snowbirds heading down this time of year."

"Snowbirds?" Suel asked.

"Folks from the northern US and Canada down there in the winter escaping the snow and ice. A guy like Dugan could just melt into the crowd and never be discovered. Well, as long as he didn't revert to his old self."

"Sooner or later, they almost always resort to their old self," Suel said.

"Yeah, you're probably right. Let me make this phone call, and then we can compare notes," Dillon said and headed out the door. He went back to his desk and dialed the number Murphy had given him.

Byrne answered on the second ring. "Hello?"

"Kevin Byrne?" Dillon asked.

"Speaking."

"Agent Byrne, I got your number from Wendell Murphy with the Boston Globe. My name is Jack Dillon. I'm a US Marshal assigned to An Garda Síochána in Dublin, Ireland."

"This wouldn't happen to be about Jimmy Dugan, would it?"

"In a roundabout way, yes, it is." Dillon went on to explain the tracking they'd done on the burner phone number. He gave Byrne the number and the address of the location in Venice, Florida.

"I'll contact a couple of people here in Boston as well as our office down in Fort Meyers. You said the guy over there, posing as Dugan, hasn't been arrested?"

"Correct. We interviewed him. It quickly became apparent he had no idea who Dugan was. In fact, he'd never heard of him until we mentioned the name. He thought the pictures were being taken for a travel agency or a tour company. The guy has been outside of Ireland exactly four days in his entire life. He was just in it for the fun weekend getaway and the two hundred euros deposited in his bank account every month. Payment for enjoying himself."

"Hmm, maybe not so strange. Let me make these calls right away."

"Anything develops, give me a call on my cell-phone," Dillon said and gave him his number.

"Many thanks, Marshal. I'd love to chat but times wasting with that burner phone."

"I hear you. Good luck," Dillon said and hung up.

He headed over to Suel's desk. Suel was on the phone and waved an index finger at Dillon. A moment later, he hung up the phone. "Billy the Butler."

"What did he have to say?"

"Nothing. It's my fourth call to him in two days, and he hasn't answered. Something's not right. His court hearing is coming up in a couple days. He would be desperate to have us put in a good word for him." Suel thought for a moment and then said, "You interested in a little trip?"

"To find Billy?"

"With any luck," Suel said. "I'm just not getting a good feel on this. Something's not right."

They were in Suel's car, driving to Cabra, an area on the north side of Dublin. Dillon had an approximate idea of where they were. The streets were lined with attached housing. The units gradually became smaller and denser as they wove through the streets.

Suel pulled onto the sidewalk next to a tall building, one of the last remaining public housing towers built back in the sixties, St. John's Towers. The parking lot for the place was actually across the street, and there appeared to be a number of open spaces. Suel fumbled beneath the driver's seat and pulled out a small stack of papers. He paged through the first half-dozen and then said, "Here we go." He placed the sheet on the dashboard and stepped out of the car.

Dillon glanced at the acronym on the sheet as they headed toward the tower and said, "What the hell is that?"

"A pass to park here, and no one will touch the car."

"You sure? Is that a county or city organization?"

"Dillon, it's from the locals. It means anyone fusses with that car, the Guards will be here making life miserable and affecting profits for a week or two. No one will go near the car, believe me."

"Mmm, interesting," Dillon said. As they entered the tower, virtually every surface was covered with spray-painted graffiti, some of which was the same acronym Suel had set on the dashboard a moment ago.

The elevator doors were spray-painted, and Suel said, "He's only up on the fourth floor. It'll be faster and probably safer if we take the stairs."

If Dillon thought the entryway was colorful, the staircase was like a nonstop show. Some of the artwork was actually very good and had clearly taken a fair amount of time. They stepped onto the fourth floor and walked down the hallway. More graffiti, not as much as the stairway, but more personalized. One of the entrances had 'WHORE' spray-painted across the door in red letters, maybe two feet high.

Suel stopped at number 411 and knocked on the door. They waited for maybe fifteen seconds, and then he pounded on the door. Still no answer.

"You want me to knock on the neighbor's door?" Dillon asked.

"Don't bother. Even if they're in there, they won't answer. I know someone we can check with. He may even be there."

They took the stairs back down to the entrance and headed out to the car. Two guys, maybe mid-twenties were sitting on the brick wall out front. A brown plastic two-liter bottle of Bulmer's cider rested between them.

"Hi ya's, lads, how youse keeping?" Suel said as he headed to the car.

Both guys nodded but didn't say anything. Suel and Dillon climbed in the car and drove off. "They making sure no one messes with your car?" Dillon asked.

"Humf, probably there to report if we hauled some-one out. Jaysus, nothing to do and all day to do it. Small wonder there's always trouble afoot here."

Suel drove maybe three blocks and pulled in front of an attached house, one of a dozen along the street. There were a couple of units that appeared well-kept. They had flowers planted. No trash was on the sidewalk outside the walls. That was not the case with the unit Suel pulled in front of and parked. He pulled halfway up on the sidewalk, effectively blocking the scraped and dented Toyota parked just inside the small area in front of the house.

A yellow and red plastic tricycle leaned to the side in the middle of the path leading to the front door. One of the rear wheels was missing. They climbed out of the car, side-stepped the tricycle, and walked to the front door. There was a hole in the doorframe where the doorbell once was. "Billy's sister," Suel said and knocked loudly.

After a moment, the door opened, and a woman in a gray sweatshirt and bluejeans answered the door. She held a little boy, not much older than a year, on her hip.

"Good morning, Gemma. Sorry to be a bother. I've been trying to reach Billy. I know he's a court case coming up in a few days and wanted to see if we could help."

"You haven't heard?"

"Heard what?"

"He was run down in the middle of the street the other night. Right out in front of St. John's. Of course, a thousand knackers living there, and no one saw anything."

"Late at night, was it?"

"Hardly, more like 7:00. He'd gone to the shops for some takeout. I talked to the Guards, but they couldn't, or wouldn't, tell me anything."

"Where is he now?"

"God Bless, they took him to the Mater. Who knows what will happen to him there."

"We'll go check on him, and I'll let you know."

"He's in a bleedin' coma. If youse really want to help, find out what worthless knacker is responsible for running him over and shoot the bastard," she shouted as tears began to run down her cheeks. The baby suddenly began to cry. She gave the door a hip check, slamming it shut. Dillon pulled out a business card and stuck it in the door.

"Wonderful," Suel said.

FORTY-ONE

ublin's Mater Hospital is located in Phibsboro, just a ten-minute drive from Billy the Butler's sister's home. Suel pulled almost in front of the hundred and sixty-year-old structure, placed a card with the An Garda Síochána logo on the dashboard, and they hurried up the front steps to the building.

Suel asked for Billy Donner's room number at the reception desk, and after waiting for five minutes, they were told no visitors were allowed. Both Suel and Dillon then flashed their IDs and were directed to the third floor.

Dillon had never heard Billy's last name. On the way up in the elevator, he asked if Billy (the Butler) Donner might be related to the Donner party.

"The Donner party? If the likes of Billy was throwing a party, I'd be the last person he'd invite," Suel replied.

Dillon saw no point in giving a short history lesson as they stepped off the elevator. They showed their IDs to a nurse at the nurse's station, who told them that Billy was in a coma. She explained that he had severe head trauma, broken bones in an arm, leg, hip, and two ribs, along with a ruptured spleen, a bruised kidney, and a ruptured bowel. "In short, he is unable to have any visitors," she said and flashed a half-second smile.

"Prognosis?" Dillon asked.

"Not good," she replied. "If you would like to leave your number, we could contact you if there is any change. He could be in this state for quite some time, unfortunately, maybe forever."

They thanked her and left.

"Bloody hell," Suel said on the way back to the station. "Poor Billy never seems to catch a break."

"You thinking the car hitting him was intentional?" Dillon asked.

"Without a doubt. Someone follows him to the take-out. Follows him home and has the perfect opportunity to run him over as he crosses the street, and then they disappear into the darkness. I'd love to catch the muppet. Just give me five minutes with 'em."

"He's got a long road to recovery," Dillon said.

Suel looked at Dillon. "Recovery? He's not going to make it."

"Well, he's definitely in pretty rough shape. I'll give you that," Dillon said.

"He's not going to make it, Dillon. No matter what you're thinking, he's done."

They pulled into the parking lot and headed up to the Special Branch office. As they stepped inside, Suel said, "I'd better give McCabe an update. This is going to set us back on the Stiles Road site."

"What if you suggest to McCabe that Billy was run over because of Stiles Road?"

"But we don't have any proof and—"

"And therefore, it's entirely possible. To be honest, it makes perfect sense. Billy the Butler mentions to someone that he's got a possible fix in on his upcoming court date. Maybe he even mentions Stiles Road. That information gets back to the wrong people, and suddenly Billy is a prime target."

"You're thinking Bertie Scallen ran him over?"

"No, although I wouldn't discount him. It just strikes me as curious that he tells you about the place. You discover that the Scallen's own the place, and suddenly Billy is knocking on death's door."

"I'm not saying it didn't happen. It's just getting the proof," Suel said.

"Maybe the first step in that is monitoring the place on Stiles Road," Dillon said.

FORTY-TWO

Sloane O'Kelly stepped into the Garden Room restaurant in Dublin's Merrion Hotel. It had been a long seven hours flying from Boston to Dublin. He had flown first class, and so he had been able to nap intermittently on the flight. He settled in at a table facing the garden and ordered a pancake breakfast even though it was lunchtime. He straightened his silverware, spacing them properly and pulled out a map of the city while he waited for his food.

He searched for Killian Graham's North Phibsboro Road address and found it in just three or four minutes. Actually, it didn't appear to be all that far from his hotel. He figured he could grab a taxi to a nearby restaurant, make a personal visit to Graham tonight, and then sightsee tomorrow.

His plate of pancakes arrived a moment later—three pancakes, accented with blueberries and raspberries. A small pitcher of maple syrup came with the pancakes, and he told the server he would need another pitcher. He limited himself to one glass of white wine, just enough to encourage an afternoon nap. He finished his breakfast in record time and returned to his room.

He sat on the edge of his bed, kicked off his shoes, and checked his watch. It was three minutes before 1:00, Dublin time, and he phoned Jimmy Dugan.

Dugan answered on the first ring. "You over there?"

"Good morning, sorry to call you so early, but I'll be napping this afternoon."

"Not a problem. Everything okay on your end?"

"Everything is just fine— nice enough place. The flight over is what it is, seven hours on a plane. But I'm here in one piece, safe and sound. I intend to meet with your client early this evening. I'm thinking, maybe six o'clock. If you could phone him, say, around 10:30 this morning, your time. Tell him I'm delivering a new credit card and maybe sweeten the deal a little, suggest you're going to increase his monthly deposit or something. I want to meet him at his place. Make sure he's alone. If anyone is there, I'm going to back out of the deal and keep your upfront payment."

"Not to worry, Sloane. I'll be texting him rather than phoning direct. It's the way we've always connected. I don't want to change anything now. Not to worry, I'll make him an offer he can't refuse, as they say in the movies."

"Good. Have him respond so you know he's on board. Once he agrees, call me at this number, so I know it's a go."

"I'll do that. I'm going to destroy this phone as soon as I hang up with you, so the next call from me will be coming from a different number."

"That sounds like a good idea. I'll talk to you in a couple of hours," O'Kelly said and disconnected. He placed the 'DO NOT DISTURB' sign on the door and stretched out on the bed. In just a few minutes, he drifted off to sleep and dreamt of maple syrup.

At exactly 10:30, Venice, Florida time, Jimmy Dugan sent a text message to Killian Graham. ***'Sorry for the confusion. Having a new credit card delivered to you. A friend bringing it 6:00 tonight to your North Phibsboro Road address. Increasing monthly deposit to your account. Please confirm you received this.'***

Killian Graham reread the text message three or four more times. A new credit card and a larger deposit in his bank account, it was almost too good to believe, he thought, and then he thought some more. After mulling things over for the better part of a half-hour, he picked up his phone and called Dillon.

Dillon and Suel were standing on Stiles Road looking at the corner where Billy the Butler told them people parked their cars and then walked up the road for two hundred meters to get to the house owned by Nora Scallen and her son Bertie.

"If we could place someone in one of those two homes across the street, we could monitor the cars being parked there," Suel said.

"How about this? We drive past every half-hour and take a photo of the area. If there's more than one vehicle, they'll have to park perpendicular to the curb. We take the picture and get the license number."

"Good idea, except that the same car driving past a couple of times is bound to attract attention," Suel said.

"Not if it's a taxi," Dillon said. "We just clamp a taxi sign to the top of the car, and we're basically invisible."

"I like the sound of that," Suel said just as Dillon's phone rang.

Dillon pulled his phone out and looked at it. "Killian Graham, probably wants to know if we'll pay the repair cost on that rental car. I don't have an answer for him, damn it," Dillon said and let the phone ring two more times. "Oh, Christ. Hi, Killian, what's up?"

Suel watched Dillon's expression change as he gave one-word answers and signaled Suel to get in the car. "What? When? You sure it's him? Yeah. Go ahead and respond. No, we're on our way. Do not open the door for anyone unless it's us. Fifteen minutes," Dillon said as he slid into the passenger seat and Suel pulled away from the curb.

"Where are we going?" Suel asked.

"Killian Graham's, North Phibsboro Road. He got a text message from Dugan," Dillon said and proceeded to give Suel what information he had.

"Your man is sending someone from the US to hand-deliver a credit card?"

"Yeah, you see any problems with that? Not to mention increasing the monthly payment."

"They're going to kill him," Suel said.

"Gee, you think?" Dillon had his phone up against his ear and a moment later said, "Yes, sir. Marshal Dillon here. I just received a troubling phone call from Killian Graham. He was the guy who— Yes, sir, exactly. He just received a text message. No, sir, but then he never does sign them. On a burner phone. We were able to trace one of the numbers to the US, a town in Florida. Suel and I are on the way to Graham's, maybe ten minutes." Dillon went on to tell McCabe what he knew.

"We'll be in his apartment. If we could have back up in the area, but not visible, that would be great. Okay. Yes, sir, once we're there. Yes."

"We're going in?" Suel said as he turned off North Circular Road. They could see the lights on in Graham's apartment above the hairdressers.

"Yeah, park anywhere on the street," Dillon said and pressed the screen on his cellphone to check the time, twenty minutes before six. "We better hurry. The text said 6:00, but just in case he shows up a little early."

Suel parked just down the street from Graham's building and then climbed out of the car. They didn't hurry, but they weren't wasting time either. As they walked toward the building, they scanned the street for anyone lingering or coming their way. Other than two women across the street carrying grocery bags, they didn't see anyone.

FORTY-THREE

Sloane O'Kelly gave a wave and slid into the backseat of the taxi parked in front of the Merrion Hotel.

"Where to?" the driver said.

"The Brian Boru Pub, in Cross Guns," O'Kelly said. The pub was maybe three blocks from Graham's apartment.

The taxi man pulled away from the curb and headed down toward O'Connell Street. "You American?" he asked and glanced in the rearview mirror.

"Canadian," the passenger replied and continued looking out the window.

He'd had them before, fares with something on their mind, not interested in the conversation. That was just fine with him. Many's the conversation he would have loved to avoid. As long as he was paid and, God forbid, left a tip, he didn't care. Across the bridge, past the GPO, he thought for half a second about pointing out the sights, but your man seemed preoccupied, so he drove on. In no time at all, he'd turned onto North Phibsboro Road and headed toward the Cross Guns bridge.

O'Kelly gave a quick glance at the hairdressers and noted the lights on in the apartment above as they drove past. It looked simple enough, almost no foot traffic at the moment. He glanced at his watch, twenty minutes. Perfect, he'd arrive just that bit early. Three minutes later, the taxi pulled in front of the Brian Boru pub. It was an eight euro fare. O'Kelly handed the driver a ten euro note and said, "Keep the change."

He slid out of the backseat and headed for the entrance to the pub. He took his time, waiting until the taxi pulled out of sight, then turned around and headed down Phibsboro road. Killian Graham would be dead after little more than a five-minute walk.

FORTY-FOUR

Kennedy's Coffee across the street appeared to have only one table occupied, two girls and a boy, maybe college students. Dillon and Suel hurried to Killian's door and pressed the buzzer.

"Yes?" he said, maybe five seconds later.

"Marshal Dillon and DI Suel," Dillon said. The door buzzed, and they could hear the lock snap open. They stepped inside, and Dillon hurried up the stairs while Suel made sure the new door closed and locked.

Dillon knocked on Graham's door and called, "Killian?"

Graham opened the door a moment later. He was holding a hurley, a wooden stick used in the Irish sport of hurling. It was about thirty-six inches long and looked a bit like a sawed-off hockey stick, only a lot heavier and more vicious. As he leaned the hurley against the wall, he said, "Jaysus, but I'm glad to see the like of youse. I can't believe that plonker thinks he can just—"

Suel appeared behind Dillon. "Right now, we need to get you out of here," Dillon said just as the buzzer on the intercom sounded.

"That can't be him. It's, it's not 6:00 yet," Killian said.

Dillon looked over at Suel and said, "Better answer it."

Suel took three steps over to the intercom, glanced back at Dillon, and then pressed the button. "Yes?"

"Killian?"

"Yes."

"Just in from the states. I've got a new credit card for you, along with a gift from your friend."

"Oh, wonderful. I've been waiting for the likes of ya's. Come on up, first door on your left at the top of the stairs. I bought a bottle of Champagne to celebrate," Suel said and pressed the button to unlock the security door.

"Get your ass in the bedroom," Dillon as he pulled out his nine-millimeter.

Suel pulled his pistol out and stood by the door, looking out the peephole. He gave Dillon a nod just before there was a knock.

Suel waited a moment, gave Dillon a quick glance, and then tore open the door with his pistol pointed at the dark-haired figure in the hall. "Don't even think about doing some—"

A foot suddenly kicked the pistol to the side, and an elbow beneath the chin knocked Suel back against the wall. O'Kelly took a swing at Suel and missed, bouncing his fist off the wall.

Dillon shouted, "Don't!" as he aimed at the back of O'Kelly's right knee and fired.

Blood splattered across Suel and the wall as O'Kelly screamed and grabbed his knee. Suel grabbed the hurley and slammed it into O'Kelly's nose. He bounced off the doorframe and laid unconscious, twitching on the hallway floor.

"Paddy, are you okay?" Dillon shouted. He kept his pistol pointed at O'Kelly as he moved toward Suel.

"You almost fecking shot me," Suel shouted.

"Sorry I missed," Dillon said as he stepped over toward O'Kelly and began to search him. He didn't find a weapon, and he told Suel to call it in. The intercom buzzer was going off, and Suel staggered over and answered it. Dillon couldn't hear what was said, but a moment later, footsteps were thundering up the stairs, and four officers appeared.

FORTY-FIVE

Down in Florida, Freddy's cellphone rang. Jimmy Dugan calling and not for the first time. Freddy let the phone ring four times, all the while cursing his luck, before deciding he'd better answer it. "Umm, Hello—"

"Where in the hell have you been? I've been calling all damn morning."

"Oh, sorry, boss. I had a doctor's appointment, and then I took Lady on a nice long walk. Guess I forgot my phone here."

"I guess you had your head up your ass, again. Get over here. I got another burner I want you to get rid of."

Another burner phone. Freddy cringed thinking about what Dugan would do to him if he ever found out a woman stole the damn thing. He shuddered with the memory of showing the picture around, telling everyone the woman had been with him. He was about to remind Dugan he could just toss the burner in a couple of the trash bins in the building but quickly decided against it.

"Yeah, sure. I'll be over in just a bit."

"Well, don't make it too long. Sarah's getting lunch ready before she heads out to her bridge game," Dugan said and hung up.

Freddy thought he had better call a taxi, but then he remembered his wallet had been stolen along with the burner phone. It was a good half-hour walk, and he figured he'd better get moving. He would have loved to bring Lady along, but if Sarah was gone, there was no telling what Dugan might do to the dog. He decided it would be best to leave her here, and he hurried out the door.

* * *

Two Federal Agents pulled in front of the one-story, six-unit structure on Ponce De Leon Avenue in Venice, Florida. They parked behind an orange Dodge Viper. "You sure this is right?" Agent Melvin Landen said. "Place looks more like subsidized housing. Jimmy Dugan lives here?"

"Supposedly, or at least his phone does. A woman named Christine Tatten is registered as the tenant. Two charges for solicitation three years ago. Let's check it out and get on to more important things, like grabbing some lunch," Agent Delton Carter said.

They climbed out of the car, and Landen said, "A 2014 Dodge Viper, I'm pretty sure it was rated the worst vehicle for 2014. I wonder who got stuck with that thing." They gave a quick glance around the quiet neighborhood while walking across the patio to the door. A sticker with the number three was stuck crookedly on the door. Carter knocked on the door. Out of force of habit, both men stepped to opposite sides and rested their hands on their weapons.

A moment later, the door opened, and a woman in blue, high-waist yoga pants and a matching sports bra answered the door. She was tan, with blonde hair and what looked like flashy diamond post earrings. Both men figured the solicitation charges were possibly justified.

"Hello, Miss Tatten, FBI," the agents said and held out their ID's.

The woman's eyes widened as she looked at the IDs. "Hey look, the man said I could just help myself, and so I did. Didn't mean no harm. Said he just wanted to reward me, is all."

"You helped yourself to his cellphone?" Carter said.

"Look, I was going to bring it back to him tonight. He told me to go ahead and use it for a day, see if I liked it, and then he'd buy me one."

"I think you'd better ask us in," Landen said.

She stepped back and let them in. They entered a small room with a fifty-five-inch tv sitting on a coffee table against the wall. A blue yoga mat was on the floor in front of the tv. What appeared to be an empty box for the tv was sitting on the couch, apparently a rather recent purchase.

"Hey, I didn't mean no harm, honest. Umm, maybe we could, you know, work something out," she said, raising her eyebrows at 'work something out.'

"That's entirely possible," Carter said. "Let's see the cellphone first."

She nodded toward the coffee table. The cellphone, along with two gold watches, a couple of what looked like diamond rings, and a set of car keys sat next to a wallet.

"This what you helped yourself to?" Landen asked.

"Yeah, but he said it was all right. Told me he wanted to make me happy. To reward me for being such a good, umm, giving him such a good back rub."

"I'm sure he did," Landen said and stepped over to the coffee table. He picked up the wallet and opened it up— a Massachusetts driver's license for a gentleman named Frederick Dwyer.

"Mr. Dwyer let you take his wallet, with his driver's license and credit cards?"

"He sort of gave me a bag of stuff. I didn't look in it or nothing, just came home, ya know. I figured I'd call him later today and bring it back to him."

"That wouldn't happen to be his car out there, would it?"

"He told me to take it. It was late, and he didn't want me to have to pay for a taxi."

"Sounds like he was a pretty nice guy. Where does he live?"

"Not too far from here."

"You got an address?"

"Not exactly."

"But you know where it is, right?"

She nodded.

"How about we take a little ride over there? You show us where he lives, and we'll bring you back here. Probably save you a lot of potential headaches, if you know what I mean."

"Yeah, umm, I guess I could do that. How 'bout I just get changed and—"

"How 'bout we just go now?"

She was in the back seat with Agent Carter sitting next to her. He was busy on the phone, getting a crew to tow the Dodge Viper and take the rings and wallet and burner phone into possession. The building she directed Landen to, the Venice Sands Apartments, was about five minutes away. A white, eleven-story building, right on the beach overlooking the Gulf of Mexico.

"He's up on the eleventh floor, number 1112," Tatten said.

Landen slowed but didn't stop. He'd seen the building before but couldn't recall ever being inside. He took the next left and headed back to Tatten's rental on Ponce De Leone Avenue.

The agents engaged Tatten in a casual conversation with the proviso that, if they were satisfied with her cooperation, no charges would be filed. She told them everything they wanted to know, along with a number of things they had absolutely no interest in.

FORTY-SIX

ollowing the arrest and hospitalization of Sloane O'Kelly, Dillon and Suel filled out the requisite forms and were assigned to desk duty pending the completion of an incident investigation. Just now, they were in a back room at the Gravediggers pub with six other officers in Special Branch. At no surprise, they were drinking Guinness, not the first, and both had a fresh pint waiting in front of them. Suel had a gauze bandage on his chin where it was split. His shirt was splattered with dry bloodstains from Dillon's kneecapping of Sloane O'Kelly.

"So you knew your man was coming?" one of the officers asked.

"We were pretty sure. Once Dillon got the call from Graham, I got behind the wheel, and we raced over. Good thing I didn't follow the speed limit. We beat him by just seconds."

The group laughed at that last line.

"He's not kidding," Dillon said. "We hadn't been there thirty seconds when the intercom rang, and it was him wanting to be let in. In fact, Paddy had literally just stepped into the apartment."

"I answered the intercom, pretending to be your man, Graham," Suel said. "That plonker O'Kelly goes on talking the good line about bringing a new credit card and a gift from your friend. That's what he said to me."

"I said something like I was all excited and buzzed him in the door. He hurries up the stairs, knocks on the door, and I answered with a pistol and a hurley. Faster than a speeding bullet, as the saying goes, he kicks the gun from my hand and splits me chin. Now I'm on the floor, and I've two crazy Americans in with me. One of 'em has a gun, and he shoots. Thank God it was Dillon, and he actually hit your man," Suel said and took a healthy swallow or two of Guinness.

Everyone chuckled, and Suel said, "I'm not kidding you lot. I said to Dillon, for lord's sake, you almost shot me. Do youse know what he said back? He looks at me, and he says, sorry I missed."

"I was sorry. I was aiming for O'Kelly's ass," Dillon interjected. Everyone laughed and took a healthy drink.

"Where's Graham during all this?" someone asked.

"I thought he'd be hiding under the bed," Suel said. "Turns out he was hiding in the jacks, in the fricking bathtub. I had the feeling it wasn't the first time he'd done that." More laughing all around.

Three more pints of Guinness made an even half-dozen. One of the Special Branch guys gave Dillon a ride home. They pulled in front of Dillon's and exchanged another joke. Dillon said thanks, and then the guy waited until Dillon unlocked the door and stepped into the house.

Lucifer hurried down the stairs as Dillon closed the door. He patted the dog on the head, let him outside. He took a biscuit from the cookie jar and tossed it out to Lucifer in the front garden. Dillon glanced across the street and spotted the black Mercedes pulled into Tara's drive and shook his head.

His alarm went off at 7:00 the following morning. He woke with a hangover and a scratchy throat and made his way into the shower. Lucifer was still asleep when he came back into the bedroom. He dressed quietly, went down to the kitchen, and took two aspirin before he put the coffee on.

The two of them, Dillon and Lucifer, had a quiet breakfast with neither the radio nor the tv on. Dillon placed his dishes in the dishwasher. He peeked out the front window in the sitting room. The black Mercedes was still parked in front of Tara's car.

Since he left his car at the station last night, he phoned a taxi and waited ten minutes before it pulled up in front. Once he gave the driver the main station as his destination, any hope of a conversation was eliminated. That was fine with Dillon. He was still nursing a hangover and waiting for the aspirin to start doing their job.

FORTY-SEVEN

reddy arrived at Dugan's apartment forty-five minutes later. He was red-faced, sweating, breathing heavily, and dreading what was to follow. He pressed the intercom, and Dugan's voice growled a moment later. "What?"

"It's me, boss."

"About damn time," Dugan shouted, and the security door buzzed.

As he took the elevator up, his breathing began to return to normal, but his heart started pounding, and sweat rolled down the sides of his face. He stepped off the elevator, hurried to Dugan's door, and knocked.

"It's open, you dumb son of a bitch," Dugan yelled.

"Jimmy, now stop that right now," Sarah said. "Come in, Freddy. How about a little lunch? We've got some smoked salmon, and I just baked a loaf of sourdough bread."

"Get your fat ass in my office and wait for me there," Dugan shouted.

"Jimmy, I'm not going to tell you again, stop that. You're upsetting me. Now, I'll be at Angelia's this afternoon. See what you can do to be in a better mood by the time I return."

Freddy was just stepping into the office when Sarah called, "I'll see you later, Freddy. Enjoy your afternoon." He heard the front door close, and all was quiet. He settled into the chair in front of Dugan's desk and waited then waited some more.

Eventually, there was a noise in the kitchen, and a moment later, Dugan stepped into the office and closed the door behind him. "You look like a piece of shit. What the hell are you sweating for? And where in the hell have you been?"

"Umm, thought I'd start getting back in shape, so I jogged over."

"You jogged over?"

"Yeah, well maybe not all the way, but—"

"How many blocks?"

"Blocks? I don't know a couple, maybe three?"

Dugan shook his head and said, "For God's sake. You'll drop dead from a heart attack you keep that shit up. Quit acting like an absolute idiot and get back in the game here." He shoved a burner phone across his desk. "Get rid of this damn thing and fast. I sent a text to Sloane O'Kelly. He was supposed to respond at noon. Something ain't right, and whatever it is, I don't want it tracked to me. I want you to get rid of this today."

"Sloane O'Kelly? He's working something for you?" Freddy asked, knowing if O'Kelly was involved, things were not going to work out well for someone, somewhere. He suddenly wondered if Dugan had called O'Kelly to deal with him just because he was late getting over here, or… had Dugan heard about Freddy last night? Maybe he knew that burner with the picture of the woman holding her blouse open had been stolen. Maybe Dugan even put the woman up to it. Set Freddy up so—

"Freddy, are you listening to what I just said? I want you to get rid of this damn thing. O'Kelly ain't called me back. He's over two hours late. Get this damn burner out of here, now!"

"Will do, boss," Freddy said. He grabbed the burner and shoved it in his pocket. "I'm on it right away."

Dugan studied him for a long moment and then said, "Go on, get the hell out of my sight."

Freddy didn't need to be told twice. He hurried out of the office, left the apartment without so much as a goodbye, and took the elevator down to the first floor.

Dugan sat and steamed for the next twenty minutes. First, he was mad at Sloane O'Kelly for not getting back to him. Next, he was mad at Freddy just on general principles. Last but not least, he was furious with himself for letting Freddy's lackadaisical attitude affect him the way it did. He decided he'd better go set things straight and double-check to make sure Freddy disposed of that damn burner phone.

* * *

On the walk back to his apartment, Freddy looked left and right and checked behind him a number of times to make sure he wasn't being followed. All the pictures in restaurants, not to mention the newspaper articles, he'd been thinking for a while that Jimmy Dugan was playing a little too fast and loose. Now Sloane O'Kelly was involved? Was he checking up on Freddy? It didn't make any sense, and none of it sounded good.

He was sweating again, profusely, as he approached his building. He glanced over at his empty parking spot, and his blood began to boil. What the hell had he been thinking? Why in the hell didn't he just dump that woman—

"Frederick Dwyer?" A voice suddenly came out of nowhere. "FBI agent Melvin Landen. Please keep your hands where we can see them."

* * *

Dugan stepped out of the elevator in the parking ramp and walked over to his car, a Chevy Impala. It was white, although officially, the color was listed as summit white. Dugan had wanted a color that would blend and not stand out. He pulled out of the ramp and drove over to Freddy's. Along the way, he looked on the sidewalks for Freddy walking. He never saw a fat guy who resembled him. He drove through Venice on East Venice Avenue. He took a left and drove two blocks down Park Boulevard to Castile Street, where he took a right and drove down to Alhambra Road.

He stopped at the corner and could see the Venice Sands apartments where Freddy lived just off to his left. Unfortunately, he could see two white Chevy Tahoes with the words FBI written on the door next to the image of an FBI badge. Behind them was a large white truck. Another FBI badge was painted on the side of the truck along with the words FORT MYERS FIELD OFFICE and, below that, FBI EVIDENCE RESPONSE TEAM.

Dugan was so shocked he just sat at the intersection and stared at the FBI vehicles and the two Venice patrol cars in the parking lot. Freddy was nowhere to be seen, but Dugan didn't need any convincing that Freddy was the person they were looking for. As a matter of fact, since the vehicles were in plain sight, he was pretty sure they already had Freddy in custody, which presented a host of immediate problems.

The horn sounding behind him brought Dugan back to reality. He looked in the rearview mirror and saw another Venice patrol car. He gave a friendly wave, put on his left turn blinker, looked right and left, and turned onto Alhambra Road. He drove in the opposite direction of the Venice Sands Apartments and Freddy. The Venice patrol car took a right and pulled into the Venice Sands parking lot.

FORTY-EIGHT

It was almost noon in Dublin. Dillon and Suel were with Eric Bergman from the American Embassy and DCI McCabe. They were in a private room at St. James Hospital. A guard sat just outside the door. They were in the process of attempting to interview Sloane O'Kelly and not getting anywhere.

O'Kelly's right leg was extended and wrapped in gauze. His nose, swollen to twice its size, was covered by an aluminum splint that ran across his cheeks, over the nose, and across his forehead. It was held in position by Velcro strips that wrapped around the back of his head above and below his ears. O'Kelly stared back at them through two puffy black eyes. Between the broken nose and the splint, his voice sounded comical.

McCabe smiled and said, "Mister O'Kelly, let me explain this to you one more time. Evidence strongly suggests you arrived in the Republic of Ireland with the intent of committing murder. To be exact, the murder of a citizen of Ireland by the name of Killian Graham. This may come as a surprise to you, but we take a rather dim view of this sort of behavior."

"Come on, man. I told you guys before. I came over for two days to enjoy the sights, maybe have a Guinness, sample some Irish hospitality. There I was, minding my own business, simply asking for directions, and these two dumb shits hit me over the head and shoot me," he said, nodding at Dillon and Suel and then grimacing with the pain his nod had caused.

"You're aware we are recording this conversation?"

"Record all you want. I didn't do anything wrong other than get lost on the street. I don't know what sort of deal you guys are running over here, but I gotta tell you, it's bullshit. I told you before. I want to talk to a lawyer." He attempted to push himself up slightly on his pillow, but with both wrists handcuffed to the bedrails, he didn't accomplish much other than another grimace from pain.

"A solicitor will be assigned. We thought, in the interest of obtaining information and arranging a better possibility for you, we would give you the opportunity to tell us your side of the story. You don't seem willing to take advantage of the offer, so a solicitor will be assigned to you shortly. That means, of course, that all offers of a lighter sentence will be off the table. I wish to stress that you will be sentenced, Mr. O'Kelly. With the offers withdrawn, you'll have a number of years to contemplate your decision."

"So go ahead and get me my solicitor or whatever in the hell you call him. Oh, and you, embassy dude, I'm filing a complaint. You're worth jack shit."

Eric Bergman smiled and said, "Thank you, I'll remember that."

"See that you do," O'Kelly said.

"It's been… interesting, Mister O'Kelly. I'm sure there will be further investigation, leading to all sorts of possibilities. Rest assured, we plan to be in close contact with the US Federal and Boston authorities. Gentlemen, it looks like we've hit the proverbial wall here. Let us be off. We've more important things to do than listen to someone ramble on."

"Yeah, that's right. I got you by the short hairs, McCob or McBob or whatever the hell your name is. Thanks for cheering me up, boys. See you in court. I'm thinking two to three million payment by the time I'm done with you," O'Kelly said.

"Enjoy your time in bed, sir. It's much nicer here than Mount Joy prison."

Dillon and Suel tossed their business cards on the food tray table alongside O'Kelly's bed. "Call us if you have a change of heart," Dillon said. "But don't wait too long. This isn't like back in the US. Your time is running out."

"Talk is cheap," O'Kelly shouted, and they headed out the door.

"Oh, just curious, Mr. O'Kelly," McCabe said at the door. "Did you enjoy Venice, Florida? Or were your conversations with Mr. Dugan merely a series of text messages? Wonderful luck on our part. Sometimes burner phones turn out not to be all your lot had hoped," McCabe said and headed out the door.

"Hey, hey, wait a minute. I don't know who you're talking about. I never been to Venice. Where'd you say it was, Florida? Who is Jimmy Dugan? He's dead, anyway. Hasn't been around for at least ten years. You hear me? Hey? I'll see you dudes in court."

"So long, Mr. O'Kelly, and you're so right. We'll see you in court. I, for one, am looking forward to it. Good day," McCabe said and closed the door behind him.

"Hey, wait a minute. Get the hell back here. What'd you mean by that?"

They followed McCabe down the hall and stepped onto the elevator. McCabe was still smiling when they stepped off. "Let's give the gentleman twenty-four hours to consider his options. His possessions are being reviewed in the tech lab?"

"Yes, sir," Dillon said.

"Excellent."

"Let me know what they find. McCabe slid behind the wheel of an unmarked vehicle. Dillon and Suel climbed into Dillon's car and took a round-about route past the house on Stiles Road on their way back to the station and their desks.

Everything on Stiles Road looked quiet. The window shades were pulled halfway down. No vehicle was parked in the front drive, and the garage door was closed, but that was the case with the vast majority of houses on the road.

Suel's phone rang, but since he was driving, he didn't answer. Just as they were pulling into the station parking lot, Dillon's cellphone rang, a call from an unknown number. He debated answering, thinking if it was someone he knew, they would leave a message, and he could call them back. In the end, he answered the call. "Hello."

"Marshal Dillon, please," a female voice said.

"Speaking."

"Yes, Marshal, this is Gemma Donner, Billy's sister."

"Hi, Gemma, any news on Billy?" Dillon asked. Suel gave him a quick look at the sound of Gemma's name. Dillon could hear a baby crying in the background and wondered if it was the one-year-old she was holding the other day when they'd stopped by.

"Yes, I'm afraid there is. I got off the phone with the Mater a while ago. Billy died early this morning. Just a little after 3:00. He never regained consciousness, which I guess is somewhat of a blessing." She sounded on the verge of crying and paused for a moment. "If you would please pass the news onto DI Suel. I know he tried to help Billy a number of times. I guess, in the end, he just didn't want any help, and now here we are." She suddenly began crying and a moment later disconnected.

"That was Gemma? What is it with the likes of Billy?"

"He passed away around 3:00 this morning. Never regained consciousness. She said she knew you tried to help him a number of times."

Suel just shook his head. "What a fecking waste of a life. Always looking for the shortcut. How the hell did that work, Billy?"

"You think his hit and run is tied to talking to you?" Dillon asked.

"I'd say there's a pretty good chance." Suel shook his head. "Billy never did learn when to keep his damn mouth shut. I'm thinking we should stake out that place on Stiles Road starting tonight."

"Need I remind you we are on desk duty for the next couple of days?"

"Well, then that will work out perfectly because when we're off duty and laying around on our own time, we can go over to Stiles road and check things out."

"I got a better idea," Dillon said.

Suel gave a sigh and frowned. "So you're not in with me on this?"

"I didn't say that. I'm merely suggesting we get a taxi sign, and we can drive past the place every ten or fifteen minutes if we want to. Take turns lying in the back seat and taking pictures of vehicles and maybe customers. Grab a couple of cameras from supply and—"

"I got a better idea," Suel said. "I know a guy we can borrow the cameras from. That erases any potential trail should the powers that be question us."

FORTY-NINE

Back in Florida, Sarah Halloran stopped at the grocery store on her way home from the bridge game. She loved getting together with the girls four days a week. It took some of the pressure off of living with Jimmy. If any of the girls suspected anything, they never mentioned it. They seemed to think of Jimmy as just a crabby recluse. Thankfully, he was never a topic of conversation, at least when Sarah was around.

She needed a half-dozen items that took all of five minutes before she was back in the car and heading home. Jimmy would be in his office, telling her he was busy, although his desk would be devoid of anything suggesting work. In the fourteen years she'd been with him, there had always been unanswered questions. She'd stopped asking years ago.

They lived a comfortable life. Other than having to cook breakfast, lunch, and dinner, he didn't require much. Nothing had happened in the bedroom in almost a decade, not that she wanted that to change.

She had her own car, regular deposits in her account, and an expensive roof over her head. Listening to the stories from her bridge group, actually, she had it pretty good. She would have loved to have children, but that never happened. She met Jimmy when she was forty-four, and he was sixty-two. Now, she was just biding her time until… Well, no point in wishing the time away.

She pulled into the underground parking and took the elevator up to their suite. She unlocked the door and called, "It's just me, Jimmy." She thought it strange the alarm wasn't on. She set her purse on the coffee table, took the grocery bag into the kitchen, and set it on the center counter.

"How you doing on coffee, Jimmy?" she called and proceeded to put the groceries away. A bag of whole wheat flour, two bottles of white wine, Brie cheese, the one-pound bag of fresh ground coffee Jimmy insisted on, two chocolate bars that she hid behind tomato soup cans. It took just a couple of minutes to put everything away.

"Jimmy," she called, heading out of the kitchen. She shook her head. She'd been after him to get his hearing tested for the past three or four years. Honest to God, it was enough to— She knocked on the office door. "Jimmy, how you fixed for coffee? Need anything?"

No answer.

"Jimmy? Jimmy?" she said as she opened the door and stepped inside. The office was a mess. Jimmy didn't keep it like this. What was going on? Drawers were open. The wastebasket was overflowing. The doors on the file cabinet open. What happened in here?

She hurried down the hall and checked in his bath-room. Nothing. She opened the bedroom door. His dresser drawers were pulled open. Piles of clothes lay scattered across the bed. Two empty suitcases were on the floor. What in the world?

She hurried back out to the kitchen, took her cellphone from her purse, and placed a call to Jimmy. She heard the phone ringing and followed the sound back to his office. The noise seemed to be coming from his desk. She lifted a stack of papers, and there was his cellphone. None of this was making any sense.

There was a sudden knock on the door. Strange. No one ever came to their suite unless they'd called first. As she hurried out, she called, "Just a moment, please," and then peered out through the peephole, two policemen and four men in suits. 'My God, something's happened to Jimmy?' she thought as she opened the door.

"Sarah Halloran," a man in a dark-blue suit and tie said as he held up a white plastic ID that she was too surprised to read.

"Yes, has something happened to Jimmy?"

"Agent Melvin Landen, Federal Bureau of Investigation. We have a warrant to investigate the premises and any storage facilities," he said, handing a sheet of paper to her with the Sarasota County letterhead.

"But what is this about? Where is Jimmy?"

"That's what we'd like to know. Now, if you'll just take a seat, please," Agent Landen said. At least a dozen individuals followed him into the suite as Sarah sat down on the couch, crossed her arms over her chest, and began to rock back and forth in shock.

They hurried through the suite going down the hall with weapons drawn. They headed into Jimmy's office, shouting, "Clear," and then stepped inside. Seconds later, three more voices shouted, "Clear," from further away. Probably the bedroom and bathrooms. She glanced into the kitchen and watched as two individuals wearing clear plastic gloves placed coffee cups and silverware from the dishwasher into plastic bags.

"Miss Halloran, it would be best for you if you told us where Mr. Dugan is," the man in the dark-blue suit said. Sarah had already forgotten his name.

"I, I don't know where Jimmy is. I just got home not ten minutes ago. Is he alright? What's this about?"

"What's this about? We had a lot of questions for Mr. Dugan. You say you don't know where he is?"

"No, I just told you. I've only been home a few minutes. I called him, didn't get an answer, and when I checked, it looked like someone had ransacked his office and our bedroom. Papers and clothes were thrown all over. What is going on here?"

He glanced at two guys in suits standing behind him and said, "Okay, take her back to the office. We'll follow once we have things moving here. Miss Halloran, I'm placing you under arrest. You have the right to remain silent…"

FIFTY

It was approaching 10:30 at night. Dillon and Suel were eating takeaway meals in the front seat of Suel's car. They were parked in front of the Macari's Take Away in Glasnevin, enjoying fish n chips. The car had a taxi sign attached to the top of the vehicle.

"I'm thinking we drive past every fifteen minutes or so," Dillon said and proceeded to lick his fingertips. "We'll switch positions. You drive, and I'll be in back. I'll drive, and you'll be in back."

Suel snickered and said, "Part of the time you're in back, you can wear that wig. You'll fit right in."

"And you're not going to wear it?" Dillon asked.

"Are you a bleeding lunatic? I put a wig like that on, and it will only attract more attention," Suel said and chuckled. Dillon had to admit he had a point. It would be the largest and probably worst looking woman anyone had ever seen. You could start with Suel's 'S' curved nose and go on from there.

"I'm thinking we do our first pass a little after 11:00. According to what Billy the Butler told us, they don't open for business until midnight. It will be interesting to see if we can catch a vehicle pulling in and unloading the Russian ladies."

"I'd like to catch sight of Bertie Scallen either going in or coming out," Dillon said. "I want to nail that guy."

"With any luck, we'll be able to do that," Suel said.

They finished their dinners. Dillon collected the bags, wrappers, napkins, and empty cups. He climbed out and tossed them into the trash bin.

"You know, it's interesting. You got Macari's and the Aberdeen, both takeout places, and they've been dealing with a steady stream of people all night. Neither place has been empty. In fact, there's always been someone waiting for their order, at least one person ordering, and someone else coming in."

"You do it right, and they both do, you'll have a profitable business. If you have good food at a reasonable price, you've got a gold mine on your hands. Don't get me wrong. They earn it. Hard work and not a lot of romance, but it can pay well."

"Yeah, and fish and chips, what could be healthier? Dillon said.

It was close to 11:30 when they made their first drive up Stiles Road. Suel was driving, and Dillon was stretched out across the back seat. As they approached the corner where Billy the Butler told them customers had to park, Suel alerted Dillon.

"Couple of seconds, and we're there. I'm taking my foot off the gas, and we'll coast past. Two lads are standing on the corner. There's one, make that two cars," Suel said. Dillon felt the car begin to coast as Suel removed his foot from the accelerator. A couple of seconds later, they resumed speed. Dillon couldn't pick up any change in the engine noise.

"You get the picture?" Suel asked.

Dillon checked the digital images. "Yeah, two shots. I think if we enlarge them, we can get the license numbers on the cars, and we could maybe run one of the lads through facial recognition and see if anything comes up."

Twenty minutes later, they made another pass. This time, there were five cars parked around the corner. The same two guys were standing on the corner.

"Yeah, they're definitely keeping an eye on the cars," Dillon said.

They switched places and drove past with Dillon behind the wheel and Suel in the back seat. The only problem was Suel was taller than Dillon, so he had to lay on his side and try to take the photos. Otherwise, his knees would be obvious, and even though it was dark, they didn't want to take the chance of alerting the two lookouts. There were as many as nine different cars parked around the corner at one time. Over the course of three hours, Dillon guesstimated there had been twenty-six different cars.

They knocked off a little after 3:00 in the morning. Suel dropped off Dillon at home. Dillon noticed the black Mercedes at Tara's house as he unlocked his front door. He got the coffee ready for the morning and picked up the remnants of paper napkins that Lucifer had torn up, but other than that, there wasn't any mess.

He tiptoed upstairs, brushed his teeth, and crawled into bed after setting the alarm for 9:00.

FIFTY-ONE

Lucifer woke Dillon at 8:30 the following morning, barking at the front door to be let out. Dillon hurried downstairs, let him out, and jumped in the shower. He filled Lucifer's food and water dishes, made a quick breakfast for himself, and was on his way to the office by 9:30. His desk phone signaled a message waiting for him when he arrived.

He listened to the recording. "Yeah, umm, Dillon. This is Sloane O'Kelly. I'm hoping we can still talk. If you can call the nurse's desk, they'll provide me with a phone, and we can chat. Their number is…" Dillon listened to the message a second time and wrote down the number. Suel wasn't in yet, but McCabe was, and Dillon knocked on his doorframe as he stepped into the office.

McCabe looked up from the stack of files he'd been reviewing. "Yes, Marshal, what is it?"

Dillon explained the phone message and finished up with, "What do you think?"

"Let me ask you the same thing. What do you think, Marshal?"

"Mmm, if he wants to talk, I'd like to do it in person with a witness and record it."

"And you don't think that will upset him and cause him not to say anything?"

"Even if it does, we're no worse off than we are now, and we've got a pretty solid case against him. I'm guessing he talked to a solicitor yesterday and got an honest assessment of his situation."

"Which is?"

"We're going to nail him."

McCabe seemed to think for a moment and then nodded. "Is Suel in?"

"Not yet, sir. He's at Dublin County offices looking up the property records on the Stiles Road property," Dillon lied.

McCabe seemed to think about that for a moment and then said, "Maybe give him a call and see if he could join you. Anything else?"

"No sir," Dillon said and hurried out the door. He fled the office and didn't phone Suel until he stepped off the elevator on the main floor.

The phone rang twice before Suel answered, "What?"

"I had a message from Sloane O'Kelly waiting for me when I got in. He seems to have had a change of heart and would like to talk. I'm heading over to James's now. McCabe told me to give you a call."

"You told him I wasn't in?"

"I told him you were at Dublin County offices checking property records on Stiles Road."

"Good lad. I'll meet you at James's in twenty minutes. Wait for me in the lobby."

"See you there," Dillon said and disconnected. He was in the lobby of St. James Hospital ten minutes later. He waited for close to a half-hour before Suel arrived.

"Too bad I'm not getting paid by the hour," Dillon said.

Suel yawned and said, "Sorry, I was in the middle of grocery shopping. I would have been here sooner, but unfortunately, I had two old ones ahead of me. Apparently, they had all the time in the world. You said you had a message from O'Kelly. Did you call him back?"

"I thought it might be better to let him sweat a little."

Suel nodded. "Good move. Let's see what he has to say."

They took the elevator up to O'Kelly's room. The uniformed guard was seated just outside the room. He was reading a copy of the Irish Independent newspaper. He glanced over the top of the paper when he heard Dillon and Suel approaching, folded the newspaper, and said, "Good morning, gentlemen," as they approached.

"Hi ya's, Timmy. Anything from your man?" Suel asked.

"No, I heard him talking to one of the nurses about getting a phone call, but nothing's happened since then."

"Was that maybe an hour ago?" Dillon asked.

The man nodded.

"Probably right before he called me. Said I'd have to call the nurse's desk and gave me a phone number."

"No point in calling if we're already here," Suel said as he opened the door to the room.

O'Kelly was still handcuffed to the bed rails. He didn't look any better than when they saw him yesterday. Maybe even a little worse because he now had two days worth of beard stubble.

"Good morning, Mr. O'Kelly," Suel said as he stepped in.

"Got your message," Dillon said, following Suel into the room. "How's the knee?"

"Let's just say, even with the meds, it's got my attention."

"You mentioned you wanted to talk," Dillon said.

"Yeah, I think we maybe got off on the wrong foot yesterday," O'Kelly said. "I wasn't myself, probably all the meds I was on."

"And you're not on them today?" Dillon asked.

"Oh, I am, but I reduced the dosage, and I maybe had a little time to think."

"Good. Two things. First, I'm going to tape our conversation. Second, you get belligerent, and we're out of here. DCI McCabe wasn't kidding yesterday."

With that, Dillon pulled out his cell and pressed record. He mentioned himself, Suel, and O'Kelly. Plus the date, time, and location. "Sloane O'Kelly, we are here at your request, is that correct?"

"Yeah."

"And you're aware we are recording this conversation?"

"Yeah."

"Let me state for the record that we are here to discuss the text messages you received from Jimmy Dugan's burner phone in Venice, Florida. You were instructed to come to Dublin, Ireland and deal with Mr. Killian Graham. Correct?"

"Yeah, that was the gig."

Dillon went through the circumstances step by step. O'Kelly gave mostly one or two-word answers agreeing with the statements Dillon made. It took no more than fifteen minutes. Suel remained quiet the entire time.

When they were finished, Dillon asked, "Is there anything else you would like to add?"

"Yeah, I'm guessing, since you haven't told me Jimmy Dugan has been arrested, that you guys screwed it up, once again. Now, you're scratching your head, wondering where in the hell he ran off to. I think I know, and I can tell you if you're interested. I'm thinking it'll be my get out of jail card."

"All right, where did he go?" Dillon asked.

"No, it ain't gonna be that easy. I want to be transported back to the states. I'm willing to do six months at home recovery from this bullshit," he said, indicating his knee. And then all charges will be expunged from my record. In return, I'll tell you where you can find Jimmy Dugan. Of course, I'll need our agreement in writing. In case you forgot, Jimmy's been in the top ten on the nation's most-wanted list since 2012," O'Kelly said and smiled.

"This is going to be above my pay grade," Dillon said.

"Somehow, I think you'll be able to find a way, Marshal. Besides, I ain't going anywhere," O'Kelly said and nodded at his knee.

"I'll take this to the powers that be," Dillon said, but this is a pretty tall order.

"Cut the bullshit. You know, and I know, this Graham guy is safe. No one is coming after him now. Dugan's hiding. Just for starters, think of the press if he's arrested. And you're going to give all that up to put me behind bars on an assault charge?"

"Umm, it was quite a bit more than an assault charge," Dillon said.

"Oh, really? The big guy there got a bump on the chin, big deal. I'm gonna be walking with a limp for the rest of my life. I never even saw that Graham guy. Couldn't pick him out of a crowd of two. And you're going to let Jimmy Dugan off the hook? The guy's murdered upwards of thirty people."

"Officially, the count is nineteen."

"Don't kid yourself. Look, I ain't gonna argue with you. You heard my offer. Run it up the pole and see what happens. I'll probably be here for a while."

Dillon thought about that for a minute and said, "The conversation has ended at eleven twenty-eight AM Dublin time." He turned off his cellphone and put it in his pocket.

"We'll see what happens," Dillon said.

"Enjoy the day, fellas," O'Kelly replied.

Other than a goodbye to the guard, Dillon and Suel didn't speak until they were outside. Dillon had parked in the ramp, and Suel's car was in the opposite direction out on James Street in front of Kenny's Bar.

"What do you think?" Suel asked.

"I think if he really could give Dugan up, there's a good chance folks will go for it. I'm glad it's not my decision. We'll run it past McCabe, and he can take it from there."

Suel shook his head. "That wanker seemed pretty sure of himself."

"It's always all about him. He should have gone into politics," Dillon said.

They headed straight for McCabe's office once they were back in Special Branch. Dillon played the recording for McCabe. When he was finished listening, McCabe shook his head and said, "All right, I want you to take that down to the tech lab. Let me call them now. They'll meet you at the door. Have them make two copies, one for safe-keeping as well as a docu copy. Once that's completed, contact your man at the American embassy—"

"Eric Bergman," Dillon said.

"Send him a copy. I want this out of our hands as quickly as possible. I'll inform headquarters here, and they can deal with it. You two are off desk duty. Get back to work. Where do we stand on Stiles Road?"

Suel proceeded to suggest they spend early morning hours photographing the suspected house and the parking area rumored to be used for 'clients.' He neglected to mention they had done exactly that the previous evening.

McCabe seemed to think on that for a few seconds and nodded. "Very well, I'd like this brought to a close as quickly as possible. Anything else?"

"No, sir," Dillon and Suel responded.

"Thank you," McCabe said, dismissing them.

Dillon was met by Emily in the tech lab. It took all of fifteen minutes for her to record the conversation with Sloane O'Kelly. She sent him a URL that he could forward to Eric Bergman. She sent a copy to DCI McCabe so he could send it on to the upper ranks.

Dillon was home just after 4:00 that afternoon. He'd planned on trying to grab a nap since he and Suel would be spending another late night driving up and down Stiles Road.

Of course, the black Mercedes was backed into Tara's drive. Dillon figured, *If the guy was there at this hour, he must have moved in with her.* He took Lucifer for a walk over to the green and let him chase the tennis ball. They played for a good forty minutes before Lucifer had enough. They took the long way home to avoid walking past Tara's home. Dillon ate leftover pizza for dinner and then dozed off, watching the six o'clock news.

Suel picked him up just after 11:00. The rooftop taxi sign was clamped onto the top of his car again. As Dillon climbed into the car, he caught Tara's bedroom lights going off and shook his head.

FIFTY-TWO

The rain was just steady enough to have to use the wipers. They had been at it for a good two hours, driving up and down Stiles Road, photographing the parked cars and the same two individuals keeping an eye on the cars. They were driving past once again. Dillon was lying in the back, taking the pictures. At the moment, there were three cars parked around the corner, a slow night probably due to the rain.

As they drove past, Suel looked straight ahead and said, "Did you see your man with the camera?"

Dillon clicked on the digital images he'd just taken and said, "Yeah, looking at it now. He appears to be taking our picture."

"Yeah, damn it, I'd say it's a pretty good chance they're onto us," Suel said.

"So what do you want to do?"

"Wait until we're out of sight, and then we're going to need some help. One squad to watch those two knackers and two more to follow us in."

"You want to raid the place? We'll need a warrant, and at this hour, it'll be next to impossible to—"

"We suspect a number of women are being held against their will and are being forced to participate in sexual acts. It would seem to be a clear-cut case of our duty to intervene," Suel said. He turned off Stiles road, parked at the curb, and looked into the rear seat just as Dillon sat up. He handed the camera to Suel with the digital image of the guy photographing them as they drove past.

"He's made us, or he's about to. I'm going to call for back up. You with me?"

"Yeah, while you're calling, I'll get the taxi sign off the roof of the car," Dillon said and climbed out. It took him no more than a minute or two to unclamp the taxi sign. He pulled the cord out of the lights and handed it to Suel through the driver's window then set the taxi sign in the trunk. He pulled out two protective vests, handed one to Suel, and slipped into the other before climbing into the passenger seat.

"You get ahold of anyone?"

"Thank God for the rain. It's a quiet night. They'll meet us here in the next fifteen or twenty minutes," Suel said.

It was less than ten minutes, and three squad cars were parked next to them. The rain seemed to be picking up. Suel was on a radio, explaining what they intended to do. "Everyone follow us. Lights on low. I'll turn into the front drive of number ninety-four Stiles Road. Desi, you two continue down to the corner, block any attempt for a car to leave. Arrest the two knackers there. One of them should be carrying a camera. The rest will pull into the drive and head for the front door. Brenden, once we're inside, you two go to the back door just in case anyone tries to go out that way. Tommy, you lot post yourselves at the top of the staircase. Anyone steps out of a room, you shag 'em back inside. Dillon and I will clear the ground floor and follow you upstairs. Questions?"

"Security?" someone asked.

"Most likely, but not sure what. I would expect at least one at the front door, another maybe in the kitchen. We move fast, and they won't know we're even in there before we're on top of them. Anything else? All right, stay safe and let's move," Suel said.

He drove down to the next corner and made a U-turn then drove past the three squad cars and took a left back onto Stiles Road. Suel had his bright lights on. The three squad cars had their low beams. Once all three cars pulled onto Stiles Road Suel said into the radio, "All right, picking up speed to sixty-five kilometers per hour." He gradually increased speed. A minute later, he said, "I'm going to take a right into the drive six doors up. I'll block the garage. Soon as we stop, we're out of the car and going to the front door."

Suel slowed slightly and pulled in through the open gate. He cut his lights, accelerated up the fairly long drive, and stopped in front of the attached garage. He and Dillon hurried out of the car, leaving the doors open. The lights appeared to be on inside the home. The heavy white shutters mounted on every window were closed. Four Garda officers hurried up behind them in seconds.

They were gathered at the front door. The door was black and had two panels of leaded glass along with a silver knocker and doorknob. Suel glanced behind him, nodded, and then reached for the silver doorknob. "Damn it, locked."

"Let me, Paddy," one of the uniformed officers said. He was larger than Suel with a thick neck and hands that looked like the size of ten-pound hams.

"Kick it in, Tommy," Suel said as he stepped aside.

Tommy sized up the door as if he was going to kick an extra point in the final second of a game. He raised his knee and growled as his foot slammed into the door just behind the doorknob. The door burst open as first Tommy, then Dillon, Suel, and the rest stormed into the front hallway.

A guy with a shaved head and a goatee was seated in a wooden chair maybe four feet beyond the door. He had just begun to stand when Tommy slammed into him with a massive forearm, knocking him back onto the chair. He tipped backward, and his head made a 'thump' sound as it bounced off the floor. Dillon and Suel moved into a room off to the side as an officer hurried up the stairs, and two hurried toward the kitchen. Tommy rolled the guy on the floor over face down.

A man in jeans and a t-shirt was asleep on the couch in the side room. As his eyes flickered open, Dillon grabbed him by the t-shirt and yanked him onto the floor.

He placed his knee on the man's back, removed the pistol wedged in the back of the man's belt, and handcuffed his hands behind his back. Suel raced through the room, into the empty dining room, and from there into the kitchen.

Dillon held onto the pistol he'd taken and stepped back into the hallway. The man Tommy had knocked over was lying face down with his hands cuffed behind his back. He was bleeding from the nose but otherwise seemed all right.

Suel, Brenden, and another officer stepped out of the kitchen. Suel pointed to the staircase, and Dillon led them up the stairs. Tommy and another officer were waiting at the top of the stairs.

The officer placed his index finger against his lips, signaling quiet, and smiled. They could hear what sounded like a woman sobbing and a man's voice groaning, "Yes, yes, yes."

There were five doors along the hallway. One was partially opened and appeared to have a white tile floor. A flickering light suggesting candles played on the wall. Tommy pointed at the flickering light and mouthed the words, 'The loo.'

They tiptoed down the hall, spreading out and taking up positions in front of the remaining four doors. Suel and Dillon prepared to enter rooms on their own. Suel gave a nod, and they burst open the doors to the rooms and turned on the lights.

Brief screams and shouting followed, which quickly changed to female voices seeming to plead in a language none of them could understand. Dillon had burst into a room with a four-poster bed and a couple asleep. The blonde woman's scream quickly turned to cries as tears ran down her face. Her hands were fastened at the wrists by a black zip tie. She lifted her hands and seemed to plead to Dillon.

The guy next to her in the bed looked like he was old enough to be her father. He coughed a couple of times and growled, "What the hell do you think you're doing in here. I'll have you know I'm in Dáil Éireann. Now step outside and wait your turn. I paid for a full night."

"Oh, you're going to pay for a lot more than that," Dillon said.

"Now you just wait a min—"

Dillon grabbed him by the arm and rolled him off of the bed. He dropped three feet onto the floor. "Uff," he grunted when he hit the floor and then decided that it might be best to keep quiet.

Suel stepped into the room a moment later with a small knife. He was followed by a woman in jeans and a soiled sweatshirt. She hurried over to the woman sobbing in the bed and wrapped her arms around her, whispering something in a different language.

"If you could undo her wrists, please," she said to Suel and then followed up with more whispers. She stroked the woman's hair as Suel carefully placed the knife blade between her wrists and cut the zip tie.

"There are eight of them all told, women," Suel said. "One of the rooms had them gagged and tied on the floor. Three customers, including your man here," he said and nodded at the naked body breathing heavily on the floor.

"Best be careful. He's in Dáil Éireann," Dillon said and suppressed a laugh.

"Interesting. I've seen enough. Help him get a pair of pants on, and we'll get everyone to the station. Your woman's clothes are in the other room," Suel said.

He stepped out into the hall and went into the bathroom, returning quickly with a large white towel. He handed the towel to the woman in the sweatshirt, and she wrapped it around the blonde woman, who continued to cry as she was led out of the room.

"They stripped the women and put them in these rooms, figured they couldn't escape if they didn't have clothes," Suel said.

"I, I think I'm going to be sick," the man on the floor said.

"That's going to be the least of your problems," Dillon replied.

"For God's sake get some trousers on this wanker and bring him down to the front room. I'll get transportation alerted," Suel said and left.

A pair of black trousers hung over the back of a red velvet upholstered chair. Dillon picked them up and tossed them on the floor next to the man.

"Let's take a moment here, lad. I'm sure I can do youse a favor," he said as he quickly pulled the trousers on.

"I'm thinking you'd better shut up before I gag you," Dillon said.

Once the man had his trousers on, Dillon led him downstairs to the front room, barefoot and shirtless. The two thugs were sitting on the floor against a couch. The one who had been at the front door had his head tilted back. Bloodied tissues were stuffed up his now swollen nose. Two other men were seated on the floor, and they looked at the older man Dillon led into the room. There seemed to be a sense of recognition, but neither said anything.

A few minutes later, the two Garda who had gone down to the corner with the parked cars stepped into the room. Each led a young guy Dillon recognized from the many drives past the corner. If they recognized Dillon, they didn't acknowledge it.

Twenty minutes later, there was a knock on the door, and two female officers stepped inside. Suel led them up the stairs, and after about ten minutes, they came back down with eight women. The woman who'd been in the room Dillon entered was dressed in slacks and a sweater with torn elbows. At least she'd stopped crying.

One of the women stepped into the room, shouted something, and spit on the guy with the bloody nose. He raised his head for a moment, looked at her, then tilted his head back, resting it on the couch.

Suel and Tommy walked out with the women and put them in some sort of van. "Just you lot left," Suel said when he came back into the room. "Transportation should be here in a few minutes. You'll be sharing a cell when you're brought to the station," he said and smiled.

It was a good half-hour before there was a knock on the door. Suel answered it.

"Oh good, you're all set. Wonderful. We'll bring them out in just a moment."

Suel stepped into the room, all smiles. "All right, I'll lead the way. An officer will lead you lot out and—"

"This has gone far enough," the guy Dillon had pulled onto the floor half-shouted. "I demand my clothes. I'll give you my name, and we can establish a time when I'll come down and discuss matters. If you must know, I was conducting an investigation of my own. Exploring why a facility such as this was allowed to operate under the supposed watchful eye of An Garda Síochána."

"Really, Eamon Conlan. Your own investigation?" Suel said.

The man had a surprised look on his face when Suel said his name, but quickly recovered. "Umm, yes, that's correct, and I should warn you, I've found some things that will not relate kindly to An Garda Síochána. It would seem to be in everyone's interest to discuss this privately at a later time when cooler heads will prevail."

Suel seemed to think about that for a long moment before he shook his head and said, "Nah, bring them out, lads. Mr. Conlan, this will be your chance to tell the world what you've learned. The press is waiting."

"The, the press? Now you just wait a—"

"Marshal, if you would be so kind," Suel said as Dillon took hold of shirtless, barefoot, Eamon Conlan's arm and led him out the front door.

The rain had stopped, and as they stepped outside, lights flashed on, and three cameras began filming. A half-dozen reporters shouting questions rushed toward Dillon and Conlan.

Conlan shouted, "No, no, no," as Dillon slowly dragged him down the drive toward the street and a white paneled van with An Garda Síochána in large blue letters next to the image of the department logo. Red and blue lights flashed back and forth on top of the van.

"Looks like you'll be riding in the 'Meat Wagon,' Mr. Conlan."

The cameramen and reporters appeared to have no interest in the two other arrestees. Conlan pulled left and right, attempting to hide his face, which only encouraged the reporters and cameramen to follow even closer. They continued to shout questions over Conlan's screeching as Dillon led him slowly toward the van and took his time chaining him onto the bench.

Dillon climbed out of the van and let the press take pictures for a couple more minutes of shirtless, barefoot Conlan chained to the bench.

FIFTY-THREE

Dillon and Suel were the last to leave. They'd se-cured the house and waited for the forensics team to arrive. Among other things, Dillon found a gray Ford Fiesta parked in the attached garage. The front of the car was severely damaged with a broken headlight, a shattered grill, and a dented hood and front bumper. Traces of dried blood were apparent on the vehicle, and he backed away from it, not wanting to leave a fingerprint.

When the forensics team finally arrived, Dillon and Suel took them into the garage and showed them the vehicle. They'd already traced the license plate, listed to a corporation, amazingly named Estate Investments. Which meant the vehicle was probably the same one Bertie Scallen had driven the day they met him at Forty-four Reginald Street. Once the forensics team began, Suel drove Dillon home. It was almost 6:00 AM. They promised to meet at the station at 2:00 that afternoon.

Dillon opened the gate and walked to his front door as Suel drove off. He unlocked the door, stepped inside, and turned to close the door quietly, only to notice the black Mercedes backed into Tara's drive. He closed the door and decided there was nothing he could or should do.

He tiptoed up to his bedroom, undressed, and decided to close his eyes for just thirty minutes. Lucifer's barking woke him three hours later. It was a lovely morning, and he let Lucifer out into the front garden. He filled his food and water dishes, placed them on the front stoop, and went back to bed. His alarm woke him at 12:30.

He showered, shaved, dressed, and encouraged Lucifer to come inside with the bribe of a biscuit. He stepped outside at 1:40, made note of the fact that the black Mercedes was nowhere to be seen, and headed for the office.

As he climbed out of the car, Suel pulled in, and they headed into the building together. "Did you get some sleep?" Suel asked.

"Out like a light. I could use a few more hours, but it looks like I'll have to wait until tonight. How 'bout you?"

"Same. I think I was asleep before my head hit the pillow." They took the elevator up. As they walked into the office, they got congratulatory calls and thumbs-up from a number of people. McCabe appeared in the door to his office and called, "Dillon, Suel, grab a tea and join me."

Dillon cleared the four plates and two mugs from his desk and carried them into the break room. Suel put the kettle on. Dillon went back to his desk and retrieved his mug. He filled it with coffee and took a sip. Surprisingly, it wasn't half-bad. He waited for Suel's tea, and they headed into McCabe's office.

McCabe was all smiles. "Interesting evening. Congratulations on your success. Not being critical, but what prompted the move?"

They went on to explain the two young men photographing the car as they drove past.

McCabe nodded as they told the story. "Very pleased with the results. The eight women will be flown back to Russia once they're examined and given a couple of days to rest." McCabe shook his head, "They've given us names, and we've a team out now looking for three individuals."

"That wouldn't happen to include Nora Scallen and her son Bertie, would it?" Suel asked.

"No, as a matter of fact. I thought I would leave that to you two. Now, I think it best they be arrested simultaneously. Which one would you gentlemen be interested in arresting?"

"Bertie," Dillon and Suel said in unison.

"I thought as much. By the way, testing came back just after the noon hour on the blood samples the forensics team gathered from the car on Stiles Road."

"The gray Ford Fiesta?" Dillon asked.

McCabe nodded and smiled. "A match with one William Donner, recently deceased from injuries received in a hit and run," McCabe said and slid a technical report across the desk.

Suel slid it between the two of them, and they studied it for a long moment. "Billy the Butler, God bless," Suel said in almost a whisper.

"I'll leave it to you two to find Mr. Scallen and bring him in. Anything else?" McCabe asked.

"No, sir, we'd better get on this," Suel said, and they hurried out of McCabe's office. Suel set his half-finished tea on Dillon's desk and said, "I'll drive."

"Home or his office?" Dillon asked.

"Home first. If he's not there, his office. If we don't find him in either one of those places, we can check St. Margaret's Rest Home down in the Liberties. Let me just pull a file with his addresses," Suel said and hurried to his desk.

Dillon gulped down his coffee, and by the time he walked over to Suel's desk, Suel had the file pulled and was headed for the door.

Dillon had to hurry to catch up. They took the elevator down to the ground floor. As it began to slow, Suel said, "Come on, come on, Jaysus, this takes all day." The doors opened, and Suel hurried out. Dillon followed two or three steps behind. As they stepped outside, a light sprinkling of rain was just beginning.

When they got to the car, Suel took a deep breath, and then another. "Okay, sorry about that. But your man killed Billy the Butler with that skanky bit of a car. I want to arrest him in the worst way."

"You want me to drive?" Dillon said.

"Na, this plonker lives almost up to Howth. Rather than give the likes of you directions, we'll get there quicker if I drive. You can sit back and enjoy the scenery."

They climbed in. Suel backed out of the parking place, took a deep breath, and said, "All right, let's go pick up your man."

They drove through Dublin, heading toward Howth. They were in Kilbarrack Lower, driving along Dublin road with attractive, unattached homes on the left-hand side and Dublin Bay on the right. Other than Suel complaining about the occasional driver, not much was said. That was fine with Dillon. Despite the rain, he was enjoying the view.

"Here we go," Suel said as he slowed and turned into a long drive leading up to a cream-colored two-story home. The six-foot-high wrought iron front gates were open, and Suel drove in. Two vehicles were parked off to the side. A bronze SUV and next to the SUV was a light blue truck with the image of a white sink, tub, and toilet on the side. The company name and phone number ran beneath the images of the plumbing fixtures.

"Well, will you look at that?" Suel said and chuckled at the sight of the truck.

"Surprise, surprise. No doubt here to fix a bathroom leak," Dillon said.

The rear door on the SUV was raised and flush with the roof of the vehicle. Suel parked behind the vehicles, basically blocking them from backing up. The SUV had two large suitcases lying in the back, one black and one pink.

"What do you think? Are they coming or going?" Dillon asked.

"I'm guessing they booked a flight about five minutes after they learned of the arrests." Suel walked over and placed a hand on the hood of the SUV. "Warm. It's just back from somewhere."

"Please, time is of the essence. We've no time to waste. Now get—" Bertie Scallen stopped halfway out the front door. He was carrying what looked like a pink makeup case, the kind with a mirror attached to the inside of the lid.

"Going on a vacation, are you, Bertie?"

Bertie plastered on a smile and headed toward them. A woman, Dillon presumed his wife, followed. She held a small brown dog in her arms and asked, "Who are these two?"

"Would love to chat, but we're going to be late for our flight, lads. Back in a few days. Can we meet up then?"

"What?" the woman said. "A few days, Bertie? I thought you said—"

"Shut up."

"— a month."

"For God's sake, will you stop talking, woman?"

"Where are you off to, Bertie?"

"Little trip to Spain, get some sun in our bones. Now, if you'll excuse us. We—"

"Oh, I'm afraid you may have to adjust your plans," Suel said.

"Adjust our plans?" the woman said.

"You wouldn't know anything about a house at ninety-four Stiles Road, would you, Bertie?" Dillon asked.

"Stiles Road? No, I don't think so, I—"

"Bertie, you do. It was your mam's. You grew up—"

"Would you please shut the hell up, Kiera?"

"Here now, Bertie. Is that any way to talk? I'm afraid you've a lot bigger problems than remembering your mam's address. Say, I'm looking around, and I'm not seeing your Ford Fiesta, that gray one. Now, I wonder where that might be," Suel said.

"It wasn't my fault. He, umm, he stepped out in front of me. Yeah, that was it. He stepped out right in front of me. I think he'd been drinking. Drinking a lot and—"

"Bertie, if you know what's good for you, you'll just shut the hell up," Suel said. He pulled a pair of handcuffs from his pocket and dangled them in front of Bertie.

Bertie stared at the handcuffs for a moment and then tossed the pink makeup case at Suel. He turned to run, took two steps, and slammed into the raised rear door on the SUV. His feet flew out from underneath him, and he seemed to levitate for a half-second before dropping onto the asphalt drive.

The woman screamed, the dog barked, and Suel rolled Bertie over into a puddle and cuffed his hands behind his back.

"Bertie Scallen, I'm placing you under arrest for the murder of William Donner. More charges to follow," Suel said and laughed. "Give us a hand, will you, Dillon?" Suel said, taking hold of one of Bertie's arms.

Dillon took hold of the other arm, and they began to hoist Bertie to his feet. Only Suel yanked Bertie up so as they raised him to his feet, his head slammed into the open rear door on the SUV.

"Oh, careful there, Bertie, you bleeding gob shite. You'll scramble what little brains you have left."

"No, wait, wait. I was going to call you. I can explain," Bertie mumbled as they dragged him toward Suel's car.

"Might be best just to keep quiet," Dillon said.

They placed Bertie in the back seat. Dillon hurried around to the passenger side while Suel opened the driver's door.

"Pleasure to meet you, Kiera," Suel said as he climbed in. He started the car, gave a slight wave to speechless Kiera, staring with her mouth open. The little brown dog was next to the SUV, lifting his leg and aiming at the rear tire.

FIFTY-FOUR

Dillon, Suel, and a half-dozen officers were at the Autobahn Roadhouse in Glasnevin. They'd been trading stories and laughs for the last couple of hours. Dillon had hoped to be home two or three hours ago, but that thought was now barely a memory. More laughs, yet another pint of Guinness, and thankfully someone offered to give him a ride home.

They pulled in front of Dillon's house, and Dillon slid out of the passenger seat, said thanks, and waved goodbye. At least the rain had finally stopped. He glanced over at Tara's house. It was after midnight, the lights were off, and sure enough, the black Mercedes was backed into the drive. Dillon told himself he didn't give a damn, but the next thing he knew, he was crouched down, letting the air out of a rear tire.

He completed his task, thought about doing the same to the remaining three tires, and in the end, staggered home and went to bed.

Lucifer barking downstairs at the door eventually woke Dillon. His mouth was dry, his head was pounding, and he'd slept in his clothes. He was still wearing his shoes. He made his way downstairs and let Lucifer out the door. He headed into the kitchen and searched the cabinet for aspirin.

He had just taken two deep breaths and prayed the aspirin would do their job, quickly, when the doorbell rang. He debated answering when it rang again. God, probably dreadful Deitora from next door, bitching about something. He took a deep breath and decided there was only one way to deal with this.

He tore open the front door, about to say something, and there stood Tara. Suddenly, it came back to him, letting the air out of the rear tire of the Mercedes. God, how did she know it was him? Did she see him? Did he leave a trail?

"Oh, Tara, umm—"

"Hi, Dillon, sorry to bother you. Thank God you're home. I didn't see your car, but I saw Lucifer out in the garden. I'm hoping you can help. I've been trying to change the rear tire on my dad's car, but I can't get the things to move. They're on so tight. My dad had heart surgery a little more than a week ago, and I don't want him near that flat tire. Can you help?"

"Your dad?"

"Yeah, he's been staying with me for a week or so. He has physical therapy during the day and all sorts of monitoring. He has another examination today. If he checks out, he can go back home to Sligo. But he's not going anywhere with a flat tire."

"That black Mercedes belongs to your dad?"

She nodded and looked over her shoulder at the Mercedes.

"I'll be right over," Dillon said. "Let me get my toolbox."

"Oh, thanks so much, Jack. I'll owe you big time."

Dillon ran out the backdoor and grabbed his toolbox from the shed. He hurried over to Tara's drive, cursing himself. He focused on the flat rear tire, and suddenly, the fog in his mind immediately disappeared.

The lug wrench hung from one of the lug nuts. Tara had her foot on the wrench and was attempting to use her weight to turn the nut. Unfortunately, she was attempting to turn it the wrong way, actually tightening the nut if that was possible.

"Stop, Tara, you're going the wrong way."

"What?"

"The direction you're trying to turn it, that actually tightens the nut."

"Oh, God, I don't believe it."

"Let me get in there and see what I can do."

He took a spray can from the toolbox, sprayed the nuts, and loosened them slightly. He slipped the jack underneath the car and slowly raised the rear of the vehicle. He removed the nuts, pulled the tire off, and leaned it against the fence. He rolled the spare over, mounted it on the lug bolts, and tightened the lug nuts by hand. He lowered the vehicle and tightened the lug nuts using the weight of his body.

The entire process took no more than six minutes.

"Oh. My. God. You did it that fast?"

"Not a problem. Tell you what. Give me the keys, and I'll get the tire repaired and changed. You don't want your dad driving all the way to Sligo on a spare tire."

"Oh, no, I can do that and—"

"Do you have the keys?"

"Yeah," she said, reaching into her pocket.

Dillon grabbed them and said, "I'll be back in thirty minutes."

"You sure? You don't have to do this."

Dillon took the keys and climbed in behind the wheel. He started the car, gave Tara a wave, and headed to a repair station a mile and a half away on Santry Lane. Fortunately, there was no one being serviced, and he was back at Tara's twenty minutes and thirty euros later.

He rang the doorbell, handed her the car keys when she answered, and got a kiss on the cheek for his trouble. He carried his toolbox back to his shed. He bribed Lucifer back into the house with a biscuit, filled his food and water dishes, and spent a good twenty minutes in the shower.

FIFTY-FIVE

He was slowly but surely working his way through a mountain of paperwork when McCabe stepped to his office door and said, "Dillon, Suel, if you could give me a minute of your time, please."

Dillon looked over at Suel, who shrugged.

As they entered McCabe's office, he said, "Grab a seat, gentlemen." He closed the file in front of him. Once they were seated, he took a manila envelope from the corner of his desk and opened it. "I've received a response to Mr. O'Kelly's offer." As McCabe spoke, he handed a two-page form to Dillon.

Dillon looked at it and read the first two paragraphs. "They're agreeing to his offer? He's not going to be charged?"

"Provided he meets the stipulations. In other words, if they arrest James Dugan, O'Kelly will be returned to the US, and his record will be expunged of this particular incident. He will remain in our custody until Dugan is arrested. If Dugan is not arrested, O'Kelly will be tried and, I've no doubt, convicted. I'd like you two to present this offer to him."

"He's still in St. James hospital?" Dillon asked.

Suel nodded. "It should be a fairly brief meeting. Either he cooperates, or he doesn't."

"I'll drive this time," Dillon said as they left McCabe's office with the manila envelope. They were pulling into the parking ramp at St. James Hospital fifteen minutes later. Sloane O'Kelly was still in the same room, handcuffed to the bed. The guard seated in front of the entrance to his room was reading his cellphone.

He looked up as Dillon and Suel approached. He flashed a smile once he recognized Suel. "Hi ya, Paddy. I got a call saying youse might be stopping by."

"Here to see your man. Shouldn't take long. You know Marshall Dillon?" Suel asked and nodded at Dillon.

"Only by reputation, nice to meet youse, Eoin McCabe," he said and held out his hand.

"McCabe? Any relation to DCI McCabe?" Dillon asked.

"Me uncle. Which means he's been cracking the whip on my arse since I was a wee one."

Dillon and Suel laughed as McCabe stood and pulled his chair off to the side. "Good luck in there," McCabe said as Dillon opened the door.

Sloane O'Kelly was staring out the window, apparently studying the brick wall just six inches away. He slowly glanced over as Dillon and Suel stepped in.

"Gentlemen, to what do I owe the pleasure?"

"You've got about ten minutes to make a decision, Mr. O'Kelly."

"It won't take that long. I think a red wine. Say a nice Cabernet with dinner."

"You want to joke around, or do you want to see the offer?" Dillon said, pulling his cellphone out. He pressed the record button, stated the date, time, and location. He mentioned their names and had O'Kelly state that he had no questions. "By the way, this is a onetime offer. Take it or leave it," Dillon said. He pulled the two page offer from the manila envelope and set it on the tray table positioned over O'Kelly's bed.

"Read the offer out loud," Dillon said.

O'Kelly studied the offer for a long moment before he began reading out loud. When he got to the bottom of the first page, he looked at Dillon and said, "Would you mind turning the page? I seem to be a bit indisposed." He raised both arms, indicating the handcuffs attached to the bedrails.

"For the record, Mr. O'Kelly is handcuffed to the bed and unable to turn the document to page two. I'm doing that for him now. Is that satisfactory, Mr. O'Kelly?" Dillon asked.

"Yeah, thanks," O'Kelly said and continued reading aloud.

When he'd finished reading, Dillon asked, "Any questions?"

O'Kelly shook his head.

"I need a verbal response," Dillon said. "Do you have any questions?"

"No, I'll agree to it. The sooner I get out of here, the better I'll be."

"I'll need your signature," Dillon said, pushing the document off the table tray and onto O'Kelly's lap. He pulled a pen from his pocket and reached over to hand it to O'Kelly. A moment later, he said, "Please state your actions."

"I'm signing the damn document so I can get the hell out of here. There, signed and dated," O'Kelly said.

Dillon reached over and picked up the document and his pen. "In order for this to be put in motion, we need the location of Mr. James Dugan. Just so you understand. If he is not at the location, if he's not arrested, this offer is null and void."

"Yeah, yeah, I get all that. He's in Florida, in the US. He's living under the name James Halloran. He was living in Venice, Florida. I believe he has since moved to Key West, Florida."

"You're going to have to be more specific than the name of the town," Dillon said.

"Okay, okay, I get it. Give me a minute to think here. It's a two-story white frame structure with a two-story front porch. It's right across the street from the big church, a Basilica, but I can't remember the name. Behind the house is the Silver Palms Inn. I spent a night there two or three years ago."

"You got an address?"

"I'm coming to that. The address is 1013 Windsor Lane in Key West. There, you guys happy now?"

"We will be once your friend Dugan is arrested and locked up. Any questions, Mr. O'Kelly?"

"No, just leave me alone."

Dillon mentioned the time and date, all of their names, and finished with, "This concludes our interview." He turned off his phone, and he and Suel left without another word. They said goodbye to Eoin McCabe and left St. James Hospital.

"What'd you think?" Suel said as they climbed in the car.

"Not sure what to think. I guess we'll have to see what happens. Is the address correct? Can they arrest Dugan? I will say this. I'm glad it's out of our hands, and we don't have to deal with it."

"Amen to that," Suel said.

Once back at the station, Dillon made a beeline for McCabe's Office and handed the document to him. Emily in tech uploaded the interview, and thirty minutes later, the interview along with the address had been sent to the higher-ups. McCabe seemed just as relieved as Dillon and Suel to get it off his desk.

Dillon went back to slogging through the stack of paperwork on his desk. It was just a little after five and Suel phoned him from his desk.

"You thinking of stopping for a pint?" Suel asked.

Dillon glanced over at Suel, who immediately gave him the finger. "Thanks, Paddy, but I'm dragging after last night, not to mention today. I think I'm going to take a pass."

"Okay. Suit yourself. I'll see the likes of you in the morning."

"Thanks for the offer," Dillon said and hung up. He headed out the door maybe thirty minutes after Suel. He stopped and bought a bottle of wine on the way home. He pulled into the drive in front of his place. He was going to run the wine over to Tara's, as an apology for letting the air out of her father's tire, although he'd never tell her it was him.

He noticed a red envelope partially sticking out of the mail slot in his front door. He unlocked the door, stepped inside, and grabbed the envelope. Nothing was written on the envelope, and he placed it on the kitchen counter along with the wine bottle and called upstairs for Lucifer.

He heard the dog jump off the bed, and a moment later, Lucifer peeked around the newel post upstairs.

Dillon waved a dog biscuit and said, "Treat, Lucifer. Outside." The dog hurried down the stairs and headed for the front door. Dillon opened the door and tossed the biscuit. Lucifer caught it on the first bounce and devoured it in a second or two.

Dillon went out to the kitchen and opened the red envelope;

'Just wanted to say thank you again for all you did this morning. If it's not too late are you interested in dinner? Call Me, Tara'

♥

Dillon thought about her offer for a second, maybe two, and called her.

"You're finally home?" was how she answered.

"Yeah, just. Is your offer still open?"

"Yes, it is. I'll bring dinner over in just a minute."

"You sure? I mean, I could come over to you and—"

"No, I've got everything ready," she said.

Ten minutes later, the doorbell rang. Dillon finished filling the wine glasses and hurried to the door.

Tara was there, smiling, with a large picnic basket.

"Come in, come in. This is so nice of you to do," Dillon said.

She smiled, raised her head, and gave him a kiss. "Just want to give you a special thank you. I made lasagna this afternoon. I've got garlic bread, a dessert, a bottle of wine, and a bone for Lucifer," she said.

"I've already got some wine poured," he said.

They chatted through dinner. He maybe got more information on her father's surgery than he wanted, but he didn't care. She eventually poured the last of the second bottle of wine into their glasses and suggested it might taste even better in bed. Lucifer seemed content to continue chewing on his bone.

Dillon made breakfast for them the following morning, scrambled eggs, toast, and coffee, and for the first time in a long time, he wasn't in a hurry to get to work.

EPILOGUE

Jimmy Dugan was sitting on his front porch, enjoying the shade. A young couple approached, pushing a stroller, just as a mail van pulled up and stopped. The mailman climbed out with a box in hand and headed up the front sidewalk. "Good afternoon, Mr. Halloran?"

Jimmy nodded.

"Just need a signature on this package," the mailman said as he climbed the four steps to the porch. A yellow tag was attached to the package.

Dugan was about to say something when the young man pushing the stroller called, "You have a very lovely place."

Dugan nodded as the young woman bent over, looking into the stroller. For a moment, he admired her perfect rear. He made note of the lines from a very small thong beneath the tight white shorts. He heard something off to the left, bushes rustling, and his first thought was *that damn dog.* A man in a bulletproof vest suddenly appeared.

The mailman pulled a pistol from the package, shoved it against the side of Dugan's head, and said, "Don't."

The woman in the tight shorts and her husband were cautiously approaching with long guns aimed at Dugan. He glanced down and saw two illuminated red dots centered on his chest. It was over.

THE END

Thanks for taking the time to read <u>Picture Perfect</u>. If you enjoyed the read please consider leaving a review. I'm indie published so your review really helps. Thank you, much appreciated…

Check out the sample of the next book in the Jack Dillon Dublin Tales series, <u>Dublin Moon</u>.

ONE

s Dillon refilled Tara's glass he asked, "More wine?"

"Not too much. There's no telling what I'll be up to," she said and raised her eyebrows. She raised her glass in a toast. Just like the previous dozen times this evening, they clinked glasses. Dillon let the wine touch his lips then set his glass on the coffee table. Tara took a couple of audible swallows.

She lived across the lane from Dillon. They'd had an on-again, off-again relationship for a couple of years. She'd been gone for the past three weeks, minding her father in the west of Ireland following his heart surgery. Fortunately, he was doing just fine. Stubborn guy that he was, surprisingly, he was following the doctor's orders. Apparently, a heart attack can have that effect on you.

"Thanks for bringing dinner over tonight and for minding the lawn while I was gone, Jack. You didn't have to do that."

"No big deal. I'm just glad your dad's doing okay. From what you told me, it sounds like it could have been a lot worse."

"You think? Chest pains for three solid days before he gives a call to the doctor, then he drives himself to the emergency room. Honest to God, we're lucky they didn't find him dead behind the wheel on a country road. A double bypass and I damn near had to lock him in his bedroom to keep him from tending the sheep," she said and took another healthy swallow of wine.

"You said you got a neighbor to watch over them."

"Aw, yeah. Alfie, he and his family have been next door for the last twenty years. Nice couple with four boys. They'll be taking good care of the sheep, and Alfie will be cracking the whip. He and his wife run a tight ship." She took another swallow of wine and raised her eyebrows again.

Dillon figured maybe a couple more sips, and they could begin what they were both looking forward to. He'd missed her, and although he'd never admit it to himself, he was thrilled that she was back in town. Hopefully, things would remain somewhat quiet in Dublin over the next seventy-two hours, and maybe they could get back on track.

"It's good to see you, Jack. I thought about you a good bit."

"Hopefully in a positive manner," he said.

"Most of the time. I really want—What the hell is that?"

"Oh, my damn phone," Dillon said, pulling his cell-phone from his pocket.

"I thought you told me you'd turned it off."

"I thought I did, I—"

"Well, don't answer it."

"Hello?"

"Dillon?"

"Yes, sir."

"Sorry to bother you at this time of night." DCI McCabe, usually unflappable. Tonight he sounded very upset.

"Not a bother, sir."

"There's been a tragic incident at Mountjoy Square. It's all hands on. We need you here."

"I'm on it. I'll see you there in fifteen minutes."

Click

"You're leaving?" Tara asked.

"I'm sorry, Tara, but I have to. There's been—"

"No doubt some dreadful situation you can't wait to get involved in. Well, go ahead. Off with you."

"It's not like that. I'm on call. That was DCI McCabe. He wanted—"

"McCabe is it? Well, when you see him, tell him to stop over. As long as you're leaving, maybe he'd be interested in coming over and attending to my needs. Hmm?"

"Tara, I'm sorry. Maybe if we hurried, we could—"

"You've got to be kidding. Save it, Jack. I've heard it too many times. Go on, git. If you stay here, you'll just be wondering what gruesome, grisly situation you're missing out on."

"Look, Tara, if there was—"

"Go on. Besides, this just leaves more wine for me," she said and grabbed the bottle. She emptied the bottle, filling her glass to the rim. The glass overflowed with a final glug, and she set the empty bottle on the floor.

"Okay, look, I'm really sorry. I'll call you tomorrow," Dillon said and stood. "Can I get a kiss goodbye?"

"Sure you can," she said and staggered to her feet. As she stepped toward him, she kicked the empty bottle under the coffee table. She smiled, placed her hands on either side of Dillon's face, and gave him a long, passionate kiss. As she pulled away, she rubbed both hands below his belt, smiled, and said, "Just to remind you what you'll be missing. Now go."

As he stepped out of her sitting room, he heard the TV come on. He crossed the lane and hurried into his place. He opened the cookie jar on the kitchen counter and took out a dog biscuit. At the sound of the cookie jar lid, Lucifer jumped off the bed upstairs and a moment later peeked around the newel post at the top of the stairs.

"Come on, Lucifer, outside," Dillon said and held up the biscuit. The dog hurried down the stairs and stood at the front door. Dillon opened the door, tossed out the biscuit, and closed the door behind him.

He raced upstairs, changed into a pair of pressed jeans and a clean shirt. He pulled on his shoulder holster and grabbed his brown leather jacket. He filled Lucifer's food and water dishes, let him back inside, and climbed in his car.

TWO

DCI McCabe's phone call had been more terse than usual, which was saying a lot. All Dillon knew was a body had been found in Mountjoy Square, down on Gardiner Street. "Need you here now," McCabe had said. No, 'Are you busy?' 'Sorry to interrupt,' or even a 'Please,' which was very unlike him.

On the ten-minute drive over to Mountjoy Square, Dillon tuned in to a number of different radio stations but never found any news. He sped down Drumcondra Road, which turned into Dorset Street. He took a right onto Gardiner Street, and two blocks later, just past St. Francis Xavier Church, the street was blocked by two An Garda Síochána squad cars. The officers were directing traffic onto a side street. Dillon pulled alongside and was fumbling to get his ID out when there was a knock on his window.

"You'll not be parking here. Now move on before we lock you up and sort things out in the morning. Hey, are you even listening, mate? Did you hear what I just said?" the uniformed officer said.

Dillon finally got hold of his ID and held it up as he lowered his window.

"Oh, sorry, sir. I didn't know. This situation is more than a bit upsetting."

"Relax, no problem. I just got the call to come down. No other information. What's happened?"

"Two of our lads, sir."

"Two Gardai? Are you sure? Two?" He shook his head in disbelief.

"Murdered, sir. Shot, apparently execution-style if you can believe it."

"Jesus Christ."

Now the officer shook his head and said, "I'm afraid Jesus was nowhere around when this happened. Let me move my car so you can drive past. When you find the bollox what did this, call me. I'll gladly kill the lousy bastard." He hurried into a squad car, turned it on, and pulled ahead maybe five feet.

Dillon backed up, gave him a nod as he drove between the squad cars and down Gardiner Street. Mountjoy Square was just that, a square park with trees, a children's playground, and St. Brigid's Daycare Center in the far corner. Lovely brick paths wound across the square. Developed in the late 18th century, the square was located in the middle of the city and bounded on all sides by four-story brick buildings that 250 years ago were homes to Dublin's wealthy. Today, the buildings have largely been converted to office space or multiple rental units.

Ahead, Dillon could see two emergency vehicles backed up to the sidewalk along the front of the square.

The rear doors were open, and an officer was standing next to them. He pulled across the street and parked. As he climbed out of his car, he grabbed his ID and draped the lanyard around his neck. With the almost full moon, it was more like dusk than a dark evening.

The officer gave him a nod and said, "They're straight back in the middle of the square. Follow the route they've taped off."

"Thanks," Dillon said and hurried along the sidewalk. The park was lined by a six-foot-tall wrought iron fence. White plastic tape with blue letters in English and Irish, CRIME SCENE NO ENTRY LÁTHAIR CHOIRE NÍL IONTRÁIL, was strung on the wrought iron fence. About a third of the way along the sidewalk, the tape followed a brick path, five feet wide, leading toward the center of the square. Maybe twenty individuals were scattered along the path. A camera was flashing, and a number of officers were slowly walking along an area with flashlights illuminating the ground. A white nylon tent was erected halfway down and just off the path; that would be where the bodies were.

As he approached, a familiar voice called, "Dillon, over here." It was Paddy Suel, Dillon's partner in the Special Branch. Standing next to him was their boss, DCI McCabe, and next to McCabe was a man in uniform. Dillon recognized the man as Drew Harris, Garda Commissioner. As Dillon approached, Harris shook hands with McCabe, placed a hand on his shoulder, and said something Dillon couldn't hear.

McCabe nodded, and Harris walked over to the tent. Two individuals in blue hazmat suits stepped out of the tent. Harris said something to them, and they responded.

"Thank you for coming so promptly, Dillon," McCabe said and cleared his throat. "DI Suel, if you'd be so kind as to bring Marshal Dillon up to date. If you'll excuse me, I've a matter to attend to," he said and headed down the brick path to the street.

"Fecking hell," Suel said as McCabe walked away.

"What'd I miss? One of the guys directing traffic told me two Gardai were killed. Is that right?"

"Afraid so. Executed would be a more accurate term. One of them was McCabe's nephew, Liam. The chief is heading to his brother's house now. God, I don't envy him the task. New recruit, barely a month out of the academy, and this shite happens."

They watched DCI McCabe as he walked down the path and out of the square. "What do you know at this point?" Dillon asked.

Suel shook his head, "Feck all. Teams are out knocking on doors as we speak. Early reports are two shots. Based on appearances, both men were shot in the back of the head."

"Executed?"

"Certainly appears that way," Suel said. "No witnesses at this point. The lads patrol the general area on foot, do a walk-through every evening, standard procedure. They were both unarmed. I can't wait to get my hands on the bastard that did this. For the love of God," Suel said.

"How long ago did this happen?"

"Call came in, mmm, maybe a couple of hours ago. Report of two gunshots, nothing about victims."

"You think they saw something?"

"The victims? I suppose it's possible. What's the worst they'd see? A drug deal? Maybe a robbery? God forbid two young ones banging away. Why in the hell would someone shoot them? They were unarmed. Shoot them in the damn foot if you have to, but this, this execution. Feck all. We're going to get the bastard that did this if it's the last thing I do."

They spent the next three hours talking to the officers from the Fitzgibbon Street Garda Station, the section where the two officers were stationed. The Fitzgibbon Street station was just a block away from the square. Both victims, Liam McCabe and Jimmy Murphy, were walking their usual route back to the station at the end of their shift. Dillon and Suel would get confirmation tomorrow on the route they took by checking the CCTV camera footage along the way. Unfortunately, the square itself didn't have CCTVs. A Garda was on the scene within minutes of the shots being fired. A few minutes after that, the area was crawling with officers.

"I'd say there's not much more we can do until daylight," Suel said and glanced up at the stars and the full moon. It was close to midnight. "Clear sky, no rain forecast. Meet back here tomorrow, say seven?"

"Yeah, we need to get copies of CCTV footage first thing. I'm with you on this. It doesn't seem to make much sense at this point unless the aim right from the beginning was to kill a member of the force."

"This was their usual routine. They'd walk through here every evening at the end of their shift, same time. Even with the full moon tonight you'd maybe miss someone hiding behind a tree. Some idiot with a gun comes out, lines them up, and pulls a trigger. It could've happened in less than twenty seconds, start to finish."

Dillon shook his head. "Killing two would almost have to be intentional rather than them stumbling onto something."

"Afraid so," Suel said.

Dillon turned toward a squeaking sound as two gurneys were pushed up the path past them and over to the tent. A folded black body bag rested on each of the gurneys.

Dillon and Suel walked over to the tent and glanced in. The bodies were lying no more than a foot apart. The two men who'd pushed the gurneys were arranging the body bags on the gurneys.

An officer was in the tent taking photos with a digital device. Dillon recognized him but couldn't recall his name.

"Any shell casings, Sean?" Suel asked.

"Afraid not, Paddy," Sean said and snapped off a half-dozen more photos, each time adjusting his position ever so slightly. A young-looking guy in a blue hazmat suit stepped into the tent. The photographer took two more photos, raised his eyebrows at Suel, and said, "See you later, Paddy. Good luck here."

"Take care," Suel called as Sean hurried out of the tent.

Suel rolled his eyes at Dillon then faced the guy in the hazmat suit and asked, "Anyone else from the examiner's office around?"

"No, sir. I'm afraid you're stuck with me. You're not with the Fitzgibbon Station, are you?"

"DI Suel, Special Branch. We'll be working with the Fitzgibbon team, not that it's any of your concern. What can you tell me?"

Dillon shot a look a Suel, wondering where the sudden attitude came from.

The young man swallowed nervously and said, "One round in each victim— no exit wounds. I'd say it's a pretty safe guess whoever did this used a small-caliber weapon. Maybe a 25ACP or a 22 short. That's just a guess on my part at this stage. Residue on both victims suggests maybe eight-to-twelve-inch distance."

"How 'bout you leave the guessing to us, and you just give me the damn facts."

The man quickly nodded and said, "Officer Murphy was shot in the back of the head and Officer McCabe just above the left ear. That suggests Murphy took the first round, and as he's shot, McCabe turned his head. Maybe he attempted to fight back and was shot. Both victims were on their knees, just off the path here. I don't know.

Once we recover the slugs, hopefully, we'll get a confirmation on the type of weapon. No signs of any altercation. I'm thinking one individual did this."

Suel shook his head and said, "Feck sake," just under his breath. "Contact me in Special Branch as soon as you have information. Clear?"

"Yes, sir," the young man said and nodded a number of times.

Suel stormed out of the tent. Dillon smiled and said, "Thanks for the information. Sorry for the attitude. This is hitting close to home for us. Appreciate your help." He stepped out of the tent and looked around for Suel.

THREE

S uel was partway down the path, just finishing up talking to the man who'd been taking the pictures. "Thanks for the update, Sean. We'll be back here in the daylight, early," Suel said.

"Good luck on the investigation," Sean said. He nodded as Dillon approached and headed out of the park.

"Let's do a quick walk around the square. There's only a couple of ways in and out of here," Suel said and headed out of the park without waiting for Dillon's response.

They walked around the square, looking, not saying much. After twenty minutes, Dillon was back near his car. He guessed it would be at least another hour before the bodies were removed. "I'll be back tomorrow morning. You still thinking seven?"

Suel nodded as he stared back into the square.

"Based on where the bodies are, it would seem someone was in there waiting for them instead of someone who just happened to pass them on the path. The place is unlit, dark. A normal sort, just out for a nighttime stroll, probably wouldn't cut through. They'd stick to the street with the lights," Dillon said.

"A bloody damn shame," Suel said and shook his head. "Now we've got that limp dick from the examiner's office in there mucking up the works."

"You were pretty rough on him, Paddy. He's doing his job. He's not going to be able to tell us much until they perform the autopsies. I know this is tough, and I'm just as determined as you to get whoever did this but reaming out someone we're going to be wanting information from tomorrow isn't going to help. Why are you so pissed off at him?"

"That's right, blame me, my fault. As if that plonker would mind. He'd love a reaming. Don't you get it, Dillon? He's a puff. Makes the whole lot of us a laughingstock. How in the hell they ever let him into the department when—"

"Wait a minute. Paddy? You were giving the guy a hard time because he's gay?"

"You're damn right. Everyone does. We don't want him associated with us."

"That's just great. He's hired because he's smart, probably was first in his class, but you don't like it because of who he sleeps with? Are you kidding me? You—"

"Save it, Dillon. You Americans, always looking out for everyone unless they have something you want, then you just march in and take whatever it is and call it your own. Whether it's oil, or land, or gold, or feck all. Save the holier than thou attitude for someone that fecking cares."

"Okay, probably be a good idea if we both head home, cool down, and come back here tomorrow morning. We need anything from the medical examiner, maybe let me handle it."

"Fine with me. See how that works out," Suel said and headed down the street.

Dillon walked back into the park and made his way to the tent. The young guy was standing outside writing something on a clipboard. He looked up as Dillon approached.

"Hey, just wanted to give you one of my cards," Dillon said and handed him a card. "Give me a call when you have some information. Any idea when the autopsy will be?"

"Not exactly. I'll probably be assisting, but I'm going to be here for at least another hour, which means they'll be scheduled no earlier than eleven tomorrow morning."

He glanced at the business card. "Oh, you're the American I've heard about. The shooting a few years back at Dublin Airport, terminal two."

"Ancient history," Dillon said. "I'm sorry, I didn't catch your name."

"Oh, I'm called a lot of things," he said and shrugged, not really making a joke. "Umm, Hugh Healy, pleased to meet you, Marshal Dillon," he said and held out his hand.

"Pleasure is all mine," Dillon said.

"I'll call you tomorrow with the autopsy time," Healy said.

"Thanks, I'd appreciate that. I'll be back here first thing in the morning, and then we're going to be tracking down CCTV footage, so you may end up leaving a message. Don't take it personally. I'd like to get those results as soon as they're available. Will you be dealing with the Fitzgibbon Station as well? I'm guessing they'll be heading up the investigation."

"Maybe. I believe DI Kinch at Fitzgibbon will be in charge," Healy said. "Dealt with him once before. He'd prefer anyone but me. I'm used to it."

"Hugh, it's been a pleasure. I look forward to chatting with you tomorrow at some point. Get home and get some sleep."

"A few things to wrap up, and then I'll get some sleep. Thank you for introducing yourself. It was nice to meet you."

"Like I said, the pleasure was all mine," Dillon said. They shook hands, and Dillon walked to his car. At this hour, now approaching one in the morning, traffic was light. He kept thinking about Suel's reaction to Hugh Healy on the drive home and suddenly found himself turning onto his lane. He drove down the short hill, past Tara's house. All the lights were off, and he wondered where he stood with her after leaving the way he did.

He pulled into the parking area in front of his house and climbed out of the car. He unlocked the door, stepped inside, and quietly closed the door. He got the coffee ready for the morning, topped up Lucifer's food and water dishes, and headed upstairs to bed.

Lucifer was asleep on the bed and didn't so much as move when Dillon entered the bedroom. He set the alarm for 5:30, undressed, climbed into bed, and was asleep in less than a minute.

FOUR

Dillon woke five minutes before the alarm was set to go. He turned it off and headed into the bathroom to shave and shower. He dressed in the bedroom, and Lucifer never so much as moved. He quietly headed downstairs, turned on the coffee, and set about making a breakfast of scrambled eggs and bacon. At 6:30, he woke Lucifer with a half-dozen calls offering a biscuit. He finally heard him jump off the bed, and a moment later, Lucifer appeared at the top of the stairs.

"Come on, boy, treat. A nice biscuit, just for you," Dillon said, and Lucifer hurried down the stairs. He bounded out the front door when Dillon tossed the biscuit. Dillon filled his travel mug with coffee, turned off the coffee maker, and let Lucifer back in the house.

He climbed in his car and drove back up the lane. He looked at Tara's house without turning his head as he drove past. There didn't seem to be any activity, but then it was only 6:45.

Gardiner Street was still blocked off, but now there was only one squad car and a very tired-looking officer directing traffic to the side street. Dillon slowed, raised the ID hanging around his neck, and got a friendly nod and wave from the officer.

He parked in the same spot as the previous night and headed into the square. The tent was gone, and there was only a handful of Gardai in the square. One of them was Suel.

"You able to get some sleep last night?" Dillon asked.

Suel nodded and said, "What about you?"

"I was out like a light," Dillon said.

"I just finished talking to a sergeant from Fitzgibbon Station. DI Garret Kinch will be leading the charge from there."

"Oh really," Dillon said and decided there was no point in mentioning Hugh Healy had told him that last night.

"Yeah, have you ever had to deal with him?" Suel asked.

Dillon shook his head and said, "Couldn't pick him out of a crowd of two."

"Bit of a plonker. Has to be the person always in complete control. Just a warning, let's be polite, smile, and keep things close to the vest."

"I'm with you. Any results from last night? A name or names? Type of weapon?"

"Nothing yet. It's still early. No shells found, which makes me think it was a revolver."

"Or they picked up the shells."

"Yeah, could be. One thing, the route the lads always walked was along Parnell Street to Hill Street. They would take a left on Hill up to Grenville Street then into the square. Kinch has someone rounding up the CCTV footage as we speak. Hope to be able to view that later this morning."

"Any history of threats against either one of the victims or the Fitzgibbon Station?"

Suel shook his head. "Nothing out of the ordinary. A woman charged with solicitation threatened to sue an arresting officer out of Fitzgibbon, and when that didn't work, she offered him a fifty percent discount."

"You're kidding, a discount to the arresting officer? How'd that go?"

"Not too well for her."

"They're going to conduct another search here in about thirty minutes. I've got a laundry list of CCTV locations along the route the victims were supposed to have taken. You interested in walking it with me?" Suel asked.

"Yeah, it'll give me a sense of the area. I've only driven through occasionally."

"It can be a bit dicey. There are some rough pockets," Suel said, and they headed toward Grenville Street. The street was one long block before it butted into Hill Street. On one side of Grenville was a relatively recent, as in maybe twenty or thirty years, five-story apartment building. "Council Housing," Suel said.

Across the street was a two-story white stucco structure that looked like it housed one-room efficiency units . The exterior of the building was covered with graffiti from the first floor up to the roof. At this hour of the morning, there was no apparent activity at either building.

"It'll be quiet around here until noon. Why would you get up if you don't have to go to a job?" Suel said.

Hill Street was more of the same, with a few businesses interspersed. Three and four-story apartment buildings and a stretch of one and two-story commercial establishments in hundred-year-old buildings, including an Asian butcher shop. The traffic picked up substantially once Hill Street ran into Parnell Street. There were more Asian grocery stores, Chinese restaurants, and a noodle house. A number of commercial establishments were housed in older two-story buildings along with restaurants and some bars. Parnell Street was busy even at this hour, and Dillon figured it would be hopping on just about any evening.

"You think someone could have followed them from down here?" Dillon asked.

"Entirely possible. I'm not aware of any calls they made to the station. Hopefully, we'll learn. Maybe they had a run-in with someone, or they were spotted and followed. With the council housing and the state of the buildings, I'd say sixty-to-seventy percent of the residents have had some interaction with the Gardai at one time or another."

"That doesn't mean they'd shoot someone."

"No, of course not, but it also means there's probably more than one individual around here that's harboring a grudge," Suel said.

"You up for a coffee or a tea?" Dillon asked as they approached a coffee shop.

"You buying?"

"Yeah, I'll buy."

They headed into the Ming Coffee Shop and were greeted with a smile from the Asian woman behind the counter.

"You go ahead, Paddy."

"Just a regular coffee, nothing fancy," Suel said.

"Make it two," Dillon said.

The woman poured coffee into two paper cups, placed a plastic lid on top of each, and said, "Seven Euro."

Dillon handed her a ten Euro note and pocketed the change.

Once outside, Suel took a sip and said, "Sweet Jesus, but that's hot. Wow."

"Seven Euros for the coffee, we should have gotten a pint of Guinness and split it," Dillon said.

"Yeah, we'll do that next time. As long as I get to drink the first half," Suel said.

They walked back to Mountjoy Square along the same route. The foot traffic along Hill Street was beginning to pick up, largely people working in the various commercial establishments and the occasional older woman dragging a cart to the grocery store.

Grenville Street was still quiet. Twice as many officers were now in Mountjoy Square. They'd fanned out in a line and were slowly combing over the area, looking for anything. It appeared they were coming up empty-handed.

"Looks like they'll be done here in the next hour or so," Dillon said.

"Yeah, and still no answers," Suel replied and took the final sip of his coffee. "What do you think? Do you want to hang around and wait, or should we move on?"

"I don't see any point in waiting here. Do you see Kinch anywhere?"

"I'm guessing he's at the station. Let's walk over there. It's just on the other side of the square."

They headed across the square and then onto Fitz-gibbon Street. Dillon expected a smaller station based on the two-story brown brick structures along the street. He was surprised by the large four-story red-brick building with the decorative stone entrance. A plaque listed the construction date as 1913.

They walked up the four stone steps and entered the building. Directly in front of them was a U-shape counter with four officers behind it. The oldest of the four, a bald man with a graying mustache and sergeant stripes on his sleeve, looked up and watched as they approached.

Suel was about to say something when the Sergeant said, "DI Suel, here to turn yourself in?"

Suel looked up and laughed, "Declan Tierney, I didn't know you were stationed here. And look, it takes three of these poor souls just to keep you in line." Everyone chuckled at that.

"I suppose you're here based on last night's activities."

"Unfortunately," Suel said. "The one lad, Liam McCabe, is the nephew of DCI McCabe heading up Special Branch. That's why we're here, although DI Kinch will be running the investigation."

"Mmm," Tierney said. "So what can we do for you this morning?"

"Well, if he's available, we'd like to see DI Kinch. Oh, by the way, my sometime partner, US Marshal Jack Dillon. Dillon, Sergeant Declan Tierney and I go way back."

"Oh, many's the pint, eh, Paddy? A pleasure to meet you, Dillon, is it?"

"Yeah, Jack Dillon. Nice to meet you, Sergeant."

"Likewise. I'd say you've got your work cut out for you," Tierney said and nodded at Suel.

"It's been a long time, Declan. You've been keeping well?" Suel asked.

"Yeah, twenty-three months and counting until retirement."

"Really, that's all? Oh, terrific, Declan. Really it is. So nice to see someone make it over the wall."

"Mmm, especially after an event like last night. God, if I could get my hands on the bastard who's responsible for—"

"You'd have to wait in line," Suel said.

"So, you said it's Kinch you're here to see. Let me place a call."

"We'll grab a seat," Suel said.

They hadn't taken six steps when Tierney called, "Paddy, I just left a message. No telling when he'll respond. You know how that bollox can be, so you didn't get this from me, but here's his cellphone." Tierney proceeded to write down a number and then handed the note to Suel.

"Thanks, Declan. You take care," Suel said, and they left the station.

TO BE CONTINUED . . .

Thanks for checking out the sample of the next Jack Dillon Dublin Tale, <u>Dublin Moon</u>. Better grab a copy and see what happens . . .

Check out this list of books by Mike Faricy.

Books by Mike Faricy
Crime Fiction Firsts

A boxset of the first four books in four crime fiction series:
Russian Roulette; Dev Haskell series
Welcome; Jack Dillon Dublin Tales series
Corridor Man; Corridor Man series
Reduced Ransom! Hot Shot series

The following titles comprise the Dev Haskell series:
Russian Roulette: Case 1
Mr. Swirlee: Case 2
Bite Me: Case 3
Bombshell: Case 4
Tutti Frutti: Case 5
Last Shot: Case 6
Ting-A-Ling: Case 7
Crickett: Case 8
Bulldog: Case 9
Double Trouble: Case 10
Yellow Ribbon: Case 11
Dog Gone: Case 12
Scam Man: Case 13
Foiled: Case 14
What Happens in Vegas… Case 15
Art Hound: Case 16
The Office: Case 17

Star Struck: Case 18

International Incident: Case 19

Guest From Hell: Case 20

Art Attack: Case 21

Mystery Man: Case 22

Bow-Wow Rescue: Case 23

Cold Case: Case 24

Cash Up Front: Case 25

Dream House: Case 26

Alley Katz: Case 27

The Big Gamble: Case 28

Bad to the Bone: Case 29

Silencio!: Case 30

Surprise, Surprise: Case 31

Hit & Run: Case 32

Suspect Santa: Case 33

P.I. Apprentice: Case 34

Rebel Without a Clue: Case 35

Puppy Love: Case 36

The following titles are Dev Haskell novellas:

Dollhouse

The Dance

Pixie

Fore!

Twinkle Toes

(*a Dev Haskell short story*)

The following are Dev Haskell Boxsets:
Dev Haskell Boxset 1-3
Dev Haskell Boxset 4-6
Dev Haskell Boxset 7-9
Dev Haskell Boxset 10-12
Dev Haskell Boxset 13-15
Dev Haskell Boxset 16-18
Dev Haskell Boxset 19-21
Dev Haskell Boxset 22-24
Dev Haskell Boxset 25-27
Dev Haskell Boxset 28-30
Dev Haskell Boxset 1-7
Dev Haskell Boxset 8-14
Dev Haskell Boxset 15-19
Dev Haskell Boxset 20-24
Dev Haskell Boxset 25-29

The following titles comprise the Jack Dillon Dublin Tales series:
Welcome
Jack Dillon Dublin Tale 1
Sweet Dreams
Jack Dillon Dublin Tale 2
Mirror Mirror
Jack Dillon Dublin Tale 3
Silver Bullet
Jack Dillon Dublin Tale 4
Fair City Blues

Jack Dillon Dublin Tale 5
Spade Work
Jack Dillon Dublin Tale 6
Madeline Missing
Jack Dillon Dublin Tale 7
Mistaken Identity
Jack Dillon Dublin Tale 8
Picture Perfect
Jack Dillon Dublin Tale 9
Dublin Moon
Jack Dillon Dublin Tale 10
Mystery Woman
Jack Dillon Dublin Tale 11
Second Chance
Jack Dillon Dublin Tale 12
Payback Brother
Jack Dillon Dublin Tale 13
The Heist
Jack Dillon Dublin Tale 14
Jewels To Kill For
Jack Dillon Dublin Tale 15
Retirement Scheme
Jack Dillon Dublin Tale 16
The Collector
Jack Dillon Dublin Tale 17

Jack Dillon Dublin Tales Boxsets:
Jack Dillon Dublin Tales 1-3
Jack Dillon Dublin Tales 4-6

Jack Dillon Dublin Tales 1-5
Jack Dillon Dublin Tales 1-7
Jack Dillon Dublin Tales 6-10

The following titles comprise the Hotshot series;
Reduced Ransom! Second Edition
Finders Keepers! Second Edition
Bankers Hours Second Edition
Chow Down Second Edition
Moonlight Dance Academy Second Edition
Irish Dukes (Fight Card Series)
written under the pseudonym Jack Tunney

The following titles comprise the Corridor Man series:
Corridor Man
Corridor Man 2: Opportunity knocks
Corridor Man 3: The Dungeon
Corridor Man 4: Dead End
Corridor Man 5: Finger
Corridor Man 6: Exit Strategy
Corridor Man 7: Trunk Music
Corridor Man 8: Birthday Boy
Corridor Man 9: Boss Man
Corridor Man 10: Bye Bye Bobby

Corridor Man novellas:
Corridor Man: Valentine
Corridor Man: Auditor

Corridor Man: Howling

Corridor Man: Spa Day

The following are Corridor Man Boxsets:

Corridor Man Boxset 1-3

Corridor Man Boxset 1-5

Corridor Man Boxset 6-9

THANK YOU!

Contact the author:

- Email: mikefaricyauthor@gmail.com
- Twitter: @Mikefaricybooks
- Facebook: Mike Faricy Author
- Website: http://www.mikefaricybooks.com

Published by

MJF Publishing